THE SECRETS OF
Paulina Bonaparte

EROTIC NOVEL

FÉLIX DARÍO MENDOZA

Print information available on the last page.
Rev. date:
To order additional copies of this book, contact:
Maple Leaf Publishing Inc.
3rd Floor 4915 54 Street Red Deer, Alberta T4N 2G7, Canada
1-(403)-356-0255

Contents

1

The Beginning

PUM-KUTUPUM-PUMPUM-KU-TUPUM! PUM-PUM!

The sunrays, like humongous swords, were coming down directly from heaven to penetrate the deep, salted, and warm waters of the Atlantic Ocean, creating an unusual spectacle. The earth was burning like a gigantic pail under the effect of an unforgiving Caribbean sun. The heat did not give a chance to the island's living things. In the last little curve of La Mulate Hill, which serves as a natural protection to the city of Cap-Haitien, the panorama was terrified.

One could see from every corner of the ocean bay the arrival of a long caravan of carriages filled with equipment and with high-caliber guns and soldiers. They were the front line of the tremendous invasion integrated by thousands of French marines. Three fronts of soldiers were coming out from the belly of the big ships that crowded the ocean entrance. The horses were running with desperation to reach the city doors as fast as they could. It seemed as if they were in a hurry to reach the city's entrance before the black blanket of the dark night reached the savanna and caught them in the open field.

The carriage that was leading the caravan could be easily distinguished among the others because of its special and colorful ornaments. It could be seen from a long distance among the others cars; two enormous flags and a big golden shield were covering the carriage. The brightness of the big shield, like an enormous mirror, never before seen in the French colony of Saint-Domingue, made the difference. It was obvious that this particular carriage was bringing in a group of special guests to the violent scenario.

Now, all the firearms were aiming and shooting to destroy the special target. People had to pay close attention to a gigantic horse that was running by himself attached to the lead carriage.

The gigantic animal, like a Trojan horse, was galloping as if an invisible expert horseman was controlling his path. Its enormous legs gave the optical illusion that the horse was not touching the ground. The beast was white like a big cloud, like Pegasus in the sky.

A lot of people who were taken by surprise with the French invasion were running like zombies in all directions to escape from the virtual massacre of the numerous and superior army that was here to kill or to be killed in the tropical island.

The side of each muscles of the animal was causing enormous attention. Most noticeable was his virile *member*, which was erected like a war cannon, ready to discharge its power under his big belly. The horse was aroused despite everything going on around him, like the sound of the drums and the impact of the cannon explosions, which was storming the long caravan.

The deadly fire guns were creating an inferno in the region. But men and horse were determined to go through to overcome the initial attack from the slaves' rebellion in the northern part of Hispaniola, which was under the name of Saint-Domingue. The place was burning in search of freedom from the Napoleonic Empire.

The scene was Dantesque. However, the French soldiers were committed to maintain at all cost the imperial pride that lifted the spirit of Le Grand Armée.

The horse caused such a commotion that a middle-aged Creole native lady ran inside the house to see the caravan passing by from a hidden and a safer place without exposing herself to the danger of the bloody fight. The Haitian woman could not believe what she was watching. Her lips were shaking. Her voluptuous body was trembling too. It seemed as if she was praying for something out of her control. Her pupils were opening and closing like a young mare. Her mind and her body were opening to a sensual encounter or at least getting ready to copulate with the best officer or with most muscled black rebel fighting to be free. The woman was watching the long military parade through a window. But the impression that caused her emotion and placed her under the spell of a greater power took her into a shock. Under that psychological pressure, she cried out with all the power of her lungs, "Oh mon Dieu, je croi que nous sont avant le finale du le monde! Voila le chevalle blanc avec le gr—!"

No one could hear and comprehend the last word of the sentence because the cannon balls and the rifle shooting were falling at a short distance. The noise like thunder was making people and animals as well to become deaf in Cap-Haitien.

When the woman was about to pronounce the word

grand, she fainted. Perhaps the horse was already excited due to the great amount of beautiful young mares that were coming, pulling the carriages that belonged to the invading army. That would probably explain the unexpected erection. However, what nobody could understand was why the woman paid so much attention to the animal, which was showing proudly his masculine organ as if he would be ready to copulate with the youngest and most beautiful female of the entire Antilles.

In the rear part of the long caravan, with less luxury and equal urgency, a group of carriages were running with the soldiers and officials along with their women and provisions to feed them. Behind them were carriages that were galloping at a high speed, leaving an impenetrable cloud of dust with dry powder of the Haitian soil. The smell was so strong that one could vomit without effort due to the combination of blood, feces, and urine left by the horses while passing through a bloody battlefield. It was a unique odor that occurs before the catastrophe. In that scenario, the most indifferent and bravest man could combat with the enemy fearlessly or wait to be demolished without minimum compassion by fierce a machete that would cut your neck in a second.

The troops disembarking in Saint-Domingue were facing a very bloody scenario. This battlefield was totally different for both contenders' forces. There had never occurred a similar event in history since 1492, when Great Britain, Portugal, Spain, and Holland that had colonies in the exotic and mysterious Caribbean region with an iron fist. This, thus far, had maintained in control a rebellion that would create the slavery system that was maintained under control during three hundred years. The great power for the era was controlling the Antilles.

The great power of the world had always assumed an arrogant position toward the colonies in the Caribbean.

The history is filled with examples. Saint-Domingue would prove to be the next victim of the imperial powers of the political and military expansion started by France and the emperor Napoleon Bonaparte.

PUM-KUTUM-PUM PUMKUTUM-PUM-PUM!

"Hurry up, nigger, dead man! The sugar mill is calling you! Listen to the bulls crying! Hurry up! Do not stop! Don't you see that a white man is commanding you? Add more wood to the fire that the *melao* is leaking out! Take this weep to make you pay attention to my orders! Don't forget that I represent the owner of this plantation! You are just an insignificant nigger! You are condemned to be a slave for the rest of your life! Hurry up before I punish you again and again and again!"

The mayor continued spitting out offensive words to the four winds. In that way, he was showing off what he had learned from the white patrons to maintain the slaves in producing richness in the plantations of Saint-Domingue, enriching more and more to the ambitious colony owners from the French nation. His deep voice was like an African tiger devouring its prey.

He had a hot belt made with the vine of the tree that cynical people named it brave pacifier. Each stroke felt like it was made of fire on the naked backs of the nigger slaves. The boss of plantation took advantage of each sound of the drums to hit the slaves with the same power of anger that an aggressive dog would have to attack slaves in the plantation.

Pum -Kutupum-pum- Pum-Kutu -pum! Kutupum! Pum! Pum!

With a diabolic motivation, with anger and frustration and infernal hate, the plantation mayor began another attack against the slaves under his command. The weak cries of desperation coming from the slaves each time the sharp belt opened the skin did not evoke any compassion nor pity from the owners of the plantations. The owners were contemplating without remorse the cruelty of the mayoral punishment. Instead of showing even the most minimum remorse or repentance toward the punishment against the slaves, the sophisticated ladies were showing the fans they used to alert the servants to ask them to prepare a good bath; that way they would reduce the heat.

The cold lemonade would also serve the purpose to keep them cold against the heat. The white women proudly calmed the heat that was burning their chests, which were white and soft like marmol, fanning themselves with arrogant poses.

However, neither the chains nor the offensive insults and the weepings changed the rhythmic of movements of the negroes who responded with mute or silent protest against the mayor. The slaves were moving in slow motion, as if they had heavy loads on their backs. Each step took an eternity to reduce the mill's speed, like the turtles. In that way, they were responding with aggressive anger and in an unlimitedly silent way to the vexation carried out by the owners of the plantation and to the *verdugos* and to the mayor and Creole bosses who served the owner of the plantation in Cap-Haitien.

Sometimes, when the burning fire coming from the Caribbean sun combined with the merciless belt of the mayor, the slave would tremble from head to toe, moving his lips with such speed that some mayors and bosses superstitiously distanced themselves from the slave under punishment in a trance, making the cross sign to expel the spirit that possessed the slave. The mayor was afraid that spirits from beyond would take his body and soul in the same way they possessed the slave. When a slave was possessed by the spirit from beyond their world, even the niggers would run like souls being taken by the devil.

They ran away repeating and praying the name La

Magnifica, which is considered the best curse to keep away the bad spirit according to the voodoo and zombie beliefs in the mysterious Caribbean island and beyond. With the magical prayer, they were confident that the spirit that was penetrating the slave's body would trap them.

The rumors of the reality were running rampant in the countries and the cities of Saint-Domingue. The rumors talking about the terror was running from mouth to mouth between the slaves and Creole people narrating the story of the spirit Metressa, who is one of the goddess that was mounted on all the living in the plantation of indigo and was of high importance in the region.

The spirit possessed the body of the plantation owner. The animals and human were under a crazy spell. You could see animals, men, and women flying like birds on top of trees since all of them fell victim of a malefic or a witch curse. All started running like crazy to jump into the cliff and the ocean in collective suicide.

The plantation owner was very famous in the island of La Tortue since she had great talents as she sang like a mockingbird and made people lose their minds with her voluptuous body. She moved around like a twister. The beautiful French woman was crying like she was goat, a white goat, who was going to the slaughterhouse. She was the most strange victim because instead of continuing to follow her husband to commit suicide, like a lot her family and friends, ending their life once and for all in Cap-Haitien, she was left by herself running alone around the city. She was naked like the day God brought her to life to the world. The landlady had lost her mind. She became crazy.

After that event, nobody had news of her whereabouts. The fear that covered the city was tremendous. Everybody turned mad. The fear took control of the mind of the white man and the slave negroes with the same intensity of terror. The mayor who had served with fidelity and faith to Madame Duesxplesir was not the exception. He was frustrated at the impossibility of reaching a high position in the colony of Saint-Domingue that helped him to be seated in the same table with the plantation owner and to attend the extravagant parties that were celebrated in Haiti. The mayor became furious when he listened to the rhythm of the drums that revolts were playing in the mountains in the middle of their fight to survive and to reach freedom. Each touch of the instrument was filling his heart that was developed in hateful labor of representing the owner of the plantation, the family Duesxplesir. Deep in his tormented soul, he was convinced that he was in the end of his life. If he would survive to edge of the machete of the revolutionaries, he was condemned to finish like all the mayors who were disbanded. They would be running here, jumping over there like wild pigs, whose hour was coming soon...soon.

After the justice catches them, they will end their lives. A steel instrument would penetrate his ass to the head to be cooked until the skin become golden due to the slow fire in the firepit, which resembled the horrific inferno. The mayor would spend his last days without resting with an open eye and the other closed, nervously watching the mortal stroke he would suddenly receive sooner or later as payment of the abusive torment that he did to the slaves.

The mayor was sure he would finish his suffering from the torments of his eternal nightmare. Waking up each night wet in his own sweat, wet as if he had urinated himself after receiving a scary dream, without repent and with the condition to continue the fullness of the macabre labor of being the boss of slaves. Therefore, stimulated by the madness, the mayor continue with the series of insults to humiliate the negro slaves.

* * *

"Metre Silis and the lords from beyond are watching you! Take this hit. You are so lazy that for taking a couple of eggs from a hen's nest, you would wait until the chicken hatches! You do not fool me. You were condemned to suffer every minute of your life. For that reason, you were brought from Africa in the black ships to Saint-Domingue! Feed the fire with pity and with dry wood. Do not stop, *carajo!* Are you deaf? Why are you not listening to the bulls crying? God damned! Feed sugar cane into the mill until it squeezes the cane before I will kill you with a whip!"

The slave, in the same way he was learning from his ancestors, did not utter a word. He said nothing. The slave complied with all the orders and instructions given by the mayor. He obeyed without apparent reaction, as if he was a zombie. In that way, he had behaved like his ancestors and during more than three hundred years since they arrived with the tide inside the belly of ships carrying black slaves from the African continent to the mysterious Caribbean islands. He was obeying in silence like all the negro slaves knowing to do it. They did not respond with a look or a glance to the multiple abuses carried on by the plantations' mayor in Saint-Domingue. He accepted with pain and impotency the whips from the mayor who, without any compassion, took out sucking blood of the naked backs of the slaves. Sometimes, when the boss or mayor was away, they would go around the sugar mill where they were squeezing the sugar cane to punish the other slaves who became careless in the working load. The negroes would be crying, humming, humming once more again and again.

He was humming in a low voice. The lament of his bad luck was passed to the other slaves with a lament to the following slave who pushed the enormous iron wheel of iron of the mill, trembling by the menaces of the mayor. It was a form of running away from his own destiny, with the bass and rasping voice repeating once or twice, mumbling the songs in the Creole of his ancestors, repeating pain painfully the condemnation of his lament, the tormented plantation.

"Ay Papa Bondyé! Donne moi force por le trabai! Moi gangu pour la eternite! Je moi allie la cai! L'Afrique est moi destine finale! Mois ancestres, Metre Silis, Bouckman, and Mackandal me va' ayudá!"

PUM-KUTUMPUM-PUM-PUM! KUTU-PUM-PUM!

The painful laments of the slave who was conducting the sugar cane mill had sufficient force and strength to resist the perfect struck-like-fire torches descending with the rabbi and forces of the implacable mayor. When the lash sound was in the high point, a whistle of pain anteceded it. The negroes were humming. He hummed without spilling a single tear. He was overwhelmed by the whips of the mayor. The slave pushed the wheels of the sugar mill to squeeze out the last tear of *guarapo* from the sugar came like he was squeezing this own blood. The implacable whip storming and sounding in the warm air of the sugar cane field could be heard seconds before hitting one or more slaves. He did it with skill and the impulse of the French colonizers of Saint-Domingue. The mayor was throwing the whip to one side and then stroking toward the other. He was reenacting what he learned from the white plantation owners. He hit, making the whip sound in the air, producing a macabre sound as if he was demisting the most robust animal in the region.

The mayor punished like the sun. The boss hit the slave without compassion until the sweat and blood oozed from the open skin for the negroes in chains. The mayor shouted to the four winds to make sure that plantation owners heard his insults and humiliation to the slaves under his orders. The mayor wanted the white colonizers to know that He was implacable with the slaves, even though they were considered his own brothers. The boss knew that he was hitting his own race. His own people.

The mayor was a Creole, of mixed blood. But in the name of the white blood, he was hitting by the blood of his father, hitting with anger to the slaves under his orders.

The man, like the devil with arrogance and anger, was insulting the slaves. It seemed that he was taking vengeance of his white father, who procreated him in an act of expressed sex, like a cock that mounts a hen although she does not open her tail. The mayor hated with all his might the macho power who bought him into this world, like a bitter fruit maybe of a violation to his black mother in the sugar cane field, in the stream of the hill, in the river of the mountain, or in the barracks of the slaves where they passed the night's slavery, the servants of the French/white patrons.

For that reason, they shouted and shouted with his wildly open eyes as two balls of fire, with eyes like the giant frog in the lagoon of Saint Jack, where the wild and domesticated animals of Cap-Haitien drink and bathe in the mood along the seven princes of Metresilis. Without detaining, the mayor shouted at the slave with the anger of a mad dog that. In the meantime, the African drums and the macabre laughter of the mayor increased the noise in the savanna.

"Don't even try to compare with me. Never forget that you are a slave. Keep that in mind—that is if you have one! Look into my eyes, which are blue like the sky, like the eyes of my boss, my patron. My eyes are blue like the sky that is up there that will not never reach it! You are a negro, dark like *el azabache*, like the carbon coming from Congo mine! Hurry up, negro, damned slave that of the devil. These are your last whips that I am giving you for being lazy! Pray to the soul of Macandal, Bouckman, and the Metresilis for intervening such the revolutionaries that will arrive soon to liberate you from the inferno of this world. Now keep on going, don't stop. Work hard.

"You are so lazy and disgraceful. *Vole Caguite! Vole coso!* Turned over like a pig in the pig pit, like the serpent in the savanna of Aiti Bonit, like the reptile in the Mulate Cave. If you make me pronounce Macandal's name again, I swear that I will burn your ass with this iron on fire. In that way you will go to wander forever to energy for the world with the gluteus on fire. In such a way you go free but stamped. You shall go to the inferno with burning ass! Ja, ja, ja, ja, ja, ja, ja!"

The macabre sarcasm of the plantation mayor was causing fear among the slaves. They were praying of the suffering lament to their gods who were left in the faraway African land to their patrons, and the mayoral would have some compassion and exterminate them right away to stop the suffering. They couldn't handle it anymore. The slaves did not have any more physical power to continue working so hard with resting and with very limited food and water. If they die, they were thinking, their pains in general would be left in the kingdom of this world. Their souls would be free, and they would fly like the birds to the land of liberty.

Each strike would provoke a cascade of blood, red as the blood of the French colonizer. But the mayor hit the slave with form and with more funny laughs in a cynical way. He was looking at the slave's contour of pain. His diabolical laughter seemed to come from beyond from a faraway place where the zombies live.

The war drums continued sounding around the region, from the countryside to the city of the Cab in the island of Hispaniola. War did not stop sounding. The winds were carrying the sound up to the mountain and down to the savanna, and the sea sounded again.

PUM-KUTUPUM! PUM-PUM-KUPUM-PUM-PUM!

The slaves adjusted themselves to the pain and suffering. But thinking about or keeping in their mind that the physical or mental torment would not last forever, they kept the flame of liberty on. The squeaking (*chirrido*) sound that kept them enchained and the sugar mills were coordinated, unified to the great battle that was getting closer with the arriving of new century. From the four sides or cardinal points, each drum was bring the message of liberty. The slaves were in revolt. Thus they did each time that the state of slavery reached the limit of the merciless exploitation of the French colonizers. The slaves were rebelling each time they were struck and were in contact with the spirits beyond this world that live in the savannas and the mountains of Africa. This was a long chain, so long, that was made of blood and pain that connected them to the three continents, forming an enormous triangle of suffering in the bodegas or belly in the ships that transported the slaves from Africa, chained in the most horrendous slavery that was getting into Caribbean through a big geographical door named the Cap-Haitien Bay.

Coincidentally, each mountain of Ayiti echoed with a perfect symmetry the liberty crying of Macandal, Bouckman, and Toussaint Louverture. The hills and the mountains that sounded around Cab-Haitien amplified the lamenting sound, clamorous sound, that each musician extracted with his rasping of his calloused hands by the forced work to the cow skin or animal skin of the drums to repeat the battle with the arriving of each night in Saint-Domingue.

Pum-Kutu –pump- Pum pum--Kutu –Pum- Pum- Pum -Pum!

In the faraway distance, one could hear the crying of the victims in the collapse of the millennium. The Caribbean nights were pregnant with the songs and the voices that were coming, announcing the falling of the colonial regime and the running in stampede of the white French colonizers in Saint-Domingue. The revolutionaries were dancing in celebration as if they were possessed by the spirits of their ancestors. Their voices were changing in tone, announcing their kingdom, the kingdom of revolution in the language of the revenge against the exploitation of their owners—white, Creole, and mixed. They were the same owners who were descending from the buccaneers and filibusters, the same ones who were born in Turtle Island. The colonial system of the plantations in Saint-Domingue was starting to collapse. The rebellion of the slaves was not stopping. They wanted to finish once and for all the regime of oppression that was exploited and chained to the black race in all the Caribbean regions. The song and the drums formed an enormous social tsunami that was accompanying the slaves with a clear message:

"Pour la liberté; pour Saint-Domingue et pour Ayiti! A l'attak a tout le colonizatours! Oh Papa Bondyié, donne moi force pour le batille finale! Vivre Metré Silis, Anaisa, Dessalinne, Macandal et Louverture!"

When the woman finished shouting the weird *grand*, the Creole lady used her left arm to make a sign resembling the morbid content indicating the size of the reproductive member of the horse. Because she was surprise of the emotion, the young woman fainted and collapsed. The woman had the eyes almost out its captivity for that shock of the muscles of the animal.

The Haitian was sweating. Her sweat was like a cascade. They were out because it caused fear and excitement at the same time of the white horse that had crossed the Atlantic Ocean to transport its proprietor in the unpaved roads of the Hispaniola Island. For pure luck or coincidence, another Haitian with the mammals like two big papayas was confused with the commotion and slid by the door behind the house.

She was running in a squat position to avoid getting hit in the same way by the shootings from the cannons from soldiers to the revolutionaries. With the closeness of a shot that passed the dress and scratched her gluteus, she remembers that was in the country of the battle where the violence was expected. When she felt the little warmth that was burning, she shouted that was more the result of a scary moment for the pain of the wound due to the bullet that was, for pure luck, scorched without penetrating the gluteus. The woman cried with the force and the belief that she was going to get killed.

After the surprise, she jumped like a *karateka* and fell, rolling over like a barrel, stopping to where the woman fainted. After, the woman, who was sweating from head to feet, lifted her skirt and ripped off the brassier, leaving her with little clothing to quell the heat of Saint-Domingue. Then she started to fan her with fresh air to lower the fever. The heat was suffocating. Everyone could see the chest and the titties of the young woman. At the same time she was applying a technique with the palms of her hands in the plant of her feet to make her come alive to revive the Creole lady. She was fretting over her, babbling a group of words that was part of prayers for the ritual performed to the falling.

The woman who fainted did not speak French because she came from Jamaica just to participate in the fair Marquette of Cap-Haitien, where she was planning to find a thing to have a ritual and to consult a fortune-teller. In Haiti, the female witches converted you to a hen laying eggs in a flash before you could open and close your eyes. Voodoo shamans have the cure for the fever, and they are experts in the bad luck of love. The Jamaican was called Anita Palmer, in reference to the Haitian immigrant called the White Witch because of the amount of husbands that she had, but also because she was very beautiful and was capable of doing a lot of rare works to change people into animals or make people disappear who did something wrong to her or went against her wishes. The Jamaican woman got trapped in the war initiated by the black revolutionaries in Saint-Domingue. No even the hotel that she was staying in noticed anything about the invasion.

Cap-Haitien was an in-and-out docking place of the many ships that were coming and going from around the world. It was a very active port. That might be the reason the invasion got everyone by surprise. Sometimes the city had ships and boats of different sizes docked near the horizon a distance from the coast, waiting for a space to dock in the pier of the bay. The Atlantic Ocean was in the pier of Cap-Haitien.

The woman had arrived three days before the invasion. For that reason, no one noticed Napoleon's army and navy were very close to the main land of Saint-Domingue, waiting for the order to disembark. Now the situation was the fainted woman, and somebody had to save her at all costs. Without worrying about the accent from Jamaica, with only the preoccupation of saving the Haitian woman, in the patois language that they speak in Jamaica, they told her, "Do not die yet, woman! You have a lot to see in the inferno of this world. Wake up and get up, the invasion just started! I am not a revolutionary. I came to do work of with and now have received a shot in my butt, which is the biggest thing that I have in my body. You are in good condition and healthy. Get up already. Drink this shot of alcohol tafia! Wake up. Close your legs and open your mind that the horse continued flying. Lucky will be the *malate*, I should say, the mare, or the horse to copulate on top of this beautiful animal!"

Meanwhile, a voluptuous Jamaican woman was spreading the mammals with alcohol and water from Florida to ensure that the fainted lady return to consciousness. Each time the mulatto lost her consciousness, the Good Samaritan from Jamaica kept her hands under her suspenders, and at the same time, she was rubbing her chest with honey from bees of seven queens and from Cleren from the Turtle Island. The massage to her breasts and the Caribbean woman's swollen protuberance produced a relaxing episode that she repeated again and again. "Voila le chevalle Blanc avec le grand miem...miem...miem..."

On her hallucination, the Creole lady did finish her pronunciation of the word member in reference to te size of the masculine penis of the big animal. At the same time, she left her left arm with the intention to indicate to the woman the position of the masculine muscle of the wild animal. There were a lot of females with tails left that simulated for the sexual drive to copulate with the gigantic horse that was running wild at a great speed for the field in the constant and intense gunfire coming from the invaders and the revolutionaries as well. Almost all the mares were lifting their tails, continuing to show, as if nothing was happening, everything they had between their legs to scare away the insects that were zooming around in the tropical environment. Maybe the horse was excited at the amount of female horses—young and old, robust and beautiful— that were coming, pulling the carriages of the invading army. What we could comprehend was why the lady paid so much attention to the animal that was running for the roads and little streets of the city, showing with pride its reproductive member. This masculine member was hard, like a stick made of *caoba* (mahogany), as if it was ready to ride on top of the most beautiful female horse of the Santo Domingo field.

The fire shots coming from the heavy artillery, rifles, and cannons continued zooming for every size, producing an echo of terror and fear. Looks like it was eternal. Forever.

The horseman in the caldarium was frantically zigzagging. They moved from one side to the other. It was a military tactic to confuse the enemies that were shooting to kill. With these movements, the officers of the high command wanted to advance and opened their pass to cross the fire lane to a safer battlefield. The drums were producing a deep and scary sound with the explosion of the firearms of all calibers that were vomiting fire right and left. The battlefield was a bloody terrain.

Behind, in the rear of the navy, with less luxury but with the same urgency of carriages pulled by horses, was approaching the formation with the officers and soldiers with provisions of all kinds for the need of the thousands of French military force, producing in its tumultuous path a foggy and bad odor for the great amount of urine of the animals. The wives, the doctors, the nurses, and the nuns of different nationalities were arriving at a metropolis of power and dirtiness. Fetid odor like what can only be felt in a battlefield where the feces of the animals mix with the sweat of the humans. It was producing an odor so peculiar that preceded a bloody catastrophe. It was precisely where one could feel the chilling of the death that was coming out in each corner of the road to produce terror and fear to death to both bands in conflict. The black slaves searching for freedom and the whites aspiring to continue their control over the plantation system that was trembling, threatening to collapse at any minute.

Death was watching with a scary look when both fronts were face-to-face in the battlefront. The troops that arrived from France got in to the final and definite combat that, at the end, would shape and redefined the commanding structure of control and ownership for the colonies until the moment, which was established after the arrival of the European conquistadors in 1492. Great Britain, Portugal, Spain, France, and Holland kept its colonial empires in the exotic region of the Caribbean with an iron fist. The emperor orders and the colonials were not subject to questioning or deaneries refutable to keep the production in the Antillean Islands. Protesting or revolting among the slaves was prohibited, and who dared to follow the order would pay either by hanging or execution or the guillotine would take care of his or her execution without trial. The master, the mayo, and the family were the law in the Antilles. The rebels of the slavery put in danger the hegemony of the real crowns in the so-called *New World.*

This, until now, had maintained in control any rebellion that would alter the slavery system that was imposed by the world potencies, controlling lives and plantations as well from the attack of slavery during a few centuries. The big potencies that, for the epoch, dominated the world could be indifferent to what was taking place and developing in Saint-Domingue. The look of the marquis was being focused to the Antilles. The crowns and marquis had already experienced the collapsing of great empires that were so caved for being arrogant and indifferent to claims of the people for better lives. The entire history was filled with examples. Saint-Domingue could be the next example for the imperial power and their insatiable ambition to expand the recently born French Empire.

The thirteen kilometers that they had to go through from the pier of the disembarking spot of the float of military arriving from the Old World until the imperial residence seemed a transcendental long league of torture. It was a route of terror for the invaders who were coming in from Paris and Marsella, completing a treasure passage of the three months that would take for them to cross the Atlantic Ocean. The welcome was given to the French Army arriving to the battlefield. They were the most terrifying assault registered in the history of the Caribbean region of the slavery in Haiti. They advanced like a tremendous tsunami, divesting everything that it encountered in its path. They burned the plantation and killed at the same time the white French colonizers without compassion as a punishment to the violent exploitation permanently of three hundred years.

Each explosion that was reared was a lash thrown for the sharp nails of the death who, like a grotesque woman, was trying to grasp the soldier and the rebels in a tremendous conflict that was bathed in blood, the occidental part of the island of Hispaniola.

The horses as well as the soldiers who were already used to deadly bloody battle marched like a perfect unit. To see the animals and soldiers riding in the battlefield in the savanna of Limonade, Dondon y La Mulate, which forms part of the geography of Cap-Haitien, one could better comprehend why the aborigines train, who were the first settlers in that encounter with the white men on top of the horses were united. For the so-called Indians, the men riding on the horses were one single figure with four legs when they came out from the Caribbean Sea. At this encounter in October 12, 1492, and December 24, 1492, in the island of Venture in the Bahamas and the Quisqueya, this created a pattern of information among the natives that the Spaniards called Indians that would expand to future encounters.

The Tainos thought that the Spaniards on horses were celestial deities. The same thing happened with the Seminoles and Juan de Soto in Florida and with Hernan Cortes in Mexico. The Indians pay reverence to the Spaniards because they believe that they were coming from heaven as their own legends and traditions had already established this: "White entities are coming from the sea to save them." Even Montezuma, the Aztec leader, was lured to be tricked by this legend.

For an unknown reason, in South America, the same thing happened when the Spaniards arrived. The Indians fought bravely to prevent the conquistadores to advance claiming land and treasures throughout the continent. The aborigines strongly believed that these men with long bears and heavy guns that spit fire by a hole were gods that, according with the legends and teaching, were announced by their ancestors from generation to generation.

The legend said that they would come and that the being will arrived from the ocean to save them, and they would be so different because instead of having two legs, they would have four legs. The natives as well as the Caribs as well as the people from the American continent have never seeing something like that. That would explain why the Indians would present them with welcome and jovial ceremony. Instead of receiving them with fierce resistance, they inclined in front of them, providing them with a lot of valuables items as they passed. The aborigines did not have a single idea of the genocide that they were planning for them. This time, the reality would be very different from the arriving and the hosts, like the one who was lighting the torch that they were devastating and burning everything that they encountered in the road to freedom.

Their mission had the purpose of liberating the slaves of the French colony as well as in Turtle Island. Now, the bullets of the cannons would not give space to fear nor to lamentation. There was no break in the middle of the fight to meditate nor to pray, even knowing that the nails of death from the left to the right, from one side to the other.

The attacks were coming from all sides: from the front,

from behind, from the left, and from the right. However, the attack that was the most devastating for the invaders was when they were under heavy artillery from behind and from the front. The fire was like being cooked like corn bread: fire under and fire on top. It was like being in a dead end without an exit. It was like entering the tunnel of death. The animals and horse riders were attached to one another. They prayed to all saints that not a bullet nor the edge of a sword would reach them.

It was an intense crossfire. The rebels were shooting to kill. Everything that moved was a secure target. The slaves in revelry had already conquered and dominated a great part of the territory of the northern part of Saint-Domingue. The mountains that were surrounding Cap-Haitien served as check towers and observatory for the protection of the revolutionaries that dominated the region from the Port-au-Prince bay until Fort Liberte. The visibility of the hills and mountains surrounding the battlefield permitted to have a perfect place to carry on vintage to the army that disembarked, who were well-armed but with little knowledge of the Haitian territory. The slaves, with strategy to impact, were burning fire to the plantations and houses of the French colonizers. A lot of were petrified and were stunned, looking impotent, sad, and frustrated at the advance of the rebellion slaves and the fires that were destroying everything, absolutely everything, including people, animals, forest, and stocks. A lot of the colonizers were not able to escape to Santiago de Cuba. The descendants of the filibusters, buccaneers, who had immigrated to a colony of Saint-Domingue, now were running desperados. They were running in fear to escape the anger and the machete of the black slaves who revolted against the French Revolution. They were looking at this opportunity as the only exit to end the exploitation and the suffering that resulted from a long colonial system established by the French for centuries. The horses and the soldiers were jumping in the air with the hope that the next shot would send them either to heaven or the inferno.

In the meantime, the *pumpumkutumpumpunear* sounds from the drums was getting inside the bones and minds of the ones who were confronting blood and fire in the savannas and the hills of Saint-Domingue. They were fighting to the death. Some were to break the chains of slavery. Others were fighting to keep the colonial domain of the plantation land, the sugar industry in the Antilles minors and mayors. Slavery was suffering for the blacks, wealthy for the colonizers, glory and power for the motherland. France was ready to risk everything for the possession of the territories that they already had acquired in the Caribbean region. France wanted to keep the control and the harmony of power of Saint-Domingue that, at the end of it all, represented the development, the power of the French Crown, and the establishment of the Napoleon Empire. Most of all, Saint-Domingue represented the richest colony of all territories under the domain of Napoleon Bonaparte.

2

The Commandant's Cannon

The officials' orders, the crying of calm for freedom of the slaves who were coming, breaking the chains by the four cardinal points, the quenching of the swords, had created an ambience of combat of extraordinary terror. It was a battlefield wherein the terrified crying and the laments of the soldiers who were falling under the impact of the bullets could be heard all around. They could pray a very short prayer before they had time for the last breath of life, gritting their teeth as if they wanted to bite away the pain. With eyes halfway out of its cavity, the mortally wounded soldiers threw a last look, a fast glance at the last aspiration that kept attached to the world of the living human beings.

While they were agonizing, they took a glance for the last time at the Caribbean sky, with the hope that the light that guided the moribund people and free them from the pain and suffering in their long trip to eternity. The horses, with desperation and confusion in the battlefield, were relaunched without horsemen that controlled them. The iron shoes of the legs produced fire when they made contact with rocks of the avenue. The carriage drivers were shooting orders that only the animals comprehended with feet in the air to make the horses keep the rhythm to the march. The explosion of the lashes in the air and the crying of the conductors scared the hell out of the horses that had their eyes closed to explode from the cavity because the heavy weight that was brought on top were expelling hot smoke, and saliva and baba-like gelatin was coming out from both sides of the mouths of the animals.

The horses were in pain from the pressure of the iron brakes between the tongue and the teeth of the mares and the horses that were pulling strength from where they did not have to relink with all the energy. Sometimes, the relinks terrified the animals, and they turned to crying in pain in the desperation of breathing without detaining the march to avoid the trespassing by the guns of the fire of slaves in revolution. The horse and the man were in danger in the encounter themselves in the battlefield. For the first time, the empire of the white French colonizer was confirming blood and fire in the new continent. The plantation system was reaching the end after centuries of exploitation of the black slaves in the Caribbean region that kept the slave system from the small island in the minor Antilles to Brazil. It seemed like the black soldiers were combating the implacable owners of the new world. The horses did not walk or trot; they wanted the enemies to know they came to Haiti to fight until the final battle until the horse riders would keep themselves on top of the horses, shooting and battling with the swords, which was a symbol of the pride of the Napoleon Bonaparte Army. The enormous beasts did not walk—they were flying.

His eyes were looking in only one direction, with his

sights to the front, like all the horses of the world look. Its legs barely touched the soil with their hooves. The *herraduras* were throwing fire to the contact with the rocks of streets. Like a trick tactic and the ability of the Napoleonic army a distance of the thirty-nine meters of the entrance to the military force, the carriages that were in line of the caravan formed a spectacular line. Six cars moved to the left and six moved to the right. This strategic trick confused the command of attack of the black rebels conducted by an official slave who ascended to First Lieutenant Jacobe Dominique. This young official, son of a Matinuen and Cimarron, was twenty-nine years and was being sent by Toussaint Louverture and accompanied by seven strong and robust rebels with the objective to surprise the mayor command of the invaders to kidnap the Countess Bonaparte.

This was a coup de grâce of the rebel Toussaint Louverture: "Bring them all alive! Everybody that goes in the biggest carriage must be in our custody without any harm. They are war detained, and we are responsible for their well-being. We want them good and healthy. I want Napoleon Bonaparte to know that this invasion will not succeed. The revolutionaries are not assassins like the plantations owners are. Also, bring me the white horse! I want Napoleon understand that our true intentions in this fight is to abolish slavery. The invaders are coming to continue with the exploitation of our people. It seems that they are not happy yet and satisfied with a system of exploitation that was established almost tree hundreds years ago. Enough with slavery system in Saint-Domingue!"

The official and his seven soldiers that complied with the important mission jumped off their horses, and they took off rapidly following Toussaint Louverture's orders to each of the carriage before it passed through the commandant's cannon that was like a natural tunnel that connected Cap-Haitien with the little savanna where the fortress general was located to serve as a military camp to the invaders' horses. These were the orders given by the supreme leader of the black rebel army.

Louverture's orders, who was famous as a great negotiator, could be contradicted for that seemed to be arbitrary. His intention was to kidnap the French delegation, especially Victor Emmanuel Leclerc, the Countess Bonaparte, and his son Dermide. Every one of them would have sufficient political value to force the emperor Napoleon Bonaparte to sit down in the negotiation table with the rebels of Saint-Domingue and find a pacific solution to the conflict between the plantation owners and the black army that was fight all over the country to get their liberation.

They represented to the just-born French Empire. Toussaint Louverture had many good conations in the French Crown due to his diplomatic abilities and his military knowledge. The revolutionary command had the information where Pauline and her family were traveling. Louverture gave the order to execute the plan. Then the especial command released their roses to attack by two sides. All of them were dressed with the same uniforms of the invaders. The officials of Napoleon kept a high speed. They were running in perfect formation, riding next to the caravans of the vanguard. For that reason, they were passing without being noticed. The rebels did exactly like Toussaint had ordered. Personally, Louverture had given the order to continue in a low-key manner to the carriage as much as they could without shooting. The plan was that that they would run in formation parallel to the caravans and produce the kidnapping in the moment exactly when the big coach was in the entrance of the tunnel.

First Lieutenant Jacobe Dominique was carrying the French flag. That confused the gendarmes who were protecting the mayor coach where the imperial family was riding in.

However, Victor Leclerc, who was a war veteran of many battles, was doing his own alertness and was doing his move in becoming vigilant. All of a sudden, by one of the mirrors of the carriages, he saw that the officer was getting too close with his horse in pure galloping fashion by the left flank. That produced some suspicions in Leclerc's mind since it was unusual that an official was riding with the French flag in the hand.

In a flash of a second, General Leclerc started wondering. In the second place, the three soldiers who were in charge of the custody were giants and black. Napoleon did not recruit in his army soldiers so tall nor so black. That was another alert for Victor Leclerc. The Creoles of Dessalines and Louverture were waiting in the right flank to take away the prisoners by the route that had being paved to carry on the kidnapping. But it backfired.

When the Commandant Leclerc noticed something that was about to happen, he told his wife, "Attention, Paoletta! Grab your son. Lay down on the floor! Do not lift your head. Keep your head down until I would give you the all-clear!"

At the beginning, the woman did not know what was going on. But she did what he asked her to do. It was an emergency of life or death.

The commandant pulled out his golden revolver. The gun was a wedding gift from his brother-in-law Napoleon when he got married to Pauline Bonaparte. General Leclerc aimed his golden revolver with his two hands because the carriage and the attacking team was already among them. He waited until they got close enough. When he had the soldier in his two holds of the revolver, rebels in a crossing position of his partner, the general controlled his respiration and shot and pulled out the man's shoulder with its arm part of his chest. The robust rebel, without having time to cry, went off flying through the air, falling and rolling down with his gigantic brown horse. The soldier and the animal went down rolling and rolling by the cliff of the hill that everybody named La Curve de La Mulate. The horse and mutilated body of the giant soldier disappeared between the forest of the tremendous abyss.

With that incident, Toussaint Louverture instructed and called off the operation. "Return if there is any wounded. I do not want a scratch on the imperial family. Pauline is a *metresa*. The Countess should not be touched, not even a hair thread. I repeat, the rebels are not assassins. We are soldiers who respect the human rights. I want Napoleon to know that our mission is to abolish the slavery system forever! The French Revolution and the guillotine were produced for changing the political establishment of the oligarchy and to abolish slavery. That is why we are fighting in Saint-Domingue: LIBERTED! FRATERNITE! EQUALITY FOR ALL! Vivre Saint-Domingue! Vivre La Patrie! La Hispaniole est pour noir!"

Nobody noticed the tragic incident except for Captain Murat, who was running very close to the carriage of Pauline and Victor Leclerc. He was given the order to protect the white horse that belonged to Napoleon. The other soldier officers thought that man who had flown through the air of a shot so effective had reached by one cannon of the French military.

Before the strategy was made, the carriage of the countess her husband encountered the free path to penetrate safely in the military fortress located outside the Cap-Haitien metropolitan area. This was an act of magic in the carriages before a signal constituting a half-moon formation. The strategy gave the chance to the mayor carriage that was bringing Leclerc- Bonaparte to enter without mayor consequence. But also, like it was expecting, it was an act of extreme bravery of the Commandant Leclerc before the soldier who was running before the dangerous run as he did, and the family that was under the search of Toussaint Louverture. That surprising military tactic of the French invaders caused so much commotion between the officials and commandants of the rebellion of Saint-Domingue, who, for the moment, believed to sing the victory in the initial tactic to kidnap the Countess Bonaparte, the General Leclerc, or Dermide, who was only fair for the French Empire.

A lot of people who were involved in the international conflict between Haiti and France—including Toussaint, Dessalines, Pauline, and Leclerc—commented with frequency the strategy to protect the Napoleon delegation from being kidnapped. For the rebel leaders and the French officers, that was a big challenge of heroic mission. That was a proof of love of the commandant for Pauline Bonaparte. If it was to have triumph, the revolution of the slaves would be terminated before its beginning. If the revisionary leaders, guided by the wise and brave Toussaint Louverture, was prepared for a kidnapped mission to circulate and create a trap for the mayor officials that were conducting the invasion, they made a big mistake too. It is probably comprehended to the strategy of the rebellion that General Victor Leclerc was truly the Supreme Command of the army of Napoleon Bonaparte. With this efficient military strategy, he demonstrated his titles and medals and other official recognitions he had earned through blood and fire. The most important for everybody was that this tactic formation cleared the route to the Countess and her husband. The way was free without complication in the big military fortress where they would pass the mayor part of time of his military campaign with the objective of destroying the rebellion of the slaves in Saint-Domingue. Thus, as for a magic trick, the seven horses lifted their front legs, showing their gigantic masculine members while they put the brakes to stop the carriages on the patio of fortress. The animals stopped all at the same time, producing an echo of triumph and defeat, of glory and power of the mysterious empire that was intent in that way, its demonstration of domain in the mysterious Caribbean region.

The Commander's cannon was imposed from the beginning of the French invasion. The rebels knew that if the commandant was aiming with his cannon, all was lost.

The horses with their strained muscles kept their legs up in the air as a demonstration to the masses that was gathering to give the welcome to the imperial family. The others were there out of curiosity before the presence of the emperor's sister and her husband the general. Now, they knew that they were in a safe place because they escaped the great ambush earlier. In the initial combat, all the officials noticed that their military leader, Victor Leclerc, had taken an ascertained measured decision of continuing the march after the disembarking operation. If the rebels would remain anchored in the open sea near the Cap-Haitien port, they would be attacked with destructive fire, or they would be torched the first night before having a chance to reach the land. Besides, the ships that were located in both of the bays would be destroyed with high numbers of soldiers perishing before touching the Haitian soil. In other words, the loss would be catastrophic for the French forces.

Commander in Chief Leclerc never underestimated the capacity of an intelligence in the military arts of the leader of the rebel Toussaint Louverture. Before arriving Haiti during the time of preparation in Europe, Victor Leclerc had studied the life and the strategies of the revolutionary leaders. The French had already studied each of the leaders, from Mackandal to Louverture. They knew the strength and weakness as well as their belief in leader capacity in their motives and in their participation in the black slavery rebellion. He knew also that he had to do his homework to understand the modem operandi of the revolutionary forces guiding the fight among the black slaves in Haiti. He knew that his triumph would depend on deciphering the military tactics in the encounter and vicinity of Toussaint and the army of blacks.

Now that the French soldiers were safe, the commandants were shouting consignations in favor of General Leclerc. He was the true leader and a true hero. Although the military in the French high command had won the first battle that allowed the rebel leaders of Saint-Domingue to give a hard punch of surprise to the military committee, they had won a great victory in penetrating with its gigantic ships inside the port and mobilizing the troop in the piers close by and occupied the Isle of the Turtle. These were important steps in the exchange that was initially employed by the French invaders that experienced triumph left by the ego of the French. But the first sign of victory in the initial part of the invasion was for the forces of Napoleon when they penetrated the Haitian territory, passing victoriously what was strategically put in practice by Toussaint Louverture.

This military encounter served as the punishment and experience to the Commandant Leclerc to comprehend that one thing was to battle with La Grande Armée, combating in the sea and in the open savanna of the European battlefield. Another thing was to fight back while being attacked by surprise within an enemy of black slaves that were coming out from any place without rules of war nor protocol negotiators. It was an unconventional war being fought by the black slaves who were tired of the French exploitation of the plantation system that treated the black slaves worse than animals who had to comply with the journal of hard work with limited food from sunrise to sunset. It was a fight without international conventions that would prevent the violation of the conquerors of the defeated. However, if Napoleon Bonaparte did not impose his wish, the slaves would dominate the entire territory of the Hispaniola. They wanted freedom. Napoleon wanted the domain of the colonials of Saint-Domingue.

The black slaves' rebellion was in its highest point at the arrival of the Napoleon military forces to Saint-Domingue. It was one thing to confront enemies in the open ocean, and it was another thing to go through the middle of an irregular army of revolutionary fighting for their freedom, with the wish of defeating and eliminating the invaders at all cost, employing the methods that are necessary with the purpose of wiping out the enemy, pulverizing them until the last standing soldier was breathing.

In the initial battlefield, the losses of te French were a lot because the attacks directed by Toussaint Louverture had taken them by surprise. The powerful free army and navy were guided by General Victor Emmanuel Leclerc. The commandant of the invaders never thought that his strategy would be uncounted with different war tactics so effective in the battlefield as the ones used in the ambush by the rebels, guided by the drums with its sound and strong rhythm that made the men and beasts crazy. One thing that left the French Army stunned was when they started shooting, the revolutionary's combatants fell, but as soon as they fell, they stood up again, fighting like nothing happened. Sometimes they were trespassed by the round cannon bullets, leaving a hole that you could see through, and mysteriously, they continued advancing in the front line. The wounded black soldiers continued shooting and advancing as if the bullets of the *trabucazos* did not do any harm to the black slaves fighting in the front line. They walked like zombies. It seemed that they were possessed by a strange force coming from beyond that was giving them power to throw the French soldiers in the air and their guns of fighters like they were paper dolls.

But the shakiness of the French commanders was that the official of the high command of Saint-Domingue in the revolutionary side wore the same uniforms and medals and decorations of the French official. This alarmed also the soldiers under Leclerc's army. The general was in shock for this detail. It is possible that Toussaint Louverture had intelligence formations of the invasion from France before the invasion started to take place. His two sons were French citizens, and they were in Paris when the invasion was in progress. But the bad tongues that are in charge of spreading the gossip said that the leader of the black revolution had spies in the power spheres of the French crown. If the commandant of the French Army though that it was an easy invasion to occupy without resistance the Saint-Domingue territory without suffering considerable lots, very soon he came to the conclusion that he calculated badly in his military plans.

If the leaders of the rebellion thought that the drums, the war crying, the prayers, and the voodoo ceremonies were enough to contain and defeat the invasion, they also calculated in the wrong way. They would think that if Napoleon's sister had arrived with the invaders, something big was about to happen to the French Crown. Obviously, the presence of Pauline Bonaparte accompanying her husband, who was the most important general of the army of Napoleon in Europe, was a sign of the importance of that invasion for the French Republic and from the expanding Napoleon Empire.

Saint-Domingue was the epoch of economic support, not to mention that the bourgeoisie was bon from the Haitian power. Haiti was the main principal to the export and import that represented the political and economic expansion of Gala Republic. At that point in history, Saint-Domingue was the richest colony of the entire French empire from the Pacific to the Caribbean region, including the Louisiana Poseidon de Nor America.

Toussaint had the details of the invasion before the invaders could start sailing from France. In the capital of Paris, the invasion was not a secret. Everybody knew that the French Army was preparing an invasion to the Caribbean. Napoleon had a lot of soldiers north of Africa without activities. They were well prepared, but they had time to be mercenaries, and Napoleon knew that incorporating them would be an important access to the regular army that was already being prepared to expand the empire. The many political and military analysts of the epoch commented that by spreading the news of the projected invasion to Saint-Domingue, it was a strategy of Napoleon because he wanted to abort the invasion. In other words, the emperor did want to send his best soldiers to fifth in the Caribbean. He, like other kings and governors from the past, did not want to intervene with a regular army in Haiti or the other islands. His plans were to be ready to invade the Russian Empire and other territories in the Far East like as if he wanted to emulate Genghis Khan, Peter the Great, Charles Magnum, Dario El Grande, and other leaders who conquered as much as they could. Napoleon was the new Julius Caesar with a bigger ego, ready to conquer and control.

At that point, the black rebellion in Haiti did not take him by surprise. Napoleon thought that the Caribbean region was under the control of his boots. In his mind, Moscow was the objective. Waterloo in Europe, Haiti in the Caribbean region, and the intention to conquer Russia was the tragic triangle.

A lot of things were happening in Europe. There was a turmoil, a political upheaval in terms of the many crowns that were falling, like a domino effect, one after the other. Napoleon Bonaparte had his hands full organizing the crown in Italy, Spain, Austria, and the commotion of the czars Russia has produced, shaking in power that gave the impression that all nations would collapse, even Italy, and Napoleon was taking advantage of the power vacuum left after the French Revolution that threatened to destroy the column that sustained the last stand of the oligarchy as the strongest layer of the economic and political structure around the world.

The future emperor would need until the last soldier to continue conquering territory after territory in the four cardinal points of the globe. All of Europe was up to the point of claudication, and surrendering to the Napoleonic Consul was the first step to become emperor of the world. Some of the crowns in Europe, only by mentioning the name Bonaparte, started running without putting any resistance to his psychological and fighting forces. Only Russia was standing.

Then came the faraway Orient in the Pacific. At present, Saint-Domingue was turning out to be the rock inside Bonaparte's boot to the aspirations of expanding his domain and power to the confines of the earth. In the distance, one could listen to a rhythmic beat of the strong drums that vibrated in the air, announcing the rebellion in that plantation:

PUM-KUTU-PUM-PUM-PUM-KUTU-PUM!   –PUM! KUTUM-PUM PUM!

The official carriage that was transporting the Countess Pauline Bonaparte was hit by that impact so big that little bit was missed so that the coach and its passengers would be thrown inside the abyss. But the seven horses that were pulling the carriage, after throwing around terror, kept firm and stable and started galloping. They maintained the directions under the command of the driver. The man was the best coach driver who saved Napoleon when he almost got killed in Paris. The night that Napoleon Bonaparte was almost assassinated in a Parisian theater, he was the same chauffeur who saved his life. The emperor never forgot their experience and made sure that this driver would never be placed elsewhere.

Napoleon was famous for being grateful to people who did him a favor. Eve, the love of his life, who was Desiree Clark from Marseille, lent him some money, and he paid her back after becoming emperor with a substantial monetary recompense.

The skillful driver conducted the carriage in a magisterial way for the streets of Paris in two wheels instead of four. In front of so much commotion and apparatus, the residents of the Avenue of Le Champs Elisee were putting out their heads with open mouths in shock to see such acrobatics. Some of the Paris neighbors in apparent franticness and shock were afraid of the worst and made the sign of the cross; meanwhile, their lives were waiting for the fatal finality of that noisy race. At beginning, they thought that the commotion of one of the spectacles was like magic to those from the Middle East and Far East who were now the residents of the City of Lights, as they called Paris. To those curious of the place, it never passed through their minds that the carriage in two wheels looked like it was about to turn over, and inside as a passenger was the Emperor of France, who just got out under the attack with bullets and swords in the theater of the French capital.

Now the skillful coach driver, in a fantastic demonstration of his abilities in controlling of the horses, had saved the life of Leclerc Bonaparte and their son Dermide. Dermide was, at the moment, the only legitimate heir of the empire that was about to be born in Europe. The Countess was in shock after she felt the noise of the bullet and the closeness of the enormous precipice that was waiting for them down the hill in the mountain called La Malate, but she was like her brother. Pauline was not afraid of anything. She feared nobody. This time she claimed and prayed for her family, saying, "Oh mon Dieu! Saint Sorro and Metresilis, faite la protection de Notre famille!"

Her husband made believe that he did not hear anything from his wife. But He felt curiosity when he heard his Pauline mentioning in a high voice the goddess of voodoo known as the Metresse. Victor was concentrated in the combat, and he was alert in case another rebel command would approach them to attack by surprise.

The Countess embraced her son Dermide, who was just five years of age, with her sense of protection that a mother shows when danger is getting close. She embraced him with such force, grasping him to her chest. The boy was sleeping under heavy medication in the moment of the attack. General Leclerc kept himself in silence, looking to the battlefield and making signs to the officers who where running in their horses surrounding the carriage to protect the imperial family from the shootings of guns from different calibers, obeying and carrying on every order sent by their commandant. They made signs of salutation and attention and continued passing the orders to thousands of soldiers and subofficers. They provided a gigantic shield of protection to the carriage of the countess under her husband and the son.

It was an ambush they had fallen into when they got out of the ships. The invaders fell under heavy arm attack forces of the rebels that were coming out from all directions. The plan was for the slaves to give a coup de grâce to the invaders coming out from the ocean. The strategy of the revolutionary was to give a hard group to surprise them without permitting the French gendarmes to establish themselves by taking position in firm land upon arriving in the island of Saint-Domingue.

"Capitan Murat! March! March right away to the back of the formation, and bring me the horse Milito! Do not forget that this horse belongs to the Emperor Napoleon. He sent the horse to serve as means of transportation in Saint-Domingue. The emperor wanted to protect the horse in good condition in case that he had to be present in the northern territory of the Hispaniola. Make sure that the horse did not suffer any harm. If it was saved from the cannon, it was a miracle. I knew that this horse was a shield. Still today the world in France says that this horse has the testicles blinded. Its balls are made of iron. Milito's muscles are made of iron. Everybody in the world in France say that this animal has the testicles of steel. It was so hard as Napoleon's brother-in-law was able to ride on top of Milito because the horse recognize Pauline's touch. Go ahead, Murat!"

"Oui, Mon Commandant!" responded the official. Then Captain Murat marched to the vanguard to search for the animal.

As a military reaction for being a critic for imitating his brother-in-law Napoleon, Victor Leclerc stood up with his head out of the carriage for the soldiers to see, and officials could see that he was without harm during the recent attack in the ambush. He wanted everyone to know that he was in good health. Without fear for the bullets that were flying from different directions, the Commandant Leclerc lifted his sword with his right hand. It was a sign of his military valor that had distinguished him up to the highest position within the military steps under the command of Napoleon Bonaparte.

At that special moment, the commandant called the soldiers' attention, and to motivate them, the commandant said, "Je, avec moi position of Commandant of the Grate Armee, Victor Emmanuel Leclerc demand your attention name de moi Imperator, Napoleon Bonaparte. Attention!

"Do not fear to the attack of the black slaves that always come from behind. They attack by surprise and singing estrange songs with drums and long futons [tube] that they pushed the air for one small hole, and the instruments make a terrifying noise for the French soldiers.

The black fighters come from behind, and they intruded the gun from behind. Do not be distracted by thinking something else. I am talking of the sharp knives that slaves use to kill. You would feel the cold steel breaking the flesh from behind. You have no chance, not even to cry or to pray. Do look back because they come like shadows at night. You're lucky if you feel his warm breath like a snake. Then they disappear in the plantation like ghosts.

"The rebels only attack from behind when you feel terrified and scared for the sound of drums from Africa and the language they use to make sure that we lose our mind. I went to conduct a fight in the North Africa, and I saw the black slaves being under the spell of being from Ultratumb, where the dead are presently living from the closer cemetery to fight. When you see them coming with holes in their body, do not run. I command you in the name of France, Napoleon, and the Revolution to fight to the end. Do forget the black penetrated from behind. As Milito bite the mare before penetrating when you are not expecting them because they are not soldiers. They are traitors. Black revolutionary vanguards at night searching for blood like they were vampires. Do not allow them to scare you with crying of wars and the drums of the slaves. Let us combat to the end for our Emperor! Pour La Patrie! Por notre famielles! The countess Bonaparte! To the attack mon gendarmes! Long live Napoleon! The victory is for ours! Baokeib us iyr cibdyctir! Freedom! Fraternity! And equality!"

If it was not for an official from cavalry that had already recovered Milito, the General Leclerc would have fallen destroyed. The official gave a spectacular jump on top of the carriage and pushed the general down seconds before the bullet hit from a cannon destroyed one of the carriages that was running in pairs. If not for the brave young official, the invasion of Saint-Domingue would have a different turn right at the first battle.

When General Leclerc noticed that he saved his life, that he was up to the point to be destroyed by the cannon of the rebels of Saint-Domingue, babbling a few foul words against the rebels of Saint-Domingue, the maledictions were against the slaves that were attacking to wipe out the carriages and French soldiers. He looked straight to the officer. He made the military salute of thanking him for saving his life. Immediately, he ordered all the columns to accelerate the march because he did not want his army to fall trapped in another ambush prepared by the disembarking slaves and soldiers of Toussaint Louverture.

Under this emotional speech, the general said, "If death demands my presence, I am prepared for the final march to encounter myself with the Creator in the hands of my Lord. Now, let us go to the battle, comrades, that the victory will be ours! The triumph is for the glory of our Patrie. Napoleon is present in Saint-Domingue like he has always been in all battlefields for the glory, the power, and the pride of the French nation. Napoleon is waiting for us to fight with pride and be brave if we have to sacrifice our life under shield and the French flag!"

Pauline knew that something gravely bad was happening. Her husband was a pragmatic officer. It was not of him to mix God with the war that he was leading in the Haitian capital.

Now he was not too talkative, except when he was arranging or giving orders to the soldiers in the battlefield. A lot of his officials talked about him being silent but calculating. He had learned the phrases and personal gestures of Napoleon in such a way that the soldiers and offices called him the blond Napoleon. Furthermore, besides being one of the most handsome and elegant officers, he was a very mysterious man because he did no talk too much. As the saying goes, "People who drink a lot talk a lot." However, General Leclerc could drink a lot, and still he was always concentrated on the next move or strategy of the military, army, and navy in his command. When he drank a lot, that was one of his favorite pastimes. His nickname was Pepe Bottle.

Victor Leclerc was in that moment when Pauline felt a chill that was not normal with her ardor in the tropical environment. The last words of her husband chilled the thirty-three vertebra of her beautiful body. Victor Leclerc never referred himself to the event of death, and neither did his brother-in-law Napoleon Bonaparte.

In the mouth of the Commandant Leclerc, these phrases he sent to the Supreme Creator had the sense of a premonition of what would come in his military carrier. For that, Pauline continued passing the counts of the rosary of white pearls that she kept as a precious gift given by her father, Charles Bonaparte, when she turned nine years of age. He gave the rosary when Pauline received the Confirmation as a Catholic in the Roman Church by the bishop of Ajaccio in Corcega Island.

Now Pauline was babbling in silence as if she was praying. Each time that her life was in danger, she pulled the rosary. For that inexplicable reason, she always had the crucifix hooked up between her breasts.

Leclerc pronounced these words to the officials and soldiers to repeat them with the objective that the discourse would be passed, rolling from mouth to mouth. In that way, his orders will get from the front of the battlefield to the vanguard and to the rear guard. The commandant wanted that his speech for all the regions was heard. They were not to give any sign of weakness and vacillation to the enemy, and neither would he shout a sign of being afraid in this moment so crucial as they were in the middle of battle with a very strong enemy with the mission to win or to be defeated, to kill or to be killed.

General Leclerc knew that the revolutionary leaders Jean Jack Dessalines and Toussaint Louverture were experts in strategy in the field of military enterprises and that they had been trained by the best experts in the European wars. He became aware of that when he noticed that the officials and some of the elite unities of the rebel armies had uniforms very similar to the ones used by the French forces of occupation. That is why Leclerc commented in between teeth his preoccupation to nobody to know: "This battle will be definite. The ferocity of the commands of slaves of Saint-Domingue is tremendous! The Haitians are worse than the devil!"

The official pulled the reins on his horse. The animal stood up on its hind legs, showing its enormous balls and reproductive member. For a very strange reason, the French horses always ran with a virile natural instrument standing like a mahogany bait. After a few second in this position, the officer gave a half round, touching the tip of his beret, and went with the regular phrase. "At your service, mon commandant!"

The young man penetrated the flesh of the horse. He ran as if he was running from the devil to comply with the mandate from his commandant. In his departure to get back to the formation, he did not notice that the horse Milito was already being recovered by Captain Francois Murat.

When the trumpet sounded, the French gendarmes that were in charge of the custody of the fortress entrance took strategic positions. The observation towers of defense to the four cardinal points covering the entire view of the fortress of the navy and army forces belonged to Napoleon Bonaparte in the invasion of Saint-Domingue. The carriages entered at high speed, one after the other. The official bandoliers jumped off their horses. The soldiers were trained to dismount the horse from behind to give the least amount of time for the enemies in case of an attack by surprise. After they stepped on firm land, they were looking one to the other, giving the hand, probably doubting what they saw in the first battle. They doubted that they were alive after the despicable ambush of the rebel army of Toussaint Louverture and Dessalines.

In the meantime, the officials and gendarmes came to the animals and reviewed each part of the horses and mare to see if they received any wounds during the violent battle. After this step, the carriage ambulance came in bringing the dead, the wounded, and some of the servants. That was the routine that they used to do as a sign that they just came out woundless in the initial battle during the entrance in Cap-Haitien, which served as the capital of Saint-Domingue.

3

Pauline Was Not Touched

The seven trumpets located in the seven observation towers of tortures began the ceremony of military occupation with the lifting of the French flag and the execution of the hymn "The Marseillaise" of France. At the long distance, a strong and rasping voice like thunder was making a speech so powerful that the echo came down the from many directions addressed to the present and absent in the French language and to the patois creole of Saint-Domingue.

"Attention! Mon soldiers, the children of Bouckman, Mackandal, Saint Socorro, and Matresilis! Nous son ici pour la Revolution! We are here for the liberation of our black slaves. We have been in chains for three hundred years! The plantation owners have no compassion for the blacks slaves, and we are here to liberate them with torch, the machete, and any gun that we can use to wipe out the white plantation that are sucking our blood with efficiency of vampires!"

It was in that ambient, that scenery of conflict and historic belligerence in which we encounter the Caribbean region in the last part of the arbores of the year 1800. The ten years of summary judgments being carried on the guillotine cut the neck without regarding the aristocrats, the nobles, bourgeois, females and male, and was repeating itself in Haiti. Pauline Bonaparte, to equal that the soldiers and the officials of invaders' army, was presented to the grand theater that was developing in Saint-Domingue, having into the center of the Cap-Haitien that had arrived with the glory and the protection of her brother, Napoleon Bonaparte. Even though they ambushed them at their arrival to Saint-Domingue, she knew that it was to transform her from Countess to Queen.

The words of her brother not only were coming out of her mind, neither out from her behind: "Go quietly to Saint-Domingue. You are my beloved sister. And you will be crowned as a Queen with all power in the Caribbean region. I love you with all my heart. Do not forget my promise, and keep in your mind that you are Bonaparte for all eternity!"

The Countess was coming accompanied by her husband, Victor Emmanuel Leclerc, that even his ascent as a rich man in the countryside of France, they did not stop escalating more and more in the Parisian society. Pauline's ambitions were compiling with her husband's being power hungry. Actually, his military ambition has taken him to advance in Napoleon's army. Victor demonstrated his ambition, risking his life to show Napoleon that he was an aggressive fighter in the battle field. In that way we encountered very close the powerful Crown of France. Now in this place, in this moment, it was a point of having a second marriage with the glory. After all, in this moment, he was a successful carrier officer accompanying his brother-in-law, Napoleon Bonaparte Ramolino.

The gran amphitheater of Cap-Haitien was to be in the form of an enormous screen in which it could see and appreciate the historic event of major relevance, as much for the colony of Saint-Domingue as for the Caribbean region with the slavery and plantation system that they had stashed by the French expansion under the leadership of Napoleon. General Leclerc was not satisfied with his military. He was also a hero of the one-thousand-war combat. But the physical scars have not dampened his volunteer and military ambition.

The official had blond hair like gold with the blue eyes of such intensity that drove the most beautiful women to lose their minds and increase a hormone hurricane, making them surrender before Victor Leclerc's presence. The paradox was that the husbands of the beautiful French ladies were fighting to next to the great commander in the battlefield under his guidance and courage. For his soldiers and officials, the elegance of Victor Leclerc had trespassed the end that people had against him. In the contrary before his presence, the men under his command inclined themselves of respect and was to distinguish in the combats how bloody the battlefield would be. Everybody respected Commandant Leclerc.

The battlefield of Saint-Domingue was the most aggressive the soldiers of the Napoleon Army had confronted. It was an amphitheater of death. They were there pushed to imminent death that produced a sensation of terror. His love for Pauline was passionate. He was a general of excellent attitudes, very gallant and a gentlemen. These qualities attracted the women that surrounded him. Pauline was jealous like a panther when her meat was in danger. She was possessive, a passionate and mysterious beast. She was very sensual and possessed a lot of special secrets that she used at the moment of making love with the most virile men of her enrolment.

The Countess Bonaparte had a rustic education. She was educated at home, so she was inclined to be more genuine and pragmatic. After all, she was the result of military formation in the years more important of his development in the many young hormones that were already reacting as a storm, and doing that journey took away years from body, making her young body vibrate and shake under the emotional reaction that was in interior flame.

The importance of this invasion of the powerful emperor Bonaparte marked his youngest sister in such a form that the events and the final result divided Pauline between the war and the death of her husband. Her spiritual transformation was profound. The new knowledge increased her erotic capacity and sensual performance to return to Roma and Paris, stunned as a zombie of pearl skin, but a controlling woman for the men who had the intention of discovering the passion and the eruption that was burning in her matrix.

Three years were enough to attribute the feminine to reach the cupid of heroism and sensualism that would accompany her until her departure to the terrain world.

The most famous artists like Antonio Canova became crazy for Pauline from the first moment, and the first night they taught some of the tricks for her to love. If they loved her or not, only Pauline would know it. A lot of her lovers preferred to believe in it before they investigated more over there if she allowed to penetrate in his body. Through her thought of Pauline, she could travel in time and come and go in the past of the events that were most important in her life. The changes and behavior in her acting in the physical as in the spiritual created a veil of the mysterious infinity of levels around her personality. If she was born like this, it is not easy to know that maybe her passion at the different hours of loving was like a volcano erupting. For inside and for outside, Pauline Bonaparte was like a tornado in a cascade of the eternal turbulence.

Suddenly, the military fortress belonged to Napoleon's soldiers in Saint-Domingue, and they turned it into a camp. It was a run of the service that was getting ready to initiate her working journal like the most efficient bees, coordinated, each working with exact symmetry. It was the manner to satisfy the queen bee that would arrive at her home. But this time she did not come alone. The Countess Pauline Bonaparte was coming, like in numerous occasions, accompanied by her husband, the general.

Far away, competing with the falling of the night, the noise created by two cannons was preceded by the lights of explosions of the artillery of French soldiers that were fighting inch by inch of the terrain to the revolutionaries of the black rebellion that was threatening to cover the territory of the island of Saint-Domingue.

The drums of the military band and the musical instruments of the mercenaries from Ireland made one feel inclined of enormous trumpets that sang the marches of the rhymes of the soldiers that marched. The sound was filling the Commack with the musical parties that were contained, motivated by the gendarmes of the country to fight until the last dropoff to defeat the movement of the black rebels in Haiti.

The battlefield was one of blood and terror. It was a Dantesque scenario. The slaves attacked the rebels (*cimarrones*) and Creoles and some that were being bought to be dressed against the white colonizer within the French plantations had being implacable. The flames and the body were expanding all around Saint-Domingue. It was burning in all the northern part of Haiti where one could reach his naked eye. Beyond the Antilles manors and mayors, the territory was covered by the drums of the slaves of Saint-

Domingue, hiding and squeezing the machete, cutting like the most efficient guillotine everything that they encountered in their path that belonged to the French colony in Saint-Domingue. Each plantation in the island was converted in infernal volcanoes. The situation in each plantation was a nightmare for the white women, mulattos, and Creoles who were humble servers of the white owners of European decadence.

The crying of terror for the infernal tragedy was confused with the wailing of the women that fell in the arms of the black slaves. They were violated (raped) without modesty and without compassion.

But with the diabolic desires of the savage beasts, the colonizers were running in shock from one side to the other to escape the fire and the edge of the machetes. The voices of black slaves searching for freedom were so strong that only the cry could make a person crazy knowing that the machete would cut the neck, and the blacks will penetrate the women without regard of the age.

The slaves were coming, crying with all the power of their lungs, "FREEDM OR DEATH! DEATH TO THE WHITE OWNERS OF THE PLANTATIONT SYSTEM IN SAINT-DOMINGUE! VIVRE MACKANDAL METRESILIS, EL CONGO, LA AFRIQUE, AND TOUSSAINT LOUVERTURE!"

PUM-KUTU-PUM-PUM-PUM-KUTU-PUM-PUM-!

The savanna and the hills looked like a tsunami of enormous black waves balancing over the city of Cap-Haitien, Port-au-Prince, and Ouanaminthe. The waves of black slaves were brightening by sporadic flashes of the metal doing their liberating work. The machetes, the swords and the mochas were opening a path in all directions that the slaves found resistance. Their minds were set to be free in the land of hills as the taino called the island of Quisqueya and Aiyiti. The leftovers of the attackers were a devastating panorama of death. Not even the animals survived the massacre. Everywhere your eyes could reach, it was destruction and death.

The first attack was enormous. Nothing white, brown, and other color animals or item belonging to the French plantation would survive, and the pass to the frontier in the Spanish territory was impossible. Crossing to the frontier to the oriental part of Hispaniola of the island was blocked. The escaping toward Port-au-Prince in the south was a nightmare. The only exit that was open passed to the dock of Cap-Haitien. In the northern bay, they got in and they got out. This was the only door to arrive to the ships angled or anchored in the dock of the Atlantic Ocean. No far away, the plantation owners of sugar with the sugar mills and their mill to take out the *melao*, guarapo, which was juice coming out after squeezing the sugar cane, the coffee grains, the cocoa, and indigo were looking impotent. The little island of the Tortuga from where they had been exiting his ancestors toward the main land named Haiti. The buccaneers and filibusters came from Europe and lived there for hundreds of years.

The colonizers that ran to the main land not only had time to consider sentimentalism and remember the mysterious Isla La Turtle that served as a nest for their ancestors converted in the colony most prosperous of the French expansionist plan. Now, no person was thinking in saving the skin. No one had time to reflect too much to detain in the road to the oriental part of Cuba. Santiago de Cuba was waiting with open arms like a mother waiting because she does not have power to save her children from the ferocity of the savage beast, the wait desperate for their protection. But the major obstacles was not the machete or the violation of the black mobs that were advancing like a tsunami of big and destructive waves of blood covering the territory of Saint-Domingue from west to east and from north to south. The greatest barrier was the ninety miles that separated Cuba from Haiti in the most dangerous stretch of the Jamaican winds. That treacherous water has swallowed big ships with the entire load and human cargo. In that stretch, it is deeper than the Canal de la Mona, la Corrientes de of Caribbean Sea, and Atlantic Ocean, reaching great turbulence from the sea.

The waves go up so high until reaching the clouds and come back down to the deep abyss, vomiting foam like the giants Poseidon and Diana making love with pleasure and desperation. The ships were breaking down in pieces as if they were made from carton. It was a mysterious force that nobody knew where the devils went to stop with its loads. In his running and desperation, a lot of colonizers that were launching with their families took it as a mercy suicide to avoid the machete of the violation of the blacks with hunger and morbidity against women of all ages. They were thrown themselves to the mercy of the turbulent waters of the Atlantic, Ocean after losing their family, their goods, and the reason. A lot of the plantation owners pushed their sons and daughters first. Then they threw themselves and their wives, and then they committed the ultimate sacrifice before the mochas, machetes, or knives cut their necks and the heads. They were crazy for the sound of the African drums and the scary and chilling sound of the machetes and mochas. They were running without stopping, not knowing where to go until their legs kept them on their feet.

In the end, they would see the light of an implacable sun that was the calcination of the skin and the mind. Others, even though knowing the sexual ambition of the rebels that aspired to satisfy as hungry dogs their sexual drives of releasing adrenaline that was running inside their luxurious bodies before the oppression, they dared not to look back to the plantation that they left behind.

The women were waiting, shaking with the unwanted sexual encounter. They were afraid of some family vein of bravery from beyond to make them go back and confront the attackers that were burning their plantations and were having sex in the open field with their wives without paying attention the age or the crying of the early penetration of an unexpected virile member with the hurry of a violation load of hates, revanchist, and revelry.

The most irresponsible and cowardly thing being there for hundreds of years when they imposed their colonizers' establishment and domain, in their departure, some of them left behind their wives and children, scalping like souls taken by the devil toward the Oriental part of Cuba that was placing distance far, regardless of the closeness. But the terrified crying of the one who fell under the edge of the sword, the machetes, and the fire flame pit made the departure more terrifying. The women, the elders, and the children were waiting in a dead-end route without exit. For them, the running of the territory was an impossible mission.

Three centuries had already passed so quickly, and it felt like the time was rushing over the region, and the slaves did not even notice after the establishment of the plantation system meddled the use of the slavery most ferric of the Caribbean region. Now as a colony of France, it was being passed of the west part of the island because Spain was not interested in the High land and Montaigne land of Ayiti, as the *taino* used to call the west of the Island. He passed on the buccaneers and the filibusters in the Island La Tortue among the development of the importance of the skin commerce, rum of sugar cane, perfume, and indigo that the just-born industry of the European modeling enterprise had created a new social cast in powerful France. The bourgeoise had a fortress with the richness of Saint-Domingue. To the great Napoleon, to contain the river of blood that was threatening with expanding by all the Caribbean region.

The colonizer owners of the plantations in the northern part of Saint-Domingue arriving to the ships were under collective and infernal craziness. They were delirious, talking to themselves and praying. Women and men were running like crazy animals while they were losing everything: animals, the possessions, the land, the sugar mills, leaving the plantation being covered with destructive fire. Nothing would survive this carnage. It happened fast like a blowing tornado. It was the tsunami initiated by the French Revolution right in the heart of the motherland. Europe was burning, and so was the Caribbean region under the domain of Napoléon *Bonaparte*. Saint-Domingue was losing its money, its wealthiest, inclining the dignity as human beings. Without stopping, the big black tsunami took the name to be registered in history as *THE HAITIAN REVOLUTION*.

Behind the terrifying sound of the African drums that continued to spread throughout the vast territory of Saint-Domingue, it was like a contagious powerful force that was calling every black slave to start the humongous journal of abolishing slavery with their own blood and flesh. Each beat of the African drums began palpitating as it was the heart of the entire Caribbean island that was under French regime. The sound was so strong and powerful that Spain was shaking while Napoléon was fighting the Haitian Revolution. Spaniards played by what they heard from the violent events in Saint-Domingue. They made believe that their kind not care about was happening.

The conquistadors were terrified for the Haitian Revolution. The Spanish Crown not only had the big island under their control like Cuba, the Hispaniola, and Puerto Rico, but they control partially or totally a great part of Latin America and part of the USA, like La

Florida and Louisiana and Mexico. Spaniards have a black population being exploited from Veracruz in Mexico, the entire Central America to Venezuela, Colombia, Peru, and Ecuador. Millions of black slaves and the oppressed indios were in chains, waiting for the sound of freedom brought by the African drums that started reaching their ears and their mind to break free from the slavery system that was established by the Europeans since the Great Encounter of the continents took place in 1492.

Behind was left the immobile bodies of their family. The women were violated; the old and the children assassinated. Lifeless. That was a Dantesque scenario filled with blood and bodies everywhere you looked. This part of the island of Hispaniola was converted into a humongous cemetery with the cadavers and dying wounded bodies covering what was supposed to be saint land. The region was in the middle of a pit of vengeance carried on in a final judgment of the black slaves who had been battling during centuries to make a change in the exploitation method established by the white plantation owners. The blacks wanted a more human treatment from the plantation patrons that the wet of the black slaves and the blood that was spilled by the workers in the sugar mills did not have a bittersweet taste, so bitter like the *retama*. They wanted that the bloody rope of the mayoral did not fall with so infernal ferocity over the naked backs and shoulders of whom was hit with its working power and energy sustaining the sugar mills drifting *guarapo*, melee, azucar, ron sudor, and suete melasse to increase the wealth of the French crown kings and queens who were living la dolce vita all over the world.

The colony of Saint-Domingue became the richest colony within the French Empire. Now it was a big trouble because the French crown remained indifferent for hundreds of years. Spain was losing territories due to selling the land to other powers, selling land that did not belong to Spain anyway. Slaves were working to empower the nobles, the oligarchies, and the bourgeoisie of the motherland. This was brutal slavery. France was the visible head of the empire. Haiti or Saint-Domingue was the central motor of this big machine of production, power, and glory, which kept the goods, money going to Europe from the Caribbean region, to feed and maintain the crowns and kingdoms of the world. Behind was left an inquisition of killing, desolation, destruction, and crying—terrifying crying, whose infernal repercussion was expanding from the mountains. Crossing the rivers and streams, everybody would listen to the terrified sounds of the chains as they were broken once and for all the tidiness of slavery.

Saint-Domingue was a battlefield where the enemies involved were combating to live or to die to conquer. They were fighting with the conviction to destroy owners of the plantation and triumph in their rebel endeavors. If on the contrary they would die in the final fight, their souls would fly toward the freedom land of their mother African land from where they had being uprooted for the ambition and avarice of the colonizers of the Antilles. It was as they wanted. They would still be winners even after sacrificing their lives fighting against the French Empire.

But now the white colonizers were running disoriented and terrorized by what was coming with drum sounds and the machetes cutting the Caribbean air in two like an efficient guillotine. Abandoned to their own luck, the white plantation owners were confused because of the ambulant instability politics that was occurring in the recently born French Republic. The slaves pushed for the airs or the French Revolution; they were coming guided, according to their beliefs, for the gods from the beyond. They were acting with fire and machetes. It was the inquisition of the Haitian Revolution to abolish slavery and impose the black nation as they dreamed.

Pum-Kutupum-Pum-Pum-Kutupum-kutum-Pum-Pum...!

The revolutionaries, libertos, and cimarrones under the leadership of Toussaint Louverture, with the contagious African drums, had created its own form of *castigo* songs and dances, jumps and rituals that represent acts of violence. It created its own way of punishment for the white plantation owners. The savage guillotine was the machetes that were moving in all directions, cutting everything that they encountered in the chaos of the rebellion. The French military forces that were arriving at Saint-Domingue have never realized that the war theater of the slaves would be so terrified. The invaders of France arrived with fury, and caused all the forces to suffocate and dominate the black rebels.

However, it was for something that the imperial army and the special forces have arrived to Saint-Domingue to comb the entire Caribbean land.

The soldiers and officials had been combating in Prussia, Spain, and all over Europe.

But those involved by the order of Napoleon had arrived to the same usual place after becoming a very skillful army of mercenaries who were coming to participate in the scenario after serving a very important and long mission in the northern part of Africa right above the Sahara Desert.

Coming to the Caribbean with nothing but the big war that was being in the battlefield of Saint-Domingue or self-motivation in preparation for the big fight with Moscow with a pack of horses and mares of pure race, which were for the commandants of Napoleon Bonaparte. The animals were used to the sound of the cannons of war and the crying of the horsemen.

The soldiers were dressed strongly armed with swords and guns of the most advanced technicality and were coming for the invincible emperor Napoleon Bonaparte. To complete the enthusiasm among the corporals and the officials of the Napoleonic forces, coming with them was the sister who was most loved by the emperor of France, Her Majesty.

62

4

The Sensual Baths for the French Countess

When the main door of the luxury carriage was opened, a bright golden rug was deployed. The rug, like an enormous serpent, rolled over slowly to detain itself one step in front of the couple composed by the Countess Pauline Bonaparte and her flamboyant husband, Victor Enmanuel Leclerc. He was dressed with an impeccable white uniform with a lot of medals and a shield made of gold insignia corresponding to his position of general and commander in chief of the imperial forces belonging to the French Grand Armée.

After moving his foot three times up and down, the general ordered two assistants to accompany his wife and their son Dermide and show them the mansion where they were supposed to live as their regular residence in Saint-Domingue. At the same time, he made another movement with his foot, and seven high-ranking officials took position next to General Leclerc. After presenting arms and making the corresponding salutations, they marched together inside the long room to initiate the study of the maps of Saint-Domingue to create the battlefield scenario in preparing the strategy to distribute the invading forces to confront the black liberation movements, which was taking place in different parts of the Haitian territory. Among these seven men, there were two engineer experts in territory layout and three medicine doctors, including one who specialized in tropical plagues who studied in France but was originally from the island of Dominica.

The general and his assistants were moving quickly to consult the last reports coming from the front line in the battlefield and other territories that were possible future targets for the black liberation army. Those reports were arriving one after the other. The firsthand reports were brought by the captains, lieutenants, and the messengers who were mapping and exploring mainly the hills closer to the fortress. La Mulate, Fort Liberte, and the Island of Turtle were places of observation for the French marines and the rangers to establish a triangle of communication to secure the surroundings of the Bay of Cap-Haitien. The marine fleet was out in the open ocean. The Gran Armee de Napoleon took complete control of the entrance of the important port of Cap-Haitien. Napoleon would feel proud of his commander in chief in the initial strategic steps taken by the brilliant mind of his brother-in-law, Victor Leclerc.

The blood of the white French was running through the streams, to the rivers, to the ocean and to the soil in Saint-Domingue. The Haitian Revolution was spreading to other territories in the region. Spain, England, Holland, and Portugal were watching closely. These powerful empires did not want their territories to fall like cards. They represented money, political power, and religious control in the Western Hemisphere.

The massacre was in progress. The sound of the African drums was getting stronger, motivated by the arrival of the French Invasion. The black slaves attacked during the night by surprise, and that created more fear and terror. Events like these had already happened in Jamaica, Dominica, and Martinique, where the slavery was brutal and the white planters had shown very little compassion for the blacks. Haiti was the turning point for the black independence. The more the plantation owners oppressed they slaves, the stronger was the sentiment by the black dreaming to be free. That already happened with Bartolome de las Casas, Jose Parne, and Antonio de Montesinos. But the crowns did not pay attention to the aborigine slaves from Mexico to the Patagonia. The blacks did not want to suffer the same for hundreds of years. Saint-Domingue was fighting to become the first black independent nation in the Western Hemisphere.

Those who had fallen under the machete edge for the slaves and cimarrones were burned like they were in the saint inquisition conducted by the Catholic Church centuries before. A lot of the white people in Haiti had to run with desperation to Cuba and other islands to save their lives. Napoleon, afraid that the liberation of the territory had taken place, urged the forces to send a contingent bigger than any power had sent to the Caribbean region before by any imperial power from the Old World.

The white colonizers who represented the economic advances and political power of the middle class in the French nation were being killed in a great number, and the one who survived the first massacre either committed suicide with their families or managed to escape to Santiago de Cuba. The French forces had to act quickly to save the last of the plantation owners still alive in Saint-Domingue. Otherwise, they would be eliminated to the last human being in the French territories in the Caribbean Region.

Even though they had confronted similar rebellions in his colonies, neither the British nor the Portuguese had sent such a big army combined with the navy to put down a revolution of slaves. The soldiers and the officials that had come from France in company of the General Leclerc, were desperately combating to contain the advances of the black revolutionaries who were proclaiming the freedom to the west part of the island of Hispaniola.

Two gendarmes closed the door of the big meeting salon of General Victor Emmanuel Leclerc and his military aides.

On her side, Pauline Bonaparte was getting by with very little clothes. She was revealing herself like nothing was happening in the territory they just invaded. Each piece of clothing was removed, which, a few hours before, were covering the feminine attributes of the almost perfect body of the sister of the emperor of France. The sensual enchantments of the Countess Pauline Bonaparte made men turn crazy and lose the dreams to any man who saw her body from a short distance, if they were lucky enough to appreciate from a short distance her svelt and voluptuous figure. In Pauline were the concentrated sensuality and warm feminine eroticism of the French woman. First she walked slowly to the bureau chair. Then the shoes fell near her bed, breaking down the symmetric perfection of her routine, measuring each step of the beautiful woman. After, the items that were spread all over her chamber. It was as if the Countess was preparing to receive the massages of the two Creoles and the robust slave named Noir Curazo. The slave was brought directly from the Brazilian court to take with careful dedication the exclusive baths that, with the excuse of releasing the stress, was provided for Pauline Bonaparte after her arrival from Europe. In reality, these were erotic baths that not only stimulated her sexual appetite but also had the aphrodisiac effect, which would conduct her lovers to passion and volcanic ecstasies, and the mind would fly free to a special place in the universe of love.

Following a trick that his grandmother had taught when Nor Curazao was just a small kid, the slave lifted the extraordinary inferior lips that made him famous among the slaves and servants. The black servant was wetting the tongue while swallowing his own saliva. Remembering his grandmother's instructions, he passed the tongue by his superior and inferior lips. He made a twisted notch and passed the tongue again the under lips. It looked like he was tasting the most delicious piece of meat because each time his tongue went through, he made a soft sound, like as if the ex-slave was in in an orgy of intermittent orgasms. The female slaves enjoyed and admired that especial way of revolving the tongue, which was a special characteristics of Noir Curazao. The women, old and young, let their imagination fly away, alleviating their hard chores of being slaves and isolated in a plantation or living in barracks close to a salvage environment at the disposition of the owners and other male servant who wanted to discharge their sexual arousal in a hot or rainy day in Saint-Domingue.

Noir Curazao knew that the women turned crazy for his presence and his amorous tricks. He did it on purpose to attract the female attention. After all, the female servants wanted to gain his attention, proving in recompense any favor. That gave them a great pleasure since the ex-slave was very close to the Countess because he was her personal male masseuse. Sometimes, with no indifference, the servants emitted sound utilizing the sensuality of Pauline as a way of pleasing the mind of Nori Curazo. Other times they got together during the period for resting, and they imitated the sensual Carole La Fontaine, who was very skilled in changing her voice to lure the black slaves and the free men to think and dream of her creole beauty. She never knew her father, but he was a white man, and her mother was black. She had olive skin, and the Countess kept her as her personal assistant.

Sometimes Carole acted like the white girls, which impressed the visitors. But when the drums were sounding, the creole and exotic young woman danced like a snake, making sure that her bottom and big breasts could be seen by men and woman in the voodoo salon. The musicians could not concentrate properly and hit the drums, dreaming that they were touching Carole's protuberances.

When Noir Curazao finished his ritual with an unholy intention, he made a very especial sound where his voice went deep and became very raspy before he would say a word. Each word that came out of this mouth was vibrant and deep, like it was coming from a gigantic tunnel. After that, one could her him saying in French altered by the influence of the Portuguese languages spoken in Brazil, "Voila, your bath, madam! Everything is perfect for your pleasure, madam!"

With an auspicious smile, the robust servant went backward, taking advances that the Countess was taking off her clothes. Paulina was on tiptoe like she was in a model stage and was being naked, and she did not notice the presence of Noir Curazo. The servant was playing innocent and took the opportunity to take a glance from his side with eyes out of its orbit like it was a tiger on the lookout. The Countess Bonaparte caused anxiety and desperation on all the muscles of the servant. She took the edge of the last interior clothing that she was about to take off. The beautiful woman took some time, which was converted to a large waiting time to for the masseuse. The madam did it with extreme caution. It seemed that she was touching with the top of her finger the softeners of her interior cloth. It was made of cold silk that her mother made for her as a wedding gift of her long trip to the hot Caribbean region.

It seemed that Pauline was listening to an aunt clash in her hearing. When Madame Leticia handed over the brags, bloomers, or panties, making Pauline alert, she told her, "Paoletta, these intimate interior clothes are for you to use on and protect yourself from the high tropical temperature. The clothes were made to your side. Do not forget, Pauline, that the tropical heat will burn your gluteus if you do not protect them well. In Paris, in Roma, in Florence, Madrid, and Milan, the weather changes. The seasons can be appreciated. But in the Antilles, the fire will get inside of your body from the top and from the bottom. You feel a cold breeze from behind and a hot suffocating heat in front. All your sensual attributes will be hot like if it was the corn bread or wheat bread. The titties of your mammaries will be like two brown grapes. Imagine that you are in the island of Corcega. Like this is Saint-Domingue, like all the islands in the Caribbean. Protect the outside and the inside as well.

"Do not forget, Pauleta, that I am the one who gave birth. I carried you inside my belly during nine months, and I could feel the heat of your body. Since you were born, Charles and I argued a lot because you were running naked inside the house in Ajaccio as well as in the farm that we had in the mountain. You were completely naked while playing with the goats and the sheep and pigs. Nowadays you enjoy being with chest to the outdoors. You don't like to use brassier because your mammaries are hard like a rock for the people who stand in front of you. Your ego goes high when the elegant men from the court approach, making all excuses to get close to you. No, you have to listen to me. Cover your body with this cotton cover for the titties so they do not get dry as it turns like the lemon without juice like it was taken care of all exterior protuberances like I have taken care of my gluteus, take care of your chest!"

Pauline listened to her mother with particular attention. The geographic details were causing curiosity in Pauline's mind. But more curious was why her mother, Leticia Ramolino, was paying too much attention to many explanations and so many advices for protecting herself. It was like her mother was feeling some kind of premonition for her daughter.

Pauline had learned how to protect herself by the order of her father, Charles Bonaparte, before he passed away, and she also had the protection of her brother Napoleon. But what stunned Pauline all the more was that her mother Leticia and herself were having a conflicting relationship that was hostile. Pauline attributed this to the jealousy of her sisters, the gossips of her family, and the attitude of her mother, who made a lot of effort in public or in private to hide the conditions both had. For Leticia, Pauline was a rebel from the moment that she was in her belly. However, her maternal condition had compelled her to continue with the recommendations to the smaller daughter.

"Paoletta, as I was saying before, your skin is soft like the marble, like the porcelain. Do not expose your skin to a lot of sunrays for a long time. Excessive heat will burn your skin and your brain too. Too much tropical sun will burn your skin and your brain too. Remember, all the islands are equal. The islands are like women, surrounded by water and fire in the center. Your father always told me that my best attributes were the gluteus and the mammary. He opened his eyes as a sign of pleasure when he mentioned these two, which, according to him, were the protuberances that he enjoyed from me. Charles was happy with the hardness of titties and inflexibility of my gluteus. He always said that my titties was like *marbles de nacar*. For him, the shape of my buttocks was like the gigantic mammals of a big Swaziland caw. I loved that compliment. According to Charles, my chest was soft on the outside and warm by inside. The same thing would be said by your brother of Josephine. Sometimes I was asking myself if Charles Bonaparte would prefer to soak the mammals or squeeze the gluteus. I only know that he turned crazy. That is for sure. He lost his mind each time that he saw me naked. He jumped over me like a hungry beast to devour me from feet to head. The same way Napoleon with Josephine. She only had to show my son part of her legs to turn him crazy. The carriage driver always said that Napoleon looked like your father in the matter of sexual encounters. Both of them attacked like tigers to submit the women with a passion that I cannot forget when I think about Charles. Like father like son. That was the reason why Napoleon got trapped with the seven *nudos* of Josephine de La Pargerie, La Martiniquen. I swear that each time that I mention her name, my guts turn over, up and down, then strips the guts, and my bilirubin goes up, up. Anyway, follow my advices, what I tell you, because the islands and the Caribbean women have a lot tricks that they carry hidden inside. Don't forget, Paoletta, the Caribbean women have lease to tide in the waist and under too."

Pauline was listening to her mother. It was rare the time that she contradicted her. Pauline remained silent listening her mother's advices. Deep inside, Paoletta (that was the name that all the family called her) was doing what she wanted.

Noir Curazao, on his own part, had listened in more than one occasion the advices of Leticia to her daughter. Although the slave never knew Leticia, the servant knew of the advices from Leticia Ramolino to her daughter. The servants who came from France to Saint-Domingue spent the night talking and gossiping of the Mama Leticia over her family, not only in Ajaccio but also in the court of Europe.

In the corridors of the courts, everybody was talking and gossiping about the power between Leticia and Josephine, whose struggles expanded to the entire family, pulling them in different directions, including her beloved brother and emperor of France. Josephine de la Pargerie, the Imperatriz Josephine, and that Mama Leticia were like fire and gasoline. They could not be in the same room. The power struggles between the Imperatriz and Madam Ramolino were very evident to everyone. The mother-in-law and her daughter-in-law were in the front line of the gossips in the palace. They could not see each other eye to eye.

The Emperor was in the middle of the storm. He was fascinated to get involved in the middle of the controversy that was produced in Paris. What was happening in Saint-Domingue during the last two decades (1780–1800) not only would change the course of history, but also would produce a lot of scientific investigations in terms of environment change, including scientific, medical, and other events that were occurring at the same time in Paris and other cities in Europe. It was after the invasion of Napoleon, which extended to the capital of France. Everything was happening in Europe, and they would know about it in the Caribbean. Cap-Haitien was the center of attention. Saint-Domingue had turned into the richest colony in the hemisphere, and they received and sent back to Europe all types of news to the world. The communication between Cap-Haitien, capital of Saint-Domingue, and the city of Paris was very fluid. That secret was told by Carole La Blanche, the masseuse and private assistant of Pauline under promise. Nothing nor nobody dear would say not even half of what was about the relationship between the Countess, Josephine, and Leticia. The female triangle that surrounded the Emperor made sure that they were separate entities about the private business of Napoleon Bonaparte. The women close to him fought like cats to gain attention, political power, personal favors to satisfy their ambitions.

The female and male servants in charge of taking care of the Countess were slaves, free blacks slaves, *cimarrones*, and mulattos forced to swear fidelity and to learn the lesson of the islanders. "Todo lo que pasa en la casa, se queda en la casa."

Even though Pauline Bonaparte did not have a violent character, her temperament was very strong. Sometimes she reached the line of being stubborn. Probably because she was the youngest girl in the Bonaparte family, she developed a spoiled attitude to get what she wanted over the other sisters and brother. It was obvious that Charles Bonaparte spoiled his youngest daughter, regardless if she was right or wrong. She did not like to be contradicted. This caused her stubborn attitude.

With a lot of caution and being extremely careful, the slaves walked through the grass with trays containing the seven types of ointment to put in the bathtub of warm water for the baths for the Countess. Immersed in his secret and silent morbidity and the wiles that tormented the mind of Noir Curazo, he walked with a wish of taking a closer glance at the nakedness of his lady owner. The servant did not notice the mulatta Juliette Du La Cascade was getting in that particular moment by the same door that the black slave was going out in same direction. He was backing off in the same position.

Suddenly, the two servants collided. Since they hit butt to butt, the jar containing the ointments were sent flying, pushed by the scary moment and the impact, caused the slave to drop the bottles he was carrying. To the mulatta Juliette, it did not even pass through her mind for one instant that the back part of the her body would impact with the hard back of the ex-slave Nor Curazao.

Before the sights of Juliette and Madam Pauline, who was naked like a French Eve in the Eden of Saint-Domingue, naked like how God brought her to this world, the robust servant was doing all kinds of acrobatic tricks to catch the seven jars that were descending to the hard floor in the fortress in Cap-Haitien. The desperation and acrobatic movements of Noir Curazo caused more satisfaction than shock between Pauline and the mulatta that they both started jumping with joy.

Noir Curazo smiled at them uncertainly. Then with his voice trembling, showing how nervouse he was, he said, "Voilá, Madame! Thank the Great Lord! Everything is perfect for your bath, Majesty."

The scared servant, shaking like a cold chicken, had goose bumps all over his body. At the same time, he was giving thanks to the God and all the saints, even to the ones who were not canonized by the chuch yet, because he was able to save all the jars with the oils for the Countess's bath.

The slave was babbling words in a very strange language of his African ancestors. "Apulayahh! Matumbahh! Apulahh Ya Bananaaa! Metresilis est moi protection! Esese seng! WooMe Joiee!"

Only Noir Curazo understood the meaning of those words that he used as a prayer anytime that he was in danger or needed the protection of his ancestors or the God who took them away from the kingdom of this world. These ointments had been blessed in the special ceremony for the use of the Countess's baths. The ceremony was conducted by Florence Tingo, and he knew the punishments that will come over his back if he had allowed these bottles to be broken for a careless act of desperation to see a naked woman. That would be an unforgivable sin. Poor of him if He would let these ointments be spilled or broke the porcelain jars, which had an invaluable price. The jars belonged to the cultural patrimony of Marco Polo as a gift from the Emperor of China that was in power in the last trip that the navigator made to the far Orient.

The lips, fat and brown like the graves of the island Dominica, turned gray like ash. He was trembling, his lips like two pieces of zolapas of getine. Pauline and Juliette were looking to each other, their faces so close, it was as if both women were about to kiss each other's mouth in the longest kiss in Paris. Both women had open mouths in shock because they could not believe what they were seeing. They looked at each other again and again. At that special moment, the Countess Bonaparte noticed that she became aware of the perfection of her mammaries, and her titties were aroused with apparent ingenuity, making believe that she had not noticed that Juliette was so close to her. Both women moved back and tried to cover her breasts until their hands could not cover anymore. Juliette, of creole and African descent, had bigger protuberances than Pauline. For that reason, she only managed to cover her breasts, leaving the rest of her body open for everyone to look at. Pauline was famous for having perfect breasts so exact that a special glass of chmpagne could perfectly swallow each.

The Countess remained looking from her side. She looked with ingenuity on her side. It was as if she was not looking at all. Like wanting but not wanting to look. However, when the hormones fogged her mind and her heart, her sin turned like a hen that was becoming ready to copulate with most robust rooster in the farm. After all, she was a woman, and her body was aroused, and her mind and heart changed suddenly. She had the skin as a crocodile. Her breasts that before she had tried to cover to hide became bigger. It was in that exciting moment when the pupils of Pauline's hazel eyes uncovered the agile musculature of the strong and robust Nori Curazo.

Juliette remained by her side, holding her hand and comforting her of the sensual spectacle that was happening before Pauline got into the big bathtub that was brought from Marseilles to serve as a little swimming pool in the mansion. During the bath, Juliette was in charge of massaging the Countess. Then Pauline would be called to take her on top of a table of mahogany for the massaging, and then her chamber next door was divided by a green curtain like the green color of the Caribbean forests.

When he saw the big eyes of Juliette go to the point of getting out of its cavity and the radiant face of His Majesty the Countess, the black servant departed from the room.

Both women looked at each other, with their eyes wide. Juliette and Pauline noticed that when Noir Curazo extended his hands to catch the jars of oils and medicinal ointments for the bath of his lady owner, he did not think to hold tight his pants. With nothing to hold on to his waist, the pan fell, leaving hin naked in the presence of the two women. With one hand in front and the other behind, Noir Curazao started leaving by the same way that he came in. He desperately tied to cover his manhood. The strong servant preferred to cover with his two hands his vulnerable part that had suffered a sudden and surprised reaction seeing Pauline nude. Juliette also was naked because that was the instruction of the Roman baths since the Roman Empire established them in public places, and everyone had to be naked when performing or receiving massages.

Nori Curazo knew the secrets of the ritual, and Juliette was trained in the court of Paris by the same master who trained all the court masseuses. Juliette was educated and trained in Europe, and a lot of people wanted to have her in the court, including Josephine Bonaparte, the

Imperatriz. In the left butt cheek of Nori was a noticeable protrusion, the stamp left by a burning iron that marked him by his owner when the Brazilian owner caught him in a squat position, with his tongue out like a dog, while he was enjoying masturbating himself. He was given free imagination to his carnal wishes of seeing a young white woman who was a princess who was taking a bath without cover except for long hair that looked like a silk blanket. Her black hair covered her until her gluteus.

The lady did waste time. She was furious by the morbid movements that the slave was performing while he was having great sexual pleasure with his eyes, his imagination, and his masculine member, erected like a wooden brown bate. Mad to the point of lowering her mind and condemning the slave with all kinds of foul language for his act, thinking that he was planning to catch the lady from behind, run to kitchen, and find an iron stamp to be used to mere coincidence being prepared to mark the property of the bulls, feeding with fire alive to the oven of the enormous oven to make cassava bread. However, this time, the Brazilian lady marked them forever.

The countess and the masseuse Juliette started laughing with while the Negro free slave was vanishing like a phantom as he disappeared in the dark and long hallway of the Countess Pauline Bonaparte's mansion in Saint-Domingue.

When the curtain was finally open, the enormous bathtub with hot water and the smell of aromatic exotic aroma that was brought from the island of the Pacific, one from the Black Sea in Russia, and water from a fountain in the Montpellier volcano in Martinique, the Countess was completely nude like Eve in paradise.

The first part of the ritual was completed. Pauline was completely indifferent to what was happening in the mansion chamber, where a pianist was refining a flute and a piano in the music salon. At the same time, she was rehearsing the last melodies that were listed for the epoch in the great salons of Marseille, the Scala of Rome, and the Opera of Paris.

"Paulinaaa! Paulettaaaaa! Paulinaaaa! Are you listening or not! Do not ignore me! Remember that I am your older brother! Our protector and your Emperor! Keep that in mind forever! Did you hear me?"

It was the strong voice of Napoleón Bonaparte that sounded like tremendous thunder amplified by the echo of the high wall of the long hall in the Montmartre Palace of Paris. Napoleon was calling his sister urgently to present herself at his desk.

"Come fast to my office and stop wasting time looking at pictures and drawings of soldiers in attention position! Do not excuse yourself saying that your eyes are only concentrating, nailed in the belt of the gendarmes. You know very well that I am not *dom tonto*. I am the Emperor, French Emperor. Let's no play games! Do not come and tell me the damn thing of that every saying that still at this age I am shocked, like it was a caramel! You, like many women, think that because I am low in size, I reach it to suck myself. There are some people that are saying that everywhere that this is the only thing that causes pleasure. No, do not think like that. I am referring to the thumb finger from the right foot. There many people who still swear that I used to suck my fingers from both feet when I was a child. It is true that I am small in size. That cannot be denied, Paoletta. But do not forget that what I do not have in size, I have it in performance!"

The trumpets of the gendarmes and sentinels announced attention before the arrival of General Victor E. Leclerc to the place where he had been summoned to receive instructions about the invasion of Saint-Domingue. He did not get to listen to the meaning of the last phrase from the imperator. In the meantime, Pauline was covering her mouth by the sexual comparison of Napoleon referring to something so intimate like it was the size of his virile masculine member. Pauline was robotized. Her cheeks were red like two tomatoes. The face was in flames. The eyes were like two fire torches. Napoleon was famous for using phrases with double sensual meanings to gain attention from the women. It was a technique that he used a lot. Pauline always acted like she did not know her brother's way of talking. It seemed like he was self-conscious about his height of five feet. Maybe Charles Bonaparte and Leticia Ramolino had something to do with the Napoleon complex. For that reason, each time that his masculinity size was in doubt, he reacted by saying, "The man cannot be measured from the feet to the head. On the contrary, he should be measured from the front head to the sky."

Napoleon continue amnestying Pauline. "Do not laugh, Paoletta. When I talk about such, I'm talking about the thumb that people are angry about because they envy me that they saw me grow up in Corcega and that I had the habit when I was a baby. Now I am a grown-up man. You have proved that because the soldiers have told you many times. I was capable of penetrating it with a point. I should say of inducing the point of my sword to the earth to stop shaking when we had an earthquake during the resting time in the battlefield before crossing the Alps Mountains. However, at this time, there are many people who are saying, gossiping like women.

"They are spreading the comment that they had to prepare house remedies in order to cure the habit of sucking my index finger. A lot of things have been said about me, and a lot will be continue to be said about me in the future!"

Napoleon was furious from the inside out like a

burning inferno by the attitude of his sister who was trying to reject his order to travel to the Caribbean region. She was terrified thinking about the humongous monsters, which, according to old legends from the conquistador sailors, inhabited the Atlantic Ocean. But the scariest was the gigantic octopus that was capable of swallowing a ship in a few seconds. That legend was imbedded in her mind because people told her the story in Ajaccio to scare the boys and girls from venturing into the Mediterranean Sea that surrounded the island of Sardinia and Corcega.

Anyway, Pauline was listening without turning herself to look at him face-to-face. It seemed that she was not paying attention. That increased the anger in Napoleon. He liked to hypnotize people when he was talking. That is why he always asked people to look straight at him. He knew his big hazel pupils would penetrate the soul of women and men who were talking to him face-to-face. This was one of his powerful talents.

Pauline was used to a routine of standing hours and hours looking at the figures of soldiers wearing their military uniforms. Since she was very little, she enjoyed playing with soldiers made of porcelain. Sometimes when Napoleon was of good humor, he would take her to the training camp. Over there, she was able to play with the real soldiers of flesh and bones.

The concern would be that some soldiers would summit her to loving training. That was a constant fear of Napoleon that he repeated to her many times, "Listen carefully, Paoletta! You must be careful with misinterpreting the compliments of the gentlemen of the French gendarmes. They treat you like a princess, but if they corner you, they stop treating you like how a woman wishes or deserves. French men are efficient in the use of their tongue. They persuade you and enable you like anesthesia in your mind with their romanticism and double-sense words. Then you start to feel a chilling arousing in the spinal cord, and your hair stands like a needle.

"If you let men and the soldiers have their way, they would pleasure you, regardless that you are my beloved sister. After all, they are men, and you are a woman who is very hot in all senses. I see how the gendarmes and officials eat while they look at you. I am not stupid. When they see you, they wet they lips with their tongue, dreaming to have you, using their imagination. Just be careful, Pauline!"

Pauline was taught by their father not to respond or contradict her mayor brother, who was in charge of protecting her. She must do as Napoleon said. In the meantime, he advised Pauline to be careful and have preoccupation with the officials and soldiers that would fight for her attention. Pauline was feeling free to let her imagination run wild and continued to let her carry on with her feminine instinct. On the other hand, she enjoyed the intermittent orgasms with only touch or the uniformness of soldiers and military men. Pauline was entertained just by observing the soldiers. Pauline was fascinated to see them in attention. She was fascinated by the pictures and the sculptures of the showing of their clothes. She never lost a single detail.

Pauline developed that habit since she was a small girl. Her father was a high-ranking official of the king. Charles Bonaparte was the representative of the crown in the island of Corcega. The man who robbed her of her virginity when she was sixteen years old was a military aide of high rank and was very close to Napoleon. A great part of her family was military. She would have gotten married with the official with whom she had her first encounter of love in her house in Ajaccio, Corcega, if not for the fast intervention of her brother. She was the youngest in the loving family of Napoleon.

Now, the emperor of France was calling her to

communicate the determination of sending her along with her husband, the general Leclerc, to combat the rebellion of the black slaves in the territory that France occupied in the west of the second island of the Caribbean. The information that was arriving from the French colonizers in Saint-Domingue was not very satisfactory for Napoleon, who was already suffer violent attempts in Paris. Everything was falling like in a domino effect. They were persuaded for the wind of freedom that made dreams the drums and the chants and songs of the slaves of the occidental part of Hispaniola.

The just-burned French empire had to act fast. There was no time to waste because the colonies of the Caribbean region were producing the money to sustain the emperor, whose head was heading toward the established Republic after the triumph of the French Revolution. It was a tremendous feat done by a man a few feet tall, who was threatening to swallow the entire world, from east to west and from south to north. Napoleon was aware that if France would lose Haiti, he would lose the central member of his power. It was like amputating its virile member to continue producing goods such as honey and sugar.

To take out Pauline of their emblements, Napoleon had to raise his voice like a commandant in chef, repeating, "Pauline! I am commanding you to be prepared to be ready on time to board the ships that are getting loaded to sail to Saint-Domingue in the morning of Saturday, thirteenth of June, to catch the winds of *sotavento* that are coming from the African Coast. The invasion cannot wait anymore. Following my mother Leticia, which is the same as yours, I am giving you a period of seven days to depart. Seven days from today! Select your court and servants of both sexes. In that way you will not be sending me emissaries from the New World. Remember that the distance between Saint-Domingue and France, you have three months of duration if the ocean is calm, and the winds would blow you from behind to take you to a good place. Thus, do not pretend that I am going to allow you to bring your goat milk to prepare your erotic baths because you want to continue being young, like a twenty-one-year-old girl forever."

Pauline was listening to her brother without responding with a yes or a no. This was like being ordered by her father. He did not want that she contradict her older brother. These were his words when he was in his deathbed. The words continue today like it was yesterday.

"Paoletta, do not contradict you brother Napoleon. Never say no to him. He is your brother, and his mission is to protect, even though he has to pay with like. Take care of him and do not contradict. Promise me this before I depart to the other side, Paoletta."

With another salt of truth, Napoleon continued, "You are very spoiled. The travel on the Atlantic Ocean lasts at least three months if the wind blows favorably. I know you very well. We are in a war with the Caribbean region. Yes, I refer that what you hear is true. I am telling you that we are going to invade the Caribbean. Saint-Domingue cannot disrespect the empire and myself. France wants liberty, equality, and fraternity. But I am not going to permit that Saint-Domingue gets liberated. When we lose Haiti, the French Revolution has no meaning. When Haiti get independence, all the islands would be low domain, and the powerful empire will ask independence! What France has gained for more than two centuries with Martinique, Dominica, Guadalupe, Saint Martin, and Saint-Domingue will fall like dominos!"

Visibly irritated by the little attention Pauline was paying, Napoleon hit the table with energy and angry rage. He stood up in attention. He introduced the right hand in the uniform lapel and raised his voice again. He knew that she was the only audience in that moment of historic event so crucial to the expansion of the French Empire.

"Never, never! While I am the Emperor Napoleon, First in France and of the world, the slaves in Haiti would never triumph! Vivre La France! For motherland we should die. Saint-Domingue is ours. We have to control the region of the Caribbean. The black revolution would triumph. Never! Long live France for eternity."

Until that moment, Pauline seemed asleep. But when she listened to the last two words, she began to stutter. At that moment, she realized that he was talking seriously. For that reason, she employed one of the more effective tricks. This was a habit that she acquired since she was an adolescent. It was how she tricked the babysitter who took care of her. She always had her way with that method. She was doing whatever she wanted, taking that habit to the rest of her life. A lot of people say that the men lose their head to see a woman so sensual to get what she wanted. The shaking in her lips always painted red added a touch of sensuality and eroticism to the innocent face of Pauline Bonaparte.

"Then we can say, my brother, that as reward to the military fidelity that my husband has for you, you pay sending us to die in the ho-ho-hot ca-ca-ca-Caribbean tropi-pipipi-calal del Ca-caca-ca-ca!"

Napoleon was between furious and impassive, irritated by the childishness of Paulina. He knew that she was coming up with an excuse and continued. "Do not make like you do not understand. Look at me. I know your little trick! That is what Josephine said when she advised me to my ear for the nights that I not trust your rare carnal ways of acting, to protect myself from the sagacity of your husband. Don't believe that I do not know the ambitions of Victor Leclerc. He is an excellent soldier. But because he is very silent, He had to use my tactics. He knows what I am capable of with the traitors who fall in love with my women, including my sisters. He speak Russians. He wanted to take with him the model Malatrava before getting married with you. That was the reason why I say yes even before of you saying yes to his proposal of marriage. Besides, he was the best candidate because he had power and money.

"However, his silence is the one which scared me. Did say I get scared because I can do that to you as well. Victor spends his time reading my movement and my way of acting. I want that I remain clear that the Emperatriz Josephine did not criticize you because she envied you like you are swaying around the court. She gave me advice because she wanted to protect me. You are very dear to say that Josephine envied you, and that is being unfair with the officials close to me. This is not tolerated. Never have my balls been shaking, less making me tremble with the bad tongues with their gossiping. If they want to give tongues, let them talk with me that I know. Liars! You all are the ones who carry on the innocent people to the edge of the guillotine of Paris. Do not forget who put the empire in order. Enough. Gossipers are like roaches that just come out the armor of power. No, I do not want more division in this moment. Now, prepare your things and the servants that would accompany you."

Napoleon was not willing to let his sister persuade him against the invasion of Antilles. The pier of France was filled with ships and boats ready to sail toward Saint-Domingue. There was no way back. The decision was made. The Leclerc-Bonapartes were ordered to pack and leave for the invasion of Saint-Domingue.

The emperor told his sister, "Your carriage and horses are in the mother ship. It is like a mansion on the sea. There goes Milita the white horse. My personal horse. I do not want that the General Leclerc put his butt on the horse. It is a delicate animal. His black fur is soft like the Chinese silk. Milita is trained for fighting only. Take care of him just in case I have to go to combat personally against the slaves. Take care of your husband that he should not drink too much. Take care of your son Dermide, my nephew. Remember that we do not have heirs to the throne. Until Josefine is with child, Dermide is the only heir to the throne."

Pauline needed to take a breath. For that reason she took three steps and got close to the window.

After running the curtain of extravagant green, they were in front to the Arc de Triomphe. She made a lot of thoughts of the possibility to become the mother of the French Emperor. But Napoleon did not waste time and took her out her daydreaming moment.

"Do the same that Josephine does to me. Before I go to the battlefield, she will wait for me, ready to give me a treatment. Do not make yourself the innocent that you know very well of that I am talking about. Remember that the women of the officials are very beautiful. Do not believe that you are the only who has sensual and beautiful attributes. Do not forget that I made Victor Leclerc general. That man also has his secrets in silence the way you see him. He makes believe that he is stupid enough and that he is not capable of killing flies. But when he drinks a drink of pure vodka, even his heart and the aspirations stop. His voice rasping like the low sounds of the horses make the women crazy, and he drinks rum and gets inspiration. Victor runs himself like a poet and with tongue and accent from the northern part of France, he emits some sounds that produce orgasms to the officials' wives. His qualities make him a special man. He is a tremendous general! Take care of Victor, Pauletta.

"Some of my assistants say Victor imitates me. I do not care. I like his style. Sometimes I believe that he thinks he is in the battlefield when he is making love to a woman. He acts like a panther. Some women have told me that he is like a lion when making love. He dances like a tornado, and to amuse the present, he likes to break plates of porcelain with his virile member. I bet you did not know that. During our training and resting in the battlefield, we do things our women cannot even imagine. My father that was your father too trained me to do everything in the countryside of Corsica. Ay, if Mama Leticia would only know. Now I understand that what he wanted for me was to learn that even for being lower, I was not cowed or stupid. That you know and the entire world!"

For pure coincidence, before finalizing his reprimand, Napoleon observed something very strange moving in the curtains. What was moving looked to him like little white rats that nobody knew how it managed to arrive to the emperor's office. Each time that he looked at the amulet, he knew that something was out of place, and he got close to. It was repeating one other time, like it was a premonition of bad news of something that was about to happen.

"Such is life and my destiny!" the emperor repeated with apparent anxiety.

Napoleon Bonaparte was passing from one side to the other side of the big salon. Each step with his bright military boots was like an alert of death for the little rat that was between terrified and anxious. It was taking out its little head in the hole to see also a funny way of the extraordinary vision of the powerful man of the earth. The rat in provocative attitude defiantly moved, coming from the edge of the curtains of the French palace.

Although he wanted to ignore the rodent that caused scare and repugnance at the same time, he could not contain the anger. Napoleon crushed his teeth as a sign of discomfort. Then he took his left hand to his chest. In that position, he was admonishing his sister. His face turned red like a tomato. The eyes were about to escape his cavity, almost wanting to go out. So much anger was caused that Pauline was squat to avoid that situation for the emperor to destroy once and for all the bad rat.

The clear yellow eyes were like honeybees to the woman. There she remained terrorized. Frozen. However, her surprise was for the value that her brother was paying to the little statue that was a present given by a Russian spy with whom people gossiped that the emperor shared his bed in moments of solitude. Many people said that the Russian spy was enslaved by Napoleon and his virile member. The emperor used to massage his legs with fire of that model up and down and up. He used the little statue like he was doing a cleanse in a ritual. In the court of Russia and in the great hall and center of reunion in Europe, people used to talk about the possible matrimony between Napoleon and the spy from Russia, who had the name of Maria Josefa Malatrava. The events were public domain in the Parisian courts.

He waited for the return of the Russian girl. She never came back. He never knew what happened to the spy because she never came back to France to satisfy the loving desires and possible marriage with Napoleon Bonaparte. The statue was built and continued sliding faceup on the floor in Ma-Maison, situated in the outskirt of Paris.

The French emperor limited to say to himself again, "Such is life and my destiny!"

5

The French Emperor's Love Affairs

It is true that Pauline Bonaparte had a very high libido to deal with the men and women in her surroundings. Nobody is capable of denying that. The French Countess was hot like a volcano in constant eruption. However, Napoleon compensated his short stature with his virile power. His fame started in the battlefield and was extended to his bed. The women who fell under his umbrella of his loving affairs in Corcega and in the South of France such as Marseille were the ones who were trapped by his influence as a hot loving impulse, contributed by spreading the news of Napoleon's lovemaking. They began by saying that his power was not only physically but also mentally. His cavalry lured them to accept his approach and invitation to love him.

That happened when Napoleon was at the beginning of his political development and persuaded Desiree Clark to lose her mind for him. The gossipers of the small Marseille community received the news that the most protected woman in Southern France had surrounded herself to arms and sold of an islander from Ajaccio in Corcega. The first encounter occurred was love at first sight. Noticing the difference between the beautiful Desiree and Napoleon, who was less than five feet tall, and the five-foot-seven-inch Southern girl tended to believe that the encounter and fast impression was an act of sorcery from the part of Napoleon. Many people, including her father and Leticia, agreed that it was witchcraft for Desiree to fall in love and surrender to Napoleon's aspirations. What she ignored was that his ambition was not only to satisfy his heart, but also to continue north of France looking for power. That was his dream.

After accepting some monetary support from Desiree and her family, he continued toward the Parisian dream. At that time his rank was of young official with very little economical power for his enormous enterprise. He could marry Desiree, but later on, Napoleon returned the service to the family and paid with interest. However, he broke her heart in pieces. He continued his quest and mission. The second big catch in terms of love was the Martican, the most protected woman. She was a mysterious widow born in a plantation in the countryside of the Caribbean Island that the *tainos* Indians called Matinoo.

The Martican woman named Josephine de La Pargerie had the courts in Europe upside down, trying to get a piece of the famous widow.

A lot of princes, counts, and kings wanted to offer Josephine "villages and castles" to gain her sexual experience. She was a Caribbean Creole belonging to the Aristocratic society in Paris. That would be a very powerful move for any gentleman to conquer Josephine's love. When Napoleon heard about that woman, he managed to know her places to produce and encounter.

After she was getting close to be the most powerful man on Europe, Josephine had her own agenda too. Her ambition was demonstrated when coming from a very small island from the smaller Antilles in the Caribbean, she got married with one of the richest men in France from the family La Pargerie, who owned coffee and cattle plantations in the Caribbean. After having two children, which secured her inheritance forever, her husband died. Now Josephine was free, and her route to fame was around the corner.

When her witch-voodoo lady in the island told her, "You were born to be an *imperatriz* or a queen." She was only twelve.

The moment had come when she met face-to-face with Napoleon. He used the same trick, looking straight to her pupils. He got into her soul through her eyes. Seconds later, Josephine was under his spell. The ambition of both was so strong that he also felt the power of her clear eyes while he was penetrating inch by inch inside her heart. Josephine recognized that she had never encountered a man so powerful than Napoleon at the moment of copulating or making love to a woman. Napoleon used a special technique for her because she was physically delicate, and his virile member gave pleasure, but he had to go inside her body using a slow-motion penetration. He would stop on his way in. He waited and turned himself around, looking at her feet. And that trick made Josephine lose her mind momentarily under the virile force and sexual approach employed by Napoleon. That fact that both of them came from a small island made them special at the time of lovemaking.

After the sexual encounter with Napoleon, she told her close confidants, female or male, that Napoleon intoxicated with pleasure, provoking from her a sequence of orgasms that made her search for air to live.

There were a lot of women who let themselves be tied by the carnal desires and succumbed to the powerful sexual virile member of Napoleon Bonaparte. Actually, he was born with a physical condition that occurred among a very limited group of men in the human population. Scientists in medicine had some clues about it, but they do not know what caused that a five-foot-tall man has a penis so long that it can reach down to his knees. In the case of Napoleon, he was born with other types of characteristics with his special way of copulating with the opposite sex.

When he was growing up in the farm of the family in Corcega, some of his childhood friends said that with his erection, he scared the heads of the four-legged animals and his friends too. He used his big penis as a whip. Being so smart, Napoleon soon learned that some girls liked that, and some were scared to allow him to penetrate them. Napoleon became an expert and practiced sex combined by the way the women cried at night like they were female wolves when they saw the moon getting full in the country. The night belonged to Napoleon during his teenage days in the island of Corcega. His sexual fame was rising like a tsunami in the Mediterranean Sea that cover his island, Sardinia, Sicilia, and the southern part of Calabria in the main land Italy.

Men and women, maybe for envy or pleasure, spread the news about the virile power of Napoleon. His virile member was extending and tiding women until where his passion and manhood permitted him. One night, he went with some friends to play in the beach. The weather was perfect, and the waves were coming in slowly to bathe the sand. A young beautiful islander who came to Ajaccio from the countryside was in the group and decided to allow Napoleon to go inside a cave with her. Because she was very narrow with a condition called *cocomordan,* Napoleon convinced her to allow him to make love to her.

When he completed the penetration without knowing that she had that sexual characteristics, he was the one who cried to be free. Her friend had to come and pull her to be liberated by that encounter. He learned a lesson because she was a virgin and had never had sex, and the size of his penis got clinched. It was an unforgettable experience for them and for their friends. It was that passion of his proud machismo that characterized the men from the island of Corcega, which he was preparing before an important battlefield, the cascade that was being realized of of his body in an explosive volcano in the culmination of a sexual act. That happened after a sexual encounter that placed him on the top of triumph of the confrontation. That was the way he saw the these moments of copulating.

His love affairs or his lovers agreed with that. His enormous appendage between his legs, he used to increase his ego. He employed his member and abilities and the trick that made him increase his confidence in himself. He was very passionate that he won over every lover. But in it was truly Napoleon who was always the winner when copulating with a woman. They always said that men and women who were born in the islands belong to the tropics, and they have special and peculiar qualities when having sexual encounters.

Josephine was ready to satisfy the rituals of the emperor in bed, like it was without using perfume to execute the *Kamasutra* that he liked a lot because it was a suitable position. More than sexual satisfaction was a ritual where the pleasure spilled like volcanic lava, erupting by the escape of the product of his convulsions. He did it in a natural way. With the odor of sugar cane of Martinique that made them crazy and gave them power to use with his pair of traveling to space while he utilized like a final strategy the sense of smelling that seduced up to the intoxication of passionate love. It was a lot of lovers to lose close to the border or edge of craziness.

For that reason, the bad tongues made running the rumor that the emperor fell in love with a Moscu model because she looked like Josephine. They looked like twin sisters. They had the same temple. Josephine de La Pargerie was the one who brought him down to his knees and acted like an inoffensive goat or sheep because she also had her way of making love and her own tricks.

In searching for satisfaction to his carnal desires, Napoleon wanted the model to have her pregnant, and she would provide him an heir for his throne. Josephine was an ardent lover but did not become pregnant, regardless of many times of loving with the emperor of France, and the man sometimes treated her that she do something for him that produced a successor to the crown. The uncontrollable sexual life was so big that at daytime, they were traveling in his carriage with two invited guests that accompanied them to the palace of Montebello, and he jumped on top of her in the back seat. The movements of the carriage, the squeaking of the iron wheels, and the horse that was speeding added to the pleasure and excitement of the imperial couple while they gave in to the passion of the fast end unexpected loving encounter.

People said then that Napoleon had passed seven months in the military campaign and was unable to see his woman. She was in the countryside on a vacation retreat with her friend and lover, Hipolite Charles. It was in this moment when the anger that he was carrying inside was converted to anxiety and passion, uncalled passion, for his loving Josephine de la Pargerie. Napoleon, lifted her long dress and silk underwear.

The libido and the desire of making love to Josephine were so big that not even the jail of Les Carmes where she was counting the hours, waiting for an imminent death with the cold edge of the guillotine, waiting for the executor to cut off her beautiful, soft, and long neck, made her avoid the suppressive love events and episodes with intense passion that would propose her prisoners and friend companions in the prison of Les Carmes. Huches e Hipolite, therefore, who were her friends and confidants, were prop friends who were waiting also the same spectacle established in Paris under the order of Robespierre.

For the Parisian society, Robespierre was acting as if he was the visible head of contemporary France and was seeing without surprise the political terror in France and all the colonies around the world belonging to the French empire.

The premonition and fortune-teller, the witch of Martinique, when Josephine went to consult because she was changing from a girl to her first menstruation, following the tradition in the island: "Do not hesitate and do not worry for the nation. Do not be afraid by anybody that you are destined to be the queen of France."

Pauline was also superstitious. She consulted the European witches and the Caribbean witches for her important decisions of her life. That was the reason why a lot of women circulated the rumor of the similarity between Pauline Bonaparte and Josephine de La Pargrie for the form in that made the men around them to become crazy when they dared to get close to their circle of interaction. Both women were from the islands and were walking like the train track. Each one was her side mounting in her track, without touching. It looked like it was a competitive betting who would got there first to the final station to reach the power and dominate the men and satisfy her carnal wishes to bathe with her lava-hot ardor that was coming from the center of the volcano of their entrances, spilling the nectar sweet and sour.

You know, the voice was sounding again in the palace

walls, from wall to wall, like the echo of the uncomfortable situation that produced the apparent indifference of his sister Pauline. She approached him holding her long dress that was being dragged on the palace floor. That was the French fashion, and Pauline liked to be in fashion.

She was getting closer and closer, like wanting and not wanting to say to Napoleon in a very low, soft voice. "My dear brother..."

For more than she wanted to simulate, this time Pauline was not able to continue and stop the tears from her beautiful eyes. She looked like an actress rehearsing her manuscript. After that theatrical acting, she pulled out her handkerchief that she had hidden between the two mammaries in the cannon between her chest in case that she had to cry. It was like this as she, in the last instant of the conversation with Napoleon, it was her murmur in a low tone with her voice soft like silk, sensual and convincing, persuasive, and she told him, "Think twice. Think it over carefully, my dear brother. No, you cannot imagine all the risks that you are exposing me with this. I resist myself to think that there is somebody behind this idea of yours, giving you bad advice in order to take me out of Paris. They do not want to see me near you. The jealousy of the women and the men are caused by this attitude with little humanity from your part. Do not tell me anything. I also have my connections in the courts of Europe. I swear for the memory of Papa Charles, may he rest in peace. Victor is the general, most fearful at that. Remember that Victor is the father of your nephew Dermide, who happens to be, for the moment, the only heir to the imperial throne. Do not forget that, my dearest brother!"

Napoleon let her talk without stopping her because Pauline was like possessed. She was talking as if she was Charles Bonaparte talking. Her voice went from a feminine tone to a deep and rasping voice. Napoleon was in shock because he knew that his sister was able to adapt different tones of voices. He was scared to think that she was telling things and advices that only Charles Bonaparte knew. Not even Leticia knew about these things. These were things that his father told him alone in secret thirteen years ago when he was in his in bed to cross to the other side.

Napoleon was also very superstitious regardless of his brave temperament. After all, he was born in Corcega, and like all men and women of the island, he was also very superstitious. For that he let his sister talk without interruption.

"You know that I am not dumb or stupid. I am your younger sister. You are my protector. Remember what our father, Papa Charles Bonaparte, said: 'Never separate of Poletta. Protect her because she will be faithful and loyal to your design until death do you both part.' I was seven years old when he told me, 'Paoletta, obey your brother Napoleon because he is going to be a great man. His name will ring beyond the oceans, beyond the sunset and the sunrise in the earth. Napoleon is going to need your support now and always. Do not leave him alone, in the good times or in bad times. Do not let him be overcome by the gossip power struggles that will defeat him without your support. Remember that we are living a complicate world. But our family has come fighting to better the humanity since thousands of years. Fight at the side of your brother because you are the feminine part of my son Napoleon. Remember what I am saying to fight against the envy. Obey him forever. Do as he tells you, Paoletta. *Est la anima mia que parla!'*

"Look as my hair stand up only when I think about these words said by our father, Charles. It was his heart talking. You must be very inconsiderate, but I have bad feelings. You know my brother that not myself nor my husband wants a high position in the French Creole. What other proof do you want from my fidelity and for the motherland?"

The emperor, as if he were negotiating with an enemy, made a joke that impeded him from standing firm. He let his guard down, slacking at Pauline's pleas. She knew she was coming out on top. She wanted to convince him to desist from sending her and her husband on the mission to invade the colony of Saint-Domingue. She felt a strange protection for her son Dermide, who, as a possible successor to the throne of Napoleon Bonaparte, should not risk himself unless it was absolutely necessary.

Taking advantage of the passage of the rat that appeared again, she made another attempt at persuasion and said to Napoleon, "My brother, now I don't want to speak to you as your sister but as my sovereign. Please don't send me to that region, for although I am not superstitious, I have a feeling that this trip to the Caribbean will not be good. Send me to any part of the world where our empire and your power are exercised over goods and vassals. But don't send me to Saint-Domingue. You know that I am terrified of the beasts of the Atlantic Ocean and the sorcerers of the Antilles. In the caves, aboriginal men come out and take the women away, and they don't come out again until they've impregnated them with triplets. Black slaves go crazy making love to white women. Those men have terrible members. They say they cause pleasure, but if they rape you, the pain is unbearable. Those black men tie white women around their waists and don't let go until they faint. That's why I don't want to go to the Caribbean region. Don't send me, little brother, to the land of the zombies. It scares me to death. I have been told that black mestizos resemble Arabian horses because of the size of their reproductive organs and because of the brutality with which women are mounted when it comes to lovemaking.

Whether it's because the woman approves or because of the strength of their big muscles.

"Do you understand my concern? Your wife knows a lot about Caribbean slaves. Josephine told many women of the court everything. She also told them, with the promise that they would keep it a secret, that one of the mulattoes almost drove her mad with love with the rocking dance on a swinging seesaw. He was the son of an Artibonite sorcerer, beautiful and big as a giant. Mama Leticia knows everything too because in Paris and in Corsica, the walls talk and the trees listen."

Napoleon didn't hesitate in his response. "I told you this is your chance. In Haiti you will be the queen. If here in Paris you are the Countess, in Saint-Domingue you will be the sovereign of the Crown of France. What's more, if things go as I'm thinking, and we manage to crush the slave rebellion, Hispaniola will be under your dominion. Your reign will extend throughout the Caribbean region, and you will reach Louisiana in North America. Can you imagine the native Indians and the Yankees kissing your feet and paying you obeisance? We are not playing here. You'll be great, Paolette. You were born to be a sovereign! In Saint-Domingue is your crown! Fight for it!"

For whatever reason, Pauline didn't show much interest in taking the trip with her husband. It was like a premonition that everything was going to change for her when she set foot in the Saint-Domingue colony. It was a sense of tragedy that she was feeling. Therefore, she implored him with the kind of sobs that would move even the most indifferent of men. The tears that slid down her face betrayed the feelings that overwhelmed her. Although she was known as a woman of strong commanding qualities in the military circles of the Napoleonic army, she had secrets that weakened her. Like all women, she had her weak point. That attribute projected her femininity even more. The sobs were moving. Tears streamed down her face like a cascade of sensual provocation.

In the meantime, Napoleon Bonaparte—with his characteristic aim—threw the golden feather into the air. The pen landed in the inkwell of the mahogany desk where the sovereign was signing the documents he had to present to the court in Paris, justifying to the people of France and its allies the coming invasion of the Caribbean region. After signing the last document and placing the official stamp on it, he looked at his sister in sympathy. He was the most powerful of the Bonaparte family, and he had to be Pauline's emperor, brother, and protector. So using a low but convincing tone of voice, he said to her, "Pauline, don't make the situation more difficult for me. You know very well that Saint-Domingue is the most important point for the expansion of the French empire. I can't risk losing this geographical bastion. That is why I have arranged for you to accompany your husband, Victor Leclerc. As general and the most trusted person in my army, I give you the honor of maintaining our hegemony in the Caribbean region, preventing the black revolution from destroying the colony. This is not a game, Pauline! So stop whining so that General Leclerc will feel supported by you in order that he will do his job, and you will be alive and well back in Europe in less than seven months. I trust that your husband will give me the honor of crushing the rebellion before it spreads like wildfire, like a seaquake through all the Caribbean colonies. The French will not be able to forget forever and ever the effects of the French Revolution. Nor will they forget that I sent you to Haiti to impose the order of the empire, crushing the rebellion of the black slaves. So stop crying. I have a surprise for you when everything calms down in the Caribbean region. Think that the power of our empire begins in Saint-Domingue. That's where the sun goes to bed! Have you forgotten that the English have their noses in the whole Caribbean?

"Oh, Pauline, if you only knew that they have been sponsoring slave rebellions in my territories! The day I have a moment, the queen, the lords, and their grandmothers will have to kneel before my empire. That's when they'll know 'where the cookies crumble.' Don't come to me with the stories and tales of the beasts of the seas and oceans or the witches of the Antilles. Those legends are false. Those are road tales. You are one of those who don't leave the meetings of witchcraft that exist in the society of Paris! I am Napoleon Bonaparte, and my power has no limit! My spies never sleep."

By instinct, his right arm went up from her thighs, past her waist, to her chest, where it stopped. They were firm as if she had his attention.

"I don't want the English to come to me with the story that we are going to negotiate. Saint-Domingue is priceless because this Caribbean jewel is a creation of France, dammit! As the Spaniards say, that's where the fish bites! Did you hear me right, Pauline? So stop crying and calm your trembling lips. I am not your husband! You are going to Saint-Domingue, and that's it. Let there be no more talk of this in France or Saint-Domingue! This is an order from the imperial court under my command!"

Having said this, the emperor did not dare to look his younger sister in the face so as not to see her so sorrowful. Napoleon was afraid that Pauline would persuade him. Now he was determined not to be overcome by his younger sister's pessimism. Even if she screamed or fought as she did when she was in a rage, he would not back out of the plans he was putting on the table to march to the colony of Saint-Domingue.

At the sound of a bell, she ordered two assistants to take her to her room to rest. In the meantime, Napoleon immediately ordered the presence of General Leclerc and the officers who would accompany him in the military enterprise toward the western part of Hispaniola. On this occasion, there were two little mice: one as white as snow and the other as black as jet that appeared slipping on the Montmartre palace's spotless floor.

Under the impression that they wanted to mount the female to copulate, the rodents accelerated their march as they passed close to Napoleon's desk. They seemed more frightened by the sound of the bell than by the presence of an exotic beauty like Pauline Bonaparte. She whimpered. She sobbed when she saw the mice afraid of being crushed to death by Napoleon Bonaparte's boots.

In the meantime, he continued with his conspiracy-worthy connivances. His military assistants were studying the plans and strategies to be followed during the course of the Saint-Domingue invasion. For her part, the model took advantage of the fact that the Emperor of France needed to have children to inherit the crown. The Russian was born in a village in the rebellious region of Siberia, mixed with Tibetans. She was rustic, a peasant girl, who became refined, thanks to her exotic beauty, in the court of the Tsars of Moscow. The beautiful woman swore she loved Napoleon Bonaparte. She had refused the approaches and gifts sent to her by a Russian prince named Peter the Handsome. He had been brought the most beautiful and refined women in all Russia. But he was still crazy about Maria Malatrava. For some reason, the model was devoted to Napoleon Bonaparte. No one knows why he bewitched her, even though the difference in height was enormous. He looked like a dwarf when he was with the model. She didn't mind because Napoleon had impressed her with his virile whip and the fame defining Napoleon as an excellent male on the whole Mediterranean that had circulated from mouth to mouth, the frustrated love of the beautiful

Marseille Desiree Clark. She let those who were curious know that she was madly in love with Napoleon. He went crazy by her beauty when he saw her pass by in the port of Marseilles. She was a monument of a woman in front of Napoleon's five feet, whose fiery desire to possess her was the force that made her lose her mind and her virginity for her beloved. Others swore that the Russian was a spy in the service of the Moscow government. The only thing that the rivalry between Josephine de LaPargerie and Pauline Bonaparte agreed on was that the Russian had come to France to spy on Napoleon's military movements and political plans and then report back to their superiors in the capital of the Tsars. Both of them didn't fall for the story that Maria Malatrava was madly in love with Napoleon. Judging by Bonaparte's sexual tricks and wiles, he could have made her fall in love as many women in the world did when they got between the sheets to make love to the peasant islander Napoleon Bonaparte.

The Caribbean Sea and the Atlantic Ocean were tossing against each other. Their gigantic waves were rocking. They rose and fell, down and up. They embraced each other with nature's strongest passion. They looked like two spirited youngsters at their first love meeting. Out of the huge waves, white-water reeds formed, rising to the heights to lick the clouds. They resembled Diana and Poseidon; they sucked each other to descend stridently into the abysses of the seas as if they were in the midst of an amorous convulsion, roaring the grandeur of a masterful orgasm. In the midst of so much passion, a frothy and whitish whirlpool emerged from the seabed as the fruit of nature that converges in the Caribbean Sea and the mysterious Atlantic Ocean that flank and guard the Hispaniola Island.

Under the pressure and orders coming from Napoleon Bonaparte, the navy produced warships with great armaments from short-range blunderbusses to huge double-barrel cannons like fire dragons and anaconda serpents to swallow up the blacks in rebellion in the Antilles. Those who saw the ship fleets of the Grand Armée sailing the seas from Marseilles with the insignia of Napoleon and waving the flags of France could only pray for the immensity of so many ships that had their bows westward to cross the Atlantic Ocean and destroy the Slave Revolution in the rich colony of Saint-Domingue. But this time, instead of sugar, they brought wildfire; instead of peacetime provisions, they came loaded with the cannons and horses of death.

The twenty-three-year-old model tested the sexual powers of the emperor who made love to her as if she was being penetrated by a horse from northern Tibet that served as her mount when she was sixteen years old.

"Vous cette como une chevalle noir de Tibet. Je te ame Napoleón avec tout la force de moi passión!"

When the Russian model finished completing this sentence, she felt in the depths of her loins the manhood of the Emperor, who, after positioning her as if she were a human ball, penetrated her again and again until the lubrication of a final orgasm made her faint with the moans of a mare that has been possessed until the space of her most intimate parts allowed it.

Napoleon answered her with silence. He penetrated her until she opened her mouth for the seventh time with the desperation of a dying man gasping for air. Agonizing. Suffocating. Intoxicated by so much pleasure. The copulation of his style and the reach of his penetration, cutting off the Russian model's breath at the moment of climax and the overflow of the waterfall reached its peak.

As had been announced to her in the vernacular religious meetings and gatherings, it was only a short time before the transformation of Pauline Bonaparte would take place. When the moon was new, she would be taken to Saint Jack's cave.

At the ceremony she would be wrapped in mud and would be welcomed by the seven priests who, by this time, would be celebrating the congress of Congo. Many of them had been infiltrated from the Congo and Benin region of Africa. Fortunately, that area of La Mermelada was under the control of the French military. Tingó had convinced her that if she went through the ritual, she would increase her feminine powers, and in the long term, she would avoid being a victim of any evil spell, bewitchment, or illness of the kind that attacked the European invaders. The spiritualists respected Pauline Bonaparte. They feared her because of her resemblance to the Voodoo saint Metresilis. Her way of acting and the recommendations of Tingó Florence had put the sorcerers of Ayití in her favor. All the *hungans*, shamans, and *lwas* of the region from Gonaive to Ouanmanthie had come to the conclusion that Countess Pauline was the same Anaisa or Metresilis in body and soul. She could not be touched under any circumstances. That was the watchword. It was a command of the voodoo gods as respect for the new goddess of the Antilles.

Pum! Pum! Kutu-Pum! Pum! Pum! Pum! Kutu-Pum! Pum! Pum!

The women wiggled their bodies with an electrifying rhythmic cadence. The sound of the drums was clear, thunderous, and contagious. It seemed as if the instruments wanted to speak. Each drum emitted a groan that could be felt in the souls of the slaves of Saint-Domingue. The peculiar tone was brought out by the strong, calloused hands that scraped the leather of Francois Casablanche's drums. He was a Maroon slave who had come down from the mountains to play the kettledrums and drums in the Voodoo ceremonies in the hope of having the honor of seeing Metresilis, represented by the beauty of Pauline Bonaparte, in the audience.

When they saw her enter, the music stopped. Casablanche's hands remained in the air as if petrified in time. The sound and the air had combined to wait for her. The presence of Metresilis and Pauline. The two had become one. The beauty of the two women fused into a feminine unity, creating around them the magic of an aura that changed colors and place with every movement. It was a rainbow like the Hispaniola Island had never seen before. One end was born in the east in the Mona Passage, and the other end drank in the Windward Passage that divides Cuba and Jamaica. The transformation was coming. The enormous rainbow that crossed the four cardinal points of Saint-Domingue announced it to the world.

"*Toute la terre, arreté avec la presence de su Santísima excelence, Pauline Bonaparte. La eternité de la belle femme est en la presence de La Contessa. Attention a toute le monde! La liberté est icí. Nois some un pay grand dans les Antilles*! Long live Metresilis! Long live Pauline Bonaparte!"

The skill of the musician slaves was put to the hardest test today. On this date, a great event is celebrated in El Alcajé, Turtle, Gonaive, Juana Mendez, La Mermelade, the Mulate, and Cap-Haitien. Because of its magnitude, the event would change the course of history. In short, throughout the Haitian nation, there was an unusual joy. It was a joy in which many sang and others cried. The slaves announced it with the music of "Raa-Raa." In this ceremony, the new queen would be presented. She was the reincarnation of Metresilis. On this date the winds announced the liberation of the slaves that had been brought from the African continent with the wildness of violent battles, bloody combats that bathed the deep valleys and plateaus, dragging in their way the rumor of the great day of the awaited confrontation, of the fulfillment of a crime-fighter pact of the first black nation that was born with the arrival of the century. It was like a great seaquake wave that threatened to engulf the Hispaniola Island. The gales seemed like spirited beasts, descending the slopes of the geography of Saint-Domingue like a collective curse. Everything was concentrated in the north. The triangle of combat had formed between Port du Paix, Artibonite, the Turtle, and Cap-Haitien. This triangle was represented by three worlds: Europe, the Caribbean, and Africa, carrying in the center the torch of the rebellion that the enslaved blacks of Saint-Domingue had ignited. The animals came pushing the chariot of a new Caribbean inquisition. The horses and their riders announced to the four corners of the world, with all the strength of their lungs, the arrival of the slaves who had broken the chains that bound them to the masters and colonizers in the plantations of Haiti. They were now facing the powerful army of Napoleon Bonaparte. The Caribbean slaves had awakened.

PUM! KUTUPUM! PUM! PUM! KUTUPUM! Pum! Pum!

6

The Moans of Passion

The trickery of her moans was extraordinary. Electrifying. The moans and sighs she produced when she entered into sexual intimacy drove her lovers wild. Every scream and every body movement was meant to soften her manly partner in the intimacy of amorous passion. Pauline was almost always the winner. Passionate and mysterious, Pauline had learned that if she concentrated on her amorous wiles, she also had to maintain the intensity of her reactions throughout the performance of the act of love. For that passion, the most virile men would melt the moment they approached the atmosphere of erotic sensuality, which began with soft instrumental music, chants so elevated that her lovers were transported to a frenzied ecstasy before succumbing to the secrets she kept to bind and dominate the arrogant men with whom they shared her heart.

Pauline was surrounded by a halo of sovereignty since she had been a courtesan in the rising empire. The Countess knew how to prepare the atmosphere of reverie for the European aristocrats, who, with their attitude, provoked the French Revolution and the bourgeois plantation owners who wanted to make Saint-Domingue a city of social power like Paris and the great cities of Europe. She did not like to lose. She was used to triumph.

The Italian actor Talma lost his head with the moans and erotic sighs of Pauline Bonaparte. The ritual she employed was as effective as it was maddening. She would throw the hat; at the same time, she emitted a soft sound that reached the ear like a lulling melody. Hypnotizing. Her voice acquired a special erotic tonality. Each scream she produced, rising and falling in time with her movements when she was making love, dislocated her lover's calm. At the climax of the moment, she bathed him with incandescent lava that emanated from the volcano of her entrails like an endless stream, like the waters of a waterfall. Her body shuddered from head to toe. Every seven minutes, her skin would bristle. Her pupils would widen, and the discharge would come in sequence. It was like a balm of soft, sticky nectar. The voice became faint like a passionate symphony. Melodious. Time lost its meaning. The male and female fell into an amorous trance. There remained the lover curled up, caressing that beautiful body, convulsed in search of oxygen. The woman remains in stupor. Asphyxiated, almost poisoned by so much passion and eroticism.

Pauline had many secrets. Each one became a hidden jewel of great value to satisfy her desire of feminine power over the men who aspired to share her erotic passion and her feminine desire in the warmth of her bed; in the warm and crystalline water of the rivers of Saint-Domingue, in the turbulent Caribbean Sea, in the bushes, or in the infinite caverns of the tropical region, they swore they were close to madness when they made love with Pauline Bonaparte.

Each secret became an involuntary event that produced an atmosphere charged with sensuality, unleashing a torrent of erotic, pleasurable experiences. Unforgettable, unparalleled. That is why the men who fell into her arms swore that they had never felt so much pleasure in making love in their lives.

For each of her seven lovers, she reserved, without intending it, a special secret, with a degree and erotic intensity adjusted to the manly personality of each man. That was her feminine cunningness and wisdom. It was like a source of satisfaction for her ego, charged with sensuality, passion, and intense love to execute the sexual act in its entire dimension. They were seven lovers, and each received a unique treatment. Every detail in the environment in the place of the events had a motive.

Sculptor Antonio Canova was struck by the surprise factor. He never thought that Pauline would be waiting for him naked at the worktable. He was trembling when he was taking her measurements to make the sketch of the sculpture that immortalized Napoleon Bonaparte's younger sister. The sculptor was unable to work the same day he first laid eyes on Pauline's feminine attributes. The sculptor needed time to recover from the emotion caused by the beautiful woman on the worktable of the famous brush artist. There he remained. He was disturbed. But what it did was to delay the passage of time. When he saw her naked, everything stopped except his heart, which leaped in his chest as if it were going to burst out of his open mouth. The craziness came later. His skin crawled like a hen's when it sees the cock that's going to step on them when it gives them the shivers. Bristly.

Another one who couldn't resist his astonishment was actor Francisco Thalma, who was so enchanted by Pauline's charm that after their love encounters, he never knew if he was acting or living the reality. He swore before many of the people closest to him that Pauline brought him back to his senses. She softened him up to follow in her footsteps like a bloodhound.

General Victor Enmanuel Leclerc, her husband and the father of her son Dermide Leclerc Bonaparte, was perhaps the one who suffered the most from falling into the vine of his destiny by falling in love with Pauline. Her love for him was strange. The woman loved his power. He was the highest ranking military man in Napoleon's army. She was fascinated by the military. When she was among the sailors of the Grand Armée, she was like a fish in water. The same happened when she was with the gendarmes of the police or the French Army. For her, the uniform was a symbol of power, organization, and respect.

The experience of Saint-Domingue had a very strong effect on Pauline Bonaparte. Fortunately, there she had the opportunity to show General Leclerc how much she loved him. To do this, she used the secret of mirrors. Some soldiers and officers told that Victor Leclerc fought more vehemently on the battlefield when his wife gave him a secret treatment, which began with the figures of both of them in the seven mirrors of the mansion of Cap-Haitien. What came next was too exciting to be told to his subordinates in the heat of the battlefield, where they fought to win or die.

For the prince who came from Egypt, she had to employ more techniques than secrets. She knew that the man came in search of adventure and power. He wanted to get close to Napoleon's crown for something that was never known for certain. What Pauline did know was that if she didn't use the same tricks that the handsome prince of Egypt used to perfection with his seven wives, she would be lost when she succumbed to his amorous desires. He came to Saint-Domingue, claiming that Napoleon had given him special permission to advise the army as he was receiving many surprise attacks in Hispaniola. It could be said that Pauline was already more advanced than the techniques the prince used to make love to the seven women. All at the same time, they were waiting for him in Morocco, covering their faces with the veil of chastity and abstinence. The man went away crying like a child, asking Pauline's servants to intercede for him so that he could stay a few more days on Turtle Island. He wanted to stay a little longer even if the rebels were to realize his sexual ability, cutting off his penis and head as punishment for his audacity for coming from so far away in search of conquering and discovering Pauline's seven secrets. After all, the prince of Alexandria was also in the midst of a revolution that threatened to raze everything that represented the invading empire represented by Pauline and her husband. Staying on the island, her skin was in danger, and so were her chauvinist desires.

Count Camillo Bourghese lived suffering in the belief that Pauline had entangled him with the technique of feinting and not giving. She learned that trick from Corsica's tutor. She would tell him to be careful if his heart was not inclined to fiery passion. Ambition and interests were in the way; the best was to offer and show feminine charms. Thus she kept Camillo, the Vatican and Rome's most stale society, swearing love to her husband but sleeping in separate beds while cuddling with some of his closest servants. Pauline Bonaparte was never in love with Camillus Bourghese. When she gave herself, the cup of her passion would open, and the nectar of love would flow with the intensity of a stream of a tropical waterfall. That was an open secret. With Camillo, it wasn't like that. Perhaps he knew that his marriage to her responded to the commercial arrangements of European society. There was also the trickery and interference of the bishop of the Holy See.

Returning to the love affairs, she answered to only one of her lovers who was an Egyptian prince and who came to Paris with the excuse of joining Napoleon in his plan to conquer the country of the pyramids. The man—owner of manly strength, great size, and a deep husky voice—stood out and impressed with his presence. He was a prince of the Egyptian court who had been attracted to her when he first laid eyes on Pauline Bonaparte. The Egyptian traveled for several months on a warship to visit Pauline Bonaparte at her mansion in Cap-Haitien. He was the only man to achieve what no one else had achieved with a spectacular Kamasutra act, which he had been taught while in India. He made love to Pauline Bonaparte in such a way that she felt compelled to employ all her amorous tricks in search of defeating the prince of Egypt. She could not hide her sexual secrets. She did it because her feminine ego and her dominant desire demanded it. The woman was opening the chests of her feminine conformation until the cup could not hold anymore. She had to teach him almost everything she knew. She taught him the enjoyment of honeycomb, sweetening his virile member by dipping it in bee honey while she rubbed it with Pega Palo leaves, rubbing it in different directions with the slime of a zebu bull. He used the position of the rocking chair whose bodies were intertwined as if they were Siamese twins penetrated by the trunk. Penetration in this act is done when one seeks to impregnate the woman, but the man can be trapped and overcome because the intensity of the encounter is strong for the man than for the woman. The mind must be clear and concentrated so that an orgasm does not come at the wrong time. Usually the male is the first to succumb and falls into a drowsy state as he is squeezed in the process, which can last up to thirty-nine minutes in that position. The Singapore punishment consists of the man kneeling in front of the woman who has been tied to a stick in the shape of a cross. The man executes the sexual act by the oral way until the woman, by the force of gravity, opens the central cup, and the man uses his tongue, waiting for the exit of a circle in the same center of the feminine intimacy. This act is called the Singapore punishment because the woman reaches a state close to dementia in which the man and the woman feel hallucinations by the amount of orgasms that come out in sequence by the force of gravity to which she is subjected while the man enjoys the bulging organs and a lifting of the reddish lips by the sense of taste treatment. That experience is lived in Singapore, Indonesia, and Bali.

The Egyptian prince's mistake was to think that he had Pauline under his macho domination, subjected to his desires and amorous tricks. What the prince did not know was that Pauline had learned the trick of "the pyramid or the Pharaoh Punishment" and the "Chechens punishment," which consists of walking on all fours as if they were dogs. The woman goes underneath as dogs perform the sexual act.

Pauline was about to beg him not to do any more sexual tricks. She was already about to be defeated when she remembered a special trick. She did it like the gambler who keeps the last card up his sleeve. It was the rope trick that consisted of tying herself around the waist with her lover until the daylight came. She learned it from a sorcerer and a witch who belonged to the tribe of Cacique Caonabo's family, husband of Queen Anacaona the First. The prince was caught in his own trap and preferred to leave for Paris, defeated by the tricks of the woman he came from the Middle East to conquer. No one has dared to doubt it. Her characteristics were so special in the female population that in the world, one could count with the fingers of one hand the women who possessed those sexual qualities. The orgasms were produced in sequence. The intermittence of the orgasms was like a trickle that descended with a deep moan that came out of her throat as if seeking air to breathe. The nectar of a juicy fruit that escapes when squeezed with nothing to stop it when the infinite cup of love and sensuality is opened. Pauline's palpitations and screams that were melodious cries of happiness completed the ritual of her specialty in the act of love. This secret of Pauline's baths, altered by the wisdom of Tingó Florence, imbued the ointment with power. It made her possessor of an extraordinary sexual capacity.

Tingó Florence was an expert in the secret of the seven powers that she had learned from a priestess in the voodoo rituals celebrated in Saint Jack's Cave. The strength of the seven powers acquired more power with Pauline Bonaparte. The Countess put them into practice while in Haiti and took them to France to put them into practice among the women of the crown. Men and women from all the courts came to see the Countess. Females and males wanted to consult her. That increased the rumors that she had orgies where all the sexual acts were practiced. The special baths revived by the Countess were the scenarios to give rise to the love legends that emerged and escaped from the place, driven by the steam of the thermal waters and the smoke of the goat's milk that was imported from different countries to bathe Pauline and her companions. A couple of courtiers who were in the place saw her when her limbs were disguised and the spirit went into a trance as if possessed by the forces of the beyond.

They say that what drove Victor Emmanuel Leclerc to alcoholic beverage perdition was not the cane rum that a Puerto Rican chemist from Mayaguez had taught him, and neither because of having tasted the five-star Babancourt rum, but when he learned a secret that his wife had kept from him. They say the general knew what Pauline had developed during her stay in Cap-Haitien.

They were extraordinary abilities that were previously

unknown to him. He realized it because one night when the moon shone with a clarity as if it were a celestial mirror of great proportions; Pauline, arguing that she was afraid because she heard the beating of drums coming from the mountains of Fort Liberté and the Turtle Island, had panicked, and she sobbed, demanding the presence of her husband the general. Frightened by the sounds of the drums, the thunder and the cannon shots imprecated the servant ordering him.

"Noir Curaçao, go quickly to the fortress and tell the general that I need his presence at once. I am very scared, and they are announcing that there are going to fall burriquitos, with the thunderbolts and lightning that can be seen coming down from the mountains of Artibonite and The Mulate. Pshshsh! Shut up, Noir Curaçao. Don't you dare say half a word. Ride the first animal you find in the stable even if it's my white horse that's tied up in the mahogany bush. If you call him three times for Milito, the horse will come to you. Be careful when you ride him. Don't forget that the steed is used to my weight, to the warmth of my legs and the metal of my voice. I am the only one who controls him when he stops to show his muscles. Milito is a very intelligent horse, and he knows when I ride him. My brother, Napoleon, trained him to kneel in front of me when I'm going to ride him."

Pauline spoke with the assurance that Noir Curaçao dared not say half a word.

"He does the same with me. Oh, if the women in France could see how Milito gets when he sees me! Their tongues would fall out. You know, don't make me mention that woman's name again. You know what the Caribbean tongues are saying. Even the Irish archbishop is being given to me as a husband. Don't play dumb, you know very well what they say in the Turtle and Fort Liberté."

The burly servant Noir Curaçao listened to his mistress with wild eyes.

"Everyone spread the rumor that he did it because of his arrogance. But I know my brother. I know well that he trained Milito to kneel down when he sees me and put his neck between my legs so that he could ride me easily from the front in my wide silk dress imported from the Far East.

"If, on the other hand, Milito realizes it is you, he will throw you like he threw Carole LeBlanche for standing in front of the Notra Damus Cathedral in downtown Cap-Haitien. Some friends told me that Carole was thrown by Milito in front of the crowd going to mass on Palm Sunday. In her fall, her insides showed. I had told her to give up this habit of riding around without her underwear on such an energetic horse. Milito launched her into flight without wings. I told her that one day they would see her like her mother gave birth to her. But she loved it when men saw her with her attributes in the air. The mulatto was fascinated by the males letting their lustful imaginations run wild. I told her it was only a matter of time before I saw her upside down. She was just one slip away from the horse for wanting to compete with me. The mulatto didn't want to know that French men are the same as Caribbean men. What they want is to be shown some intimate part to go behind the trees to hide like dogs while they masturbate over and over again. What they want is to make love to you to eat the forbidden fruit.

"I don't want the horse to throw you up in the air like he threw Carole so that the women would be amazed by her nakedness and her charms. The men's manhood and breathing stopped. So don't forget to ride him from behind so he doesn't recognize you. Remember to mount from behind. Get on fast. Get on the white horse. If you see the black mare, she can ride you wherever you want because she makes no distinction between men and women who ride her. She is a very docile and cooperative beast. The mare doesn't care if it's a slave, a pure black man, a French mulatto, a white man with underpants, or a runaway slave with a petticoat."

The black Curaçao knew that when Pauline spoke in patoi, she was speaking to be understood. She spoke French, Italian, Corsican dialect, and Creole from the Haitian plantations.

"The black beast knows you very well because you're the one who bathes her and massages her every time the general feels like riding her and walking around the region of La Mermelade. She has no preference. The mare loves to be ridden from the front, but she also likes to be ridden from behind. Have you already forgotten what my husband did to make an officer's wife ride the mare when she was being tamed? Lucky I wasn't there.

"Oh, Noir Curaçao! You better shut up and don't say anything. Tingó told everything that was going on. You were the one who grabbed the mare's tail for the woman to mount. Meanwhile, my husband took her and lifted her up by the waist. With my left hand, I knew all the details, Curaçao. Anyway, I have to admit that this is the most docile mare I've had since I arrived from Paris. Don't forget that Milito is a very intelligent animal with excellent training in the best stables in Marseille. No wonder he was the favorite white horse of my brother, the Emperor of France. Did you hear me, Noir Curaçao? Look at me straight and don't pretend you don't understand. I know you very well. I know you're giving me the side eye to see if you can see some hidden part. This is not the place for that. Don't forget, we're in a battle between the French Empire and the slaves of Saint-Domingue."

The servant listened to his mistress attentively. It was not customary for servants to raise their heads or talk back to their masters. If Noir Curaçao displeased her, she could give him punishment to the sun kettle, or he could be taken to a form of "pleasurable punishment." It was an unforgettable experience that happened to her when the seven jars of bath ointments and massages from the Countess Bonaparte fell on her.

The slave, confused and surprised by the explanations of his mistress in the language of the slaves, wanted to open his mouth to tell her that he could leave in the carriage in case Commander Leclerc wanted to come and cover himself from the rain. The rain did not stop since the early morning. The storm that was announced was falling with intensity.

As Pauline Bonaparte knew him so well, she guessed the servant's thoughts by saying to him, "Don't even think of asking me what you're thinking. Go quickly and don't try it. That carriage will not move in such a storm. Besides, that carriage and the steeds that pull it were brought from France for my exclusive use. Not even my mother, Doña Leticia Ramolino, had ever put her buttocks in that carriage. It was brought here for Napoleon Bonaparte to ride in and be driven around the cities he would visit in Martinique, Port-au-Prince, Guadeloupe, and Dominica. The first thing he told me was to keep the horses and the carriage in all its luxury to take it to Louisiana. That carriage is for the official ceremonies of the empire. Remember that not even the Prince came from Egypt to eat me. Do not think in a wrong way, what I mean was that he came to eat my brains so that I would leave Cap-Haitien and my husband the general. He offered me villas and castles if I would elope with him to the Middle East. He told me he was going to put in my name the most beautiful castle on the river Nile. Not even he put his bulging buttocks and his..."

The last part was not heard because the storm was

about to start with thunder and lightning. The thunder was rumbling all over the county.

"Hear me well, Noir Curaçao! Don't let the thought of driving the carriage cross your mind. Do not think I'm going to let you ride alone because of the fact that I allowed you to give me massages before I went to see the archbishop. Have you gone mad, Noir Curaçao?! Hurry the horse. Don't stop for nothing in the world and bring me the general. I mean my husband! I have a surprise for him that he will never forget when I show him one of my best secrets. I am not jealous, but I know that there are many of the officers' wives who are going crazy over my husband's blue eyes. Many say they are taking baths of Maria La Blanca, Vini-Vini, and Florida Water to take him away from me. But they are wrong because I am Napoleon's dearest sister, and I am Haiti's sovereign. *Al revoir! Allez fu! Vole caguite, volé cosó*, Noir Curaçao. Do not forget that you are my slave. I bought you and brought you from Brazil to live with me. I mean in my court, or better said, near me. I brought you here because you were recommended by King Maximilian's cousin. I am your mistress as long as you live. *No obliez to vous cette moi pour tout la vie*, Noir Curaçao. I swear I'll stop calling myself Pauline Bonaparte Ramolino. If you fail me, I'll rip off your...I swear by Saint Socorro and Saint Jack that..."

The last sentence uttered by Pauline was not heard by Curaçao because a thunder foreshadowing the storm traveled in all directions of northern Haiti, producing an enormous noise. She did not realize that she had let slip a few bad words against the masseur-servant in the Creole language. Pauline Bonaparte's servants knew that when she became uncomfortable, everyone had to be quiet until she had finished her rhetoric, until her anger had passed, until she would run out of anger. To some servants, she was delirious about being the queen of France, and so she would go on at length berating the slaves as if she were speaking to the members of the court in Paris. Deep inside, the ex-slave knew that if she brought him from Brazil and paid a sum of money in gold for his freedom, it was because Pauline had "the mouth of the devil and the heart of God."

Noir Curaçao had many skills to work with the Countess Bonaparte, but his specialty was massages and the limited use of his tongue, which he used with care, dedication, and great pleasure to give the Countess the Turkish massages that relaxed her so much. His skills and trust for his fidelity was carte blanche to accompany Pauline on her return to France. Those who knew him, including Pauline, believed him to be mute. He was rarely heard to speak even when he was among the slaves in the plantation barracks. He would tell the other servants that his tongue could not be used for hollow words. Its use was reserved for softening and relaxing Pauline Bonaparte's body.

The servant Curaçao left without finding out more. His only concern was to comply with the order. He obeyed his mistress and, with a karate jump, fell mounted on the horse used by Pauline so that the soldiers would not stop him. He took off like the devil takes the horseman. Noir Curaçao was so black that it seemed that the animal was riding alone toward the headquarters in search of the commander of Napoleon Bonaparte's army. The most incredulous soldiers swore that this animal was Lucifer himself coming to impose his mediation between the slaves and the invaders of France.

The rebels who saw the milk-white horse ran, some of them terrified and others threw themselves to the ground, crying out to the African saints to protect them from the evil spell. The superstition of those who saw the huge beast riding at such speed swore that the animal carried a message from beyond. Those who saw the steed swore and perjured that the beast was without a rider. Others even dared to say that the four legs of the animal were not touching the ground. That it was flying over the bushes in its race along the road of La Mermelade toward the mansion of Pauline and General Leclerc. The mysterious mansion was near a hill called Mount Joli in the vicinity of Cap-Haitien.

The drums were beating seven times seven.

Pum-Kutupum!

Pum-Pum-Kutupum-Pum-Pum-Pum-Pum!

The drums of the slaves followed their beats. Sometimes clamorous and sometimes excited by the magic in the scraping of the calloused hands of the drummer musicians in the mountains and hills of the Turtle Island.

Kutupum-Kutupum! Pum-Pum! Kutupum! Pum-Pum!

As the distance between the Mulate hill and the barracks at Cap-Haitien was less than seven leagues, it took the slave little time to arrive. Despite the warning not to dig his spurs into Milito, he continued to dig his spurs into his mistress's horse so that he would not be caught in the night. The black man was very suspicious and was afraid to go through a ravine called Chorrera de Anacaona. They say that the queen wanders through that gully because it is close to where the *areitos* were celebrated when Hatuey came from Cuba to meet the aborigines in the Indian's Cave. Noir Curaçao was afraid of the place because, according to what he said, a very pretty woman would come out, singing a song that drove the riders crazy. The horses would fly through the air at the sight of the Indian showing off her charms before hiding in the endless cave behind Saint Jack's creek.

Noir Curaçao and his twin brother, Francois Casa Blanche, had an encounter with the Indian. His brother lost his mind for the long-haired aborigine when she invited him to enter the infinite cave of Anacaona. The slave did not want to suffer the same fate as his brother if he met the mysterious woman making provocative signs for him to approach the waterfall that covers the entrance to the mysterious place.

General Leclerc arrived at the gate, and Pauline had instructed the servants to go to bed early, under the pretext that a storm with heavy rain and much thunder was expected from Gonaive, Port-au-Prince, and Cap-Haitien. Countess Bonaparte knew that slaves and servants were very superstitious. She also believed in superstitions. Therefore, she expanded her beliefs and knowledge; she put them into practice whenever she could. The slaves knelt down and prayed every time there was thunder or lightning that came after the outburst in the firmament. Landed by the mysterious force of Caribbean nature, all, slaves and masters alike, would pray in an act of own guilt for the sin they were about to commit. Afterward, they knelt down and prayed to Saint Blessed Barbara so that the lightning would go away for the day the other side. "It better arrive there and don't hit here," they said in fear, promising to be better people.

Although Pauline had not been introduced to the voodoo religion, Haitians and freed men throughout the region believed and swore that she was Metresilis herself. The previous week, a storm had fallen so heavily that the region from Artibonite to La Mermelade had been cut off from land communication by the excessive and intermittent downpours; the rivers had flowed out of their flow. This storm had prevented the slaves from encircling the white settlers, forcing them to postpone surprise attacks. These were a tactic of warfare that had worked well for them. The slaves aspired to declare independence from the French colony and waited for the year to end. It was January 1800. The arrival of the new century had encouraged the slaves who had been under the yoke of the French for almost three hundred years. All of Europe was in a state of alert because whatever happened in Saint-Domingue would have repercussions in the other Caribbean colonies they dominated: Holland, England, Portugal, and France.

Napoleon was losing sleep over the problems that were occurring in Haiti. The economic and military might of the nascent French empire was at stake. If Haiti became independent, so would the slaves of Martinique, Dominica, and Guadeloupe. That is to say, from the Saba Island to Monserrat, the blacks would break their chains that prevented them from freedom.

General Leclerc arrived riding up with a group of helpers, and when he reached the gate of Pauline's residence, he signaled, and they all galloped back down the road they came. They put their buttocks where their faces were. The commander signaled Noir Curaçao to lead his mount to the stable of the house. He walked a few steps and caught a glimpse of his wife's figure waiting for him on the threshold of the mansion. He smiled at her. But he was confused by Pauline's urgent call. That was not typical of her neither in France nor in the military campaign of the general in Italy where he was accompanied by his mistress. She seldom called him with such haste.

With the fire and passion that characterized her, Pauline led her husband down a long corridor in total silence. For the occasion, which she would turn into a special, unforgettable night, she had adorned the house with thirteen giant mirrors she had brought that week from Paris. Her husband was on the front lines. She took advantage of the occasion to have the mirrors and other supplies unloaded without him or any of his trusted officers noticing. She was prepared for a unique night. Unforgettable.

Later, rumor had it that Josephine, who had spies in Pauline's circle in Saint-Domingue, learned that she wanted "to transfer the general's goods into her name in case he dies on the battlefield." The best sorcerers in Europe and the powerful Caribbean sorceresses had predicted to Pauline Bonaparte the misfortune that was coming at the end of her husband's military campaign on the tropical island of Saint-Domingue.

Victor Leclerc had not seen the remodeling that Pauline had done to the house at Cap-Haitien. She had hired the best masons and architects in Port-au-Prince. Her husband was in the fields fighting the slave rebellion. Pauline was more concerned about behaving like a queen of Haiti and not as the general's wife who was fighting hand to hand with the rebels of the colony of Saint-Domingue in search of freedom. She did not believe she was in danger, or at least that was the impression she gave to the people who were spying on her to send firsthand information to her dangerous enemy, Josephine Bonaparte. If she felt she was in a battle, it was in her combat against the sister-in-law who dominated Napoleon and France with her charms and sexual tricks, imported from her unforgettable Martinique that the aborigines had always called Martinóo.

Now what mattered to her was to unfold, with all the force of her passion, the demonstration of love she had prepared for her husband. Her sensuality slid with the softness of her wardrobe. Pauline wore a Chinese silk robe that partially covered her protuberances. Her nipples protruded from her tits like two Puerto Rican *quenepas* or two Dominican lemongrass. It was a transparent gown that defined her charms by the light of a lamp she carried in her hand, drawing her figure in every mirror. They were a display of erotic provocation. Incidentally, Pauline had left all the windows half open so that the Caribbean breeze would lift her clothes, making them float and giving the impression that she was in front and the robe behind. At the same time, the mirrors reflected a multiplication of the figure of General Victor Leclerc. He with his manly, muscular figure and his curly blond hair, as if his head was dipped in gold. Pauline was looking at herself in the mirror a thousand times, walking provocatively. Slowly. Gently. Making magic with the dim light of the lamp that her delicate hands held and passed, with desperate haste, over every part of her body. Her breasts, her navel, and a very fine chain of very small diamonds, which descended from her waist to the middle of her thighs, turned and rigid, completed the figure of a goddess in a state of transformation toward the highest part of eroticism.

Victor changed without haste. He watched her as she walked. She circled around to give him time to see her in her complete nakedness. Quietly. In search of every detail that, in his years of marriage, he hadn't been able to appreciate because of his military occupations. At this crucial moment, the general was changing rank. It was not for less because he was in front of the most sensual body that human eyes had ever seen. Victor Leclerc's ocean blue eyes bulged; they opened with intensity. He wanted to see more. A little more of his beloved's fabulous body. His general's medals jingled every time he saw an image of another dimension of his wife's body. Pauline was also excited watching the multiplication, which, as if by magic, appeared in the mirrors, observing every detail of her elegant husband in his brigadier general or field marshal of Napoleon Bonaparte's powerful army.

Man and woman, now transformed into male and female, walked with desperate slowness to pass into a dimension where the real and the fictitious mingled. A place of paradise where the animal instincts of nature dominated the most ardent bodies to give free rein to the most daring passions between two beings. Beings that meet with one foot outside and the other inside to initiate the erotic dance of lovers. It was a matter of minutes for

Countess Bonaparte and General Leclerc to shed their inhibitions. The time had come to hang up the medals of imperial protocol, to begin to sigh in search of the passionate exit of the climax with which culminate the desires that have become naked reality.

Excited as he was, General Victor Emmanuel Leclerc could no longer hide his astonishment. He took a deep breath. He looked at his beloved. Pauline knew she had magnetized him. She had him tied up. He looked like a zombie. Fascinated.

Pauline took both of her husband's hands. She opened the curtain and showed him the bed, which she had ordered her assistant, Carole LeBlanche, to position in a westernly direction. She wanted the bed to be facing where the sun would lie when it gave its last kiss to the Atlantic Ocean. "Metre la chambre en la tété de La Tortue." The Countess was fascinated by Turtle Island. That's why she ordered a holiday home to be built for her on the paradisiacal island. The Countess was fascinated by the hidden beach in front of her house.

"This room is for you." The room was spotless. "I prepared it especially for you! *Cette Chambre est pour vous, mon amour*. I promise you that tonight will be so special that you will feel better than the first time when you made me your wife! I will always remember the straw bed and the neighing of the horses. I was driven crazy by the restless mares. They were nervous as they sighed for the breeding limbs of the colts and horses in your parents' stable in Brittany City and Normandy. *Je ne oubie pa cette moment!*"

The general did not know what to say. He opened his mouth to utter a few words. His lips trembled at the beauty of his wife.

"Don't say anything!" she said to him with softness. "Ne parlez paz, monsieur! Silence, Mon amour! Je te aimez de tout Mon coer! Pour toute la eternité! Cette nuit est pour vous solament!"

The general stared at her. He was amazed. Her blue eyes grew wider as the seconds and minutes passed. Her pupils looked like two huge belugas of azure blue. Not since he had come from France had he seen his wife perform a dance of beauty and sensuality with every movement of her voice and hands.

"She's beautiful!" the officer muttered quietly. His lips vibrated as she showed him the giant tub of warm water she had prepared. Victor Leclerc couldn't believe his eyes. It was one surprise after another. Pauline had decided this time that the mulatto Carole LeBlanche did not bathe her husband, as had been the custom since they arrived in Cap-Haitien. Even though she supervised the baths given to her son Dermide and her husband, the Countess was covertly jealous of the beautiful mulatto Carole LeBlanche. But as much as she tried to hide her distrust of the voluptuous Haitian Creole, she could not hide it. On many occasions, she questioned her son Dermide to know where she was putting her husband's hand when she was massaging him with the ointments. There's no doubt, however, her high feminine ego prevented Pauline Bonaparte from demonstrating in public the envy she had for the Caribbean mulatto who massaged both her and her husband, the general.

At that hour, the atmosphere was special. If Pauline was excited by the multiplication of figures in the mirrors and the enormous bathtub with the ointments of the seven powers, the military man was driven crazy by the torrential rain falling on the roof of the mansion. Before developing the martial skills that made him the highest officer in the army of the Napoleonic Empire, he learned to enjoy the rain while riding in the fields of France and watering himself in the horse stables.

It was in the midst of a torrential downpour of lightning and thunder that he was drawn by a strange force to the family stable. Instead of going into the father's mansion, Victor went, horse and all, into the animal stable. To his astonishment, there was Pauline Bonaparte, who had come to pay him a surprise visit. As she was fascinated by horses, she stayed in the stable caressing the horses that had attracted her so much since she was a child. The storm took her by surprise. Calculated or not, that love encounter was not fully consummated because Victor Leclerc's father found the couple as God brought her into the world minutes before he hitched her up like a mare who wanted to be a woman. Pauline was already ready to jump and adjust her naked body to her beloved Victor Leclerc. They were both ready for the copulation. The neighing of the mares and horses was not enough to alert them that someone was running toward the stable. The jump was interrupted by the surprising presence of the young military man's father. Victor Leclerc came from a wealthy family in the rural Gallic Republic. But now he found himself in the north of Hispaniola, fighting a battle to the death against the fiercest slaves. If he had fought at the head of the most powerful army in Europe, he was now the commander of Napoleon Bonaparte's army that had come to the Caribbean to suffocate the slave rebellion in Haiti or Saint-Domingue.

Tonight, he had been wormed by the wisdom of his wife to keep him company on a special and unforgettable night, which, by the way, was the birthday of his marriage to Countess Bonaparte. The rain, the movement of the trees by the force of the torrential downpour, the bursting of the thunder that seemed like cannon shots to which he was accustomed in the great battles, and the lightning that cut the sky like huge golden swords created an ideal environment for the mind and body of the general to unify on that special occasion. It was as if a déjà vu was taking place between Victor and Pauline. By mere coincidence or for whatever reason, similar episodes had occurred in Corsica and in Paris. But tonight, Pauline had the bull by the horns—or rather, she had him by his manly member.

The anniversary of his marriage to the love of his life, the mother of his beloved son Dermide, and nature had combined to make Victor surrender to his wife's carnal desires. To complete the atmosphere in the love bed, the scent of a perfume that lifted his spirits had arrived in the ship's mail that had just docked at the Cap-Haitien pier that rainy morning. In secret, Pauline had sent for the perfume to surprise her husband. He smelled the scent, but in his military occupation he did not realize that inside the official suitcase from the French capital had arrived the perfume with which she conquered forever the sense of smell of Victor Emmanuel Leclerc. It was a special perfume made with the urine of a developing chimpanzee and seven drops of the pheromone from a Mamba snake. It was considered an aphrodisiac of great power. She imported the perfume as a state secret. It was brought as slaves were transported, smuggled from the jungles of the African Congo to the Caribbean islands. The power of that perfume was as old as it was expensive. But above all, it was very difficult to obtain. The woman used her power to get what she wanted. The force of her will knew no bounds. Almost always, she got her way. She got what she wanted. He was the most coveted officer in Napoleon Bonaparte's army.

Countess Bonaparte was speaking confidently when she repeated to him, "Mon amour, on this night so special for you and for me, I will show you something I have kept for you. It is a secret that you will never forget. I wish you to feel the happiest man in Cap-Haitien, Europe, and the world. It will be superior to the first time. *Je te aime de toute mon coer*, Monsieur Le General."

Her melodious voice already had control over Victor Leclerc's mind and body. His willpower had abandoned him. He wanted her to give him the bath she had prepared for him to enchant him once and for all. Intrigue was consuming him to know what was the secret she was going to teach him on this rainy lightning-filled night. The sooner the better.

He waited in desperation, but she wanted to make sure his dominance was total. She didn't want to take the slightest risk in her feminine plans. She wanted him tied up as women say when they want to have a man under absolute control. She wanted Victor to be like a little lamb. Meek. Meek! In the palm of her hands. That's why she told him, "I know very well that the crown of France has failed you by not sending you the supplies, weapons, and men that you have asked my brother for. That makes you really tense. But I am going to take it out of you. I swear I'm going to get it out of you. After the baths and the ointment treatment, you'll feel like a bull in the savanna. When we're done, you won't have a drop of bitterness left. Trust me. I will send you to the battlefield as light as a feather. You'll walk away triumphant with your tail spread like a peacock. I will make you happy until death. *Mon amour, te aimez de toute mon coer*!"

The line "I'll take it out of you, mon amour" pronounced seven times was enough for General Leclerc to be taken to the big bathtub, led like a little sheep that goes straight to its mother's tit to drink her milk. He walked as if he was numb by the sensual and melodious voice of Pauline, who repeated over and over again, "I'm going to squeeze every last drop out of you. I'm going to squeeze out what's causing you so much tension. Your battle is in my hands, General. Look at the mirrors. Look at me, listen to the crickets and the cicadas. Look at the mirror on the ceiling. That's it. Smooth. Gentle. Don't be afraid. I'm with you in war and peace."

The French soldier looked like a zombie. His will was at the mercy of her will, Pauline. She had him now in her hands. In the palms of her hands. Surrendered. Powerless against his wife's strength. Her transformation into the Metresa was paying off. The two of them had shed all inhibitions. The skins of the male and female warmed as they had the first time. The dance of love began, and the stormy night became eternal.

For whatever reason, Pauline wanted that night to be unforgettable for her husband. The final battle of the slaves and the soldiers was very close. She sensed something strange. It was a premonition of danger because she had spent most of her life in the midst of wars. Her sixth sense and experience told her so. It was a perception of what was coming. First with his parents on Corsica Island, then in France and in the other territories that her brother Napoleon conquered in the expansion of his empire, she learned to look beyond. The atmosphere in Haiti was no different. The drums and the roar of the cannons told her so.

After the French Revolution, the world was in constant war. There would never be peace again. Her brother had taught her that before going to the war camp, she had to make love. She spoke to the general in a melodious, breathy voice. She looked at him again and again. She remembered the first night of love when they were still in Paris after the wedding celebration. She had led him to make love to her under a raspberry tree in the courtyard where it would later become a hotel of her property in the north of the French capital. For him, it was a special and unforgettable night because Pauline shed tears of happiness and of satisfaction when he fulfilled her wish of marriage. They now completed the act of intense love, leaning against the leafy tree where the doves of Paris were perched.

The countess had followed her brother's teaching. To have intercourse before combat. But she had added another ritual. Before any love encounter, Pauline used to take baths prepared with peppermint, vini-vini, arrasa con todo, rompe saraguey, albeaca de muerto, sesame, juana la blanca, and bejuco de indio. The quantity varied according to the man's virile record. It is well known that Pauline Bonaparte's fame would define her as a woman of uterine fire, which is a condition in which when the man penetrates her, he feels such intense heat that he is quickly transported to a quick, fleeting ejaculation. Each time he tries to penetrate her again, the effects are hotter. At the same time, they have the sensation that something very deep burns his virile member and melts his mind. The men who possessed her lost their heads when they could not extinguish so much fire from such a desired woman. The males say that the secret of these plants is neither in the leaves nor in the roots, but in the pure waters of the seven seas, mixed in the bath of bejuco de Indio. But Tingó Florence had another method in the preparation of the concoction for the ointment that was used in the baths of passion and love. Tingó would lock herself in a room under the pretext of soothing the ointment before handing it over to the servants. Behind closed doors, she would take out a jar and pour the contents into the tub. She did this without anyone seeing her. There were thirty-three drops of a white liquid very similar to men's semen that turned out to be a gelatinous liquid from a segmental zebu from the mountains of Switzerland. It was a special substance from the most vigorous bull, capable of impregnating seven cows with a single ejaculation.

Before the soft, dominant voice of the Countess,

the man yielded. He surrendered to seduction with the obedience of a slave. The custom of placing mirrors in the matrimonial room was a way of increasing the erotic and sensual atmosphere. This custom had developed in antiquity and had taken hold since the time of the Phoenicians. The Chinese, the French Empire, and the Russian Empire had brought it to the Caribbean colonies. In Cap-Haitien and Port-au-Prince, mirrors were used for eroticism to lift the spirits and libido of women. Cleopatra was perhaps one of the most powerful women in the world who came to use mirrors in all her feminine dimensions. But it was also used to practice acts of magic and amorous conquest. The tradition of mirrors in the Caribbean became so powerful that when a mirror was broken, the family was cursed with seven years of bad luck. When a burial happened, the mirrors in the house had to be tucked in to prevent the ghosts of the dead and bad luck from being trapped and reflected in the lives of the family members. The first passion concoction was used by the indigenous princesses of the Polynesian islands in the mysterious Pacific Ocean. The semen was taken from the testicles of the hottest seven men on the region, and they were multiplied by seven moons when the moon rose for the seventh time. The reserve of manly semen was placed in the shade of a tree that turned out to be the Pega Palo tree. It was place in the shadow of that trunk for thirteen hours. Not a minute more, not a minute less. Then she would mix it with seven turkey eggs and seven eggs from Florida's legs.

All those ingredients became a special cream that permeated Pauline's pores as she soaked for seven sessions of thirty-three minutes each. Her skin became like pearl. The envy and the enigma of not knowing how to decipher that secret, that enigma, that mystery killed the women of France with curiosity when they saw that delicate body as if it were a Chinese porcelain statue. Envy and jealousy would eat their insides. Her sister-in-law Josephine, being from the Caribbean, knew many tricks that she had learned from the witches and midwives of Martinique and from the Caribbean aborigines of the Dominican island. They were tricks with which the Antilles women enchanted the most powerful, vigorous, and manly men they met in their love affairs.

Though she was dying to know them, Josephine could never know the power and origin of the secrets and tricks that Pauline Bonaparte possessed. Pauline's secrets had become so famous that her brother, the emperor, had placed a spy both in France and in Haiti to learn more of his sister's secrets with which he dominated, like meek lambs, the men who had loved his sister. In the corners of the Europe courts where the empire exercised power, it was a mystery that Pauline's lovers were sent to the front lines of the battle even if they were from the French military elite. Very few of them got out alive. Other evil tongues spread the rumor that a very handsome prince from Egypt, with a reputation for subduing seven women in the same room with his sexual strength, had come to Saint-Domingue to spy on Pauline. But his intentions, as we will see later, were different. It is said that when he saw her in Haiti, transformed and tanned by the tropical sun, he swore silently that his plans had changed. Pauline had charmed him one night when he saw her in Paris. Now she had dazzled him under the mystery of the Caribbean region. Pauline's seven lovers, including the two she married, Victor Leclerc and Camille Burghesse, lost their senses every time they fell into her sensual nets. There were many who lost their lives to the love and the intensity of Pauline Bonaparte's love.

7

The Sweet Sixteen Birthday

When Pauline turned sixteen, the most sensual moans were heard on the shores of the Corsica Island. They were the screams of a military commander of Napoleon's army who, like a wounded wolf, was moaning for the love of the most sensual woman that the history of court life has ever known. The soldier was attracted by the beauty and eroticism of Pauline, who led him like a little lamb to scream with pleasure as if he were a madman behind the curtain of Napoleon's mansion.

When the emperor found out what had happened, he did not lack of want to send him to the firing line. He did not lack the desire to shoot him and send the daring commander to the beyond. The man was twice the age of the young woman.

Pauline was fascinated by older men. For that reason, the officer fell madly in love with the sensual power of Pauline and proposed to her, offering her villages and castles. This infuriated Napoleon further when he learned from the servants that in his absence, Pauline had been found completely naked, moaning, sighing, hooked in the arms of the handsome military man who had lifted her into the air. He had fallen into the nets of her sexual powers. If she moaned with the mixture of pain and pleasure that the first copulation produced, he screamed and sighed for more. Pauline came down from his sturdy body as if descending from a mahogany tree. The man held her behind the wide curtains that covered the walls of Napoleon Bonaparte's abode.

There are many who say that the standing position in which she made love for the first time caused her so much pleasure that she swore that from then on, whenever she met a man for sex, she would always be standing. As she always selected the tallest men, she would stand seven feet away. She would wait for the man to present his erection and give the signal to walk, climb up, and receive penetration in a position that was practiced among the nomads of the Sahara desert. Evil tongues say that when one goes to the Corsica Island and walks through the dark alleys of Ajaccio City, one is attracted by the moans of a woman in the final part of the sexual act. They also add, for those who want to believe it, that one can hear the desperate cries of an officer of Napoleon's army who could never erase from his mind the tricks of that hot and sensual young woman called Pauline Bonaparte. They add that if the night is silent, that man goes hallucinating and desperate. He marches along the roads, moaning like an agonized calf that roars like a lion. His groans are for not being able to defeat in unequal battle the most erotic and sensual woman of France and its territories.

The truth is that Pauline had taken advantage of her stay in the convulsed Cape Town City in Haiti to learn and develop in a relatively short time the implementation of the experiences she had brought from France to the Caribbean, receiving in return the due instructions through which she perfected her tricks and secrets to increase the legendary fame she would carry until the day of her death. One of the rituals she adopted was the use of the scents of different plants of the tropical region. The aroma of Pauline Bonaparte's baths became a balm of an erotic reaction that when the man immersed himself in love, he felt a strange transformation on his skin. He dreamed as if he were hallucinating. They were erotic dreams that followed one after the other. At the end of the ritual, the man lost his strength and had to last several hours in a somnolent state. It was tiredness as if he was drunk with pleasure.

Another ritual that was incorporated by Pauline to her love tricks was the use of Pega Palo, eucalyptus, and mint leaves. These leaves were ground for thirteen minutes. Then they were added to a very potent drink called mamajuana, which also contained seven turtle eggs, a sea turtle member to retain ejaculation and prolong the sexual act. The sea turtle member had to be processed when the moon was full. The ritual included vinegar and hay salt baths to constrict the uterus to tighten the cervix. Pauline did not need these rituals because she was born with the cocomordan condition, meaning that she was born with a vaginal tightness that very few women in the world have. That discovery explains her desire to make love in an upright position, which she discovered as if by magic when she was barely sixteen. She perfected the tricks with the help of midwife Tingó Florence and her niece Carole LeBlanche, who taught her how to take advantage of her skills. Pauline was an excellent pupil who used her skills and sexual secrets to drive those who fell into the nets of love and passion crazy with her womb and erotic charms.

Many readers wonder, how is it possible that Pauline

Bonaparte developed a way of seducing and trapping men at such a young age? This can be explained by the fact that Pauline was probably advanced for her time. Her limited schooling made her possess an education that was suggestive for her lovers. They saw in her a woman of extraordinary beauty that made up for her academic deficiency. Pauline was a combination of a beast with wild characteristics and a passionate woman at the moment of making love. Her personality was a magnet for the male sex. So being so beautiful and at the same time so rustic, she created an interesting mix in men and intrigued the wives of the military and civil servants who served the ladies of the western courts and crowns.

Most of the femme fatale women, instead of living with passion, passed through the great palace corridors as if they were peacocks, wagging their tails as if they were walking in slow motion, on the tips of their shoes, like zombies walk. Their hands were long and delicate as if they were opera pianists. Pauline Bonaparte's erotic strength had broken the traditional protocols that women in the courts of the Western world had exhibited. When one of them stepped out of the protocol norms, the gossips and rumors of society dragged them to the bottom as if it were a tsunami, a destructive tsunami. From Eve to Marie Antoinette to "the Crazy Juana," they were women out of the ordinary; they probably had powers of suction and some special secret. But Pauline handled herself with wisdom. She used the secrets and tricks she possessed to achieve power. She used them with all her feminine strength. This is demonstrated by the fact that many of the husbands and lovers who fell at her feet found death or glory near her. Pauline's erotic powers had led them like lambs to a state of irreversible madness. Her way of seducing and the eroticism that she implanted in her amorous relationships surpassed the tricks that came from lands of the Far East. Especially the skills of Indian women and men who used seduction by suggestion and the creation of an atmosphere without taboos: without light, in the sea, in rivers, in hammocks, in trees, and riding fine horses. Where the seduction will reach and the desire, the consummation of the amorous encounter took place, which was transformed into the melting of the bodies, cupping up to the climax, up to the most passionate orgasm.

Pauline and Doña Leticia, her mother, had similar characteristics. Their temperaments were strong. Their presence was felt wherever they went. Imagine these two women vying for power, for a share of power that Napoleon achieved. It was a battle of female titans. It was like putting Joan of Arc and Marie Antoinette together in a palace circus.

8

The Crowning of Pauline

As if to confuse people, he gave a dramatic touch to his performance, and after a fleeting cough in his throat, he refined the tone of his voice. Then he began to imitate the voices of those who, according to his oath, possessed him. His intonation became effeminate, increasing his theatrical drama: "Let me go, I'm no spy. Do not mistreat me in the name of Papa Bocó and Saint Socorro! No obliez pas que nous some dans la meme bató."

The tramp could not finish the sentence, mixing Creole with French, because his lips were trembling as if they were the soles of a broken shoe.

At that moment, a bossy voice was heard shouting at the top of its lungs, "Get that bastard! Get him! Don't let the intruder escape! He must be a spy coming from France! Get him right now before he goes with gossips at Napoleon's Court! Take him in! Tie that *vole cosó, volé caguite! Languet tu mamau!*"

That bossy voice said many more things containing curses and bad words for the intruder that could not be heard over the din that erupted on the site. There was great jubilation when they caught the double agent who had infiltrated the place despite the huge surveillance.

Many said they saw a black-and-white cat coming down from the ceiling of the room where they were gathered. Others dared to say that the man entered amid a swirl of dust, through the big door, and that everyone threw themselves on the floor with their asses up and their faces down. Everyone thought that the summoned Baron of the Cemetery was arriving on the scene. No one dared to look by Metresa rule. Obviously, the intruder had employed a trick of black-and-white magic to get in unseen. But since nothing lasts forever, the power of his magic trick only lasted thirteen minutes. He must have, in thirteen minutes, gathered his information to fulfill his mission and put his face where he brought his buttocks at full speed. Perhaps the intelligence agent wasted a lot of time entertaining the voluptuous mulattoes who were showing off their attributes with bewitching magic and sensual dexterity, half-naked as women dance at carnivals, driving the men crazy and drawing angry murmurs from the female spectators.

When the unfortunate man realized that he had nowhere to escape because he had run into a dead end, he began a zigzagging flight. He was going in curves from one side to the other. As he was confused, he saw an open space and accelerated, without hesitation, in that direction. It was the arched legs of Madame Duexplasir. Without knowing it, he passed very close to the matron of the place who had ordered his capture. She waited for him with a cane, and having him so close, she put the wood between his legs and told him, "Take this blow. Stupid scoundrel so that you learns how to respect the L'organization du le zombie! Don't you realize that we are at war with France? Saint-Domingue will be free, whatever it takes! Take this blow with a stick so that you respect the slaves. So that you will not serve the oligarchs of France nor the bourgeois of Haiti who mistreat our brothers in Africa. Take this whip so you don't look lustfully at the dancers. Stupid man! Only the chosen ones can look her up and down. Windbag! You entered this sacred place in disguise. You tricked us with those tricks, stupid sorcerer. Woe to your hide, Toton Macute, Loparde, Calie, or aguizote! You're fucked!"

The blow he received in his flight, combined with an unexpected trip from one of the bystanders, threw him off balance. The meddler tumbled to the ground, where he was left shaking with terror. He looked like a cold chick. The truth was uncovered when a burly black man, instructed by a respected priestess known by the surname of Madame La Macanne for her ability to use with efficiency a black wooden stick morbidly shaped like a horse's reproductive member, fell on him. The man was writhing. He was struggling. His cries of despair reached the sky.

"Hit him hard, Bouckman! Hit him hard! Hit him hard, he's a pretender, dammit! Don't forget that zombies don't fuck around! Especially when we're fighting the forces of Napoleon Bonaparte. Stick the baton where it hurts, that's a *jabao* who thinks he's a blond European belonging to the Caucasian race. Put the tourniquet on him to squeeze!"

The last part could not be heard because the drums did not stop beating.

PUM! KUTU-PUM-PUM-PUM! PUM-PUM! KUTUM-PUM-PUM! PUM!

As he had him with a lock between his legs, the executioner obeyed without flinching at all. It was a blind obedience. He did it as all slaves do when their masters give them an order. They obey blindly without caring that the victim is one of their own. That's why they hit him harder. To make him an example. It's a lesson for the others. For that reason, he hit and hit him. With hatred. He beat the intruder of the ceremony of Madame Duex Tetes mercilessly.

Moreno Quitasueño knew that his mistress was implacable. That is why he did not hesitate to follow orders to punish the intruder in order to give a lesson to all those who aspired to serve as double agents for the invader of France in Saint-Domingue.

At a signal from the matron, he dragged him to a bonfire. She took out a lit firebrand and stuck it across his buttocks. She branded him with a spell. For being a traitor to the cause of the slaves. The screams were desperate. Those present began to chant loudly. The chants sounded like cries for the possible deceased to suffer his punishment. That's why they sang in slow motion. Like giant turtles. Slowly. The ups and downs of the voices and the beating of the drums were swallowed the moans of the infiltrator in the ceremony. The man was rolling around like a dog with fleas, itching and aching from the beating the sturdy servant was giving him. The scoundrel paid dearly for his audacity. His despair led him to run with lightning speed toward a huge precipice where he left his last cry of life suspended in the air.

In the kitchen of the place, meanwhile, a mulatto woman dressed in white, who knew the unfortunate man, was slyly preparing a pot of black coffee. She lifted the container. She turned it three times to the left and three times to the right. She lowered the carafe. She took a long gulp of the contents. She looked at the crowd out of the corner of her eye. She took another drink. She moved. Her eyes bugged out like a startled goat. From her throat came the sound of a gargle. Then she tossed the rest of the concoction into the air in a circle for "the tranquility of the deceased." At the same time, the woman hummed a song with her mouth almost closed in which she narrated the story of a man who died because of his weakness for human flesh. Those present at the ceremony limited themselves to respecting the ritual of the black woman who, at the end of her song, jumped up and down. She shook her skirt, showing to the public present the underwear the color of the flag. There was a surprising smoke that blinded for an instant to those who were there. In the blink of an eye, the mysterious woman vanished from the place in a spectacular act of magic.

When the curtain of smoke passed, she had already disappeared. Neither male nor female of the people there dared to say a word about what had happened at the Coronation ceremony.

Pauline, who was hidden in the place waiting for her opportunity of the call of the gods as demanded by the protocol of the Congolese sorceress congress, was in total amazement. She was accompanied by a delegation of maidens from the African Republic of Benin, whose Voodoo religion came to the Caribbean region with the first slaves that arrived tied to the holds of the slave ships. The Countess could not believe what she was seeing. In Paris, they were saying something else for despising the slaves of Saint-Domingue. Petrified, she was still there, covered with a transparent veil. Now she began to understand what was happening in the witchcraft center of La Mermelade.

She now believed more what her friends in Paris had told her. She would become more receptive from what she was witnessing. Initiation into the mysterious organization of the zombies was easier than she thought. Now she wouldn't mind being accused of being a pagan or a believer or a voodoo priestess. Since it was a special congress, Pauline didn't notice that in the room closest to where she was, she was receiving a remedy consisting of seven different healing herbs that would transform her that night. She saw a figure pass by wearing a long robe and a cloak like the one she was wearing to cover her head and face. For some reason, she felt strange vibrations. It was as if she guessed that this man had once been hers. He was also there to transform himself into a priest of the voodoo religion.

The Countess felt a shiver. It was a special shiver that ran up and down her spine. From the smallest bone of contentment to the last vertebra of the back of the neck, where the strength of the hormones that initiate the desire for sensual copulation is concentrated. That figure was about to reveal itself. When Pauline would see who was the person hiding behind that cassock, she would see the purple color, she would need extra strength to not lose her senses or her balance.

Pauline and the Irish Archbishop were not able to resist more the emotions that they felt in the Cape Cathedral Haitian. That's why they were there, in the Infinite Cave. He had arrived first at Saint Jack's ceremony and had escaped incognito in a disguise he had brought to the place. In the cave, he was safe. He had no fear now of the inquisitive gaze of the parishioners nor of the church beatitudes, who, with aspiration to go to heaven to be right with God and the devil, commented on the gossip of the aristocratic ladies who, following the example of French high society women, sought slaves with members the size of Milito the horse to receive a sexual discharge that the blacks fulfilled with servile surrender so that their mistresses might enjoy the Caribbean mystery and the sensual characteristics of mixed races. Also, like the noises heard in some bourgeois houses when they put the slaves in their beds while the wives carefully cultivated the garden of their mansions. Nor was he afraid of the army officers who went religiously to the temple to be at peace with God if death surprised them on the bloody battlefield.

As the hill of La Mermelade was of great height, the religious man had left the mount as black as the night. The mare was called Jet. He left her tied up on the edge of a ravine. With her he left the cassock and all the trappings he had taken with him to calm the curious, telling them that he was on a religious mission on those remote roads. The catholic priests, as well as the priests of other religions such as voodoo and Protestants, have tools of ceremonial representation as a product of the mixture and syncretism of beliefs in every corner of the world. There were many who suspected the carnal preferences and desires of the Irish Archbishop and the Countess Bonaparte. No one dared to say half a word about the importance of the two lovers both in the society of the colony of Haiti and in the European cities, especially with regard to the control exercised by the Vatican of Rome over its subjects wherever it wants them to be on the globe. The Pope's rules and laws are implacable. Neither the archbishop nor the Countess wanted to fall into the evil tongues of the "grand societé."

When the moon began its descent behind Turtle Island, the religious man heard the neighing of an animal that was undoubtedly Pauline Bonaparte's gigantic horse, which answered to the name of Milito. By the intensity of the neighing and the response of his black mare that he had left in the glen, he realized that Pauline was already approaching the place where she had promised to teach him one of the best kept secrets in her sexual life that had served as an intrigue for many men, much more for the burly Archbishop of Ireland.

"*Je te va montré une secrete sexual* that will make you hang up your cassock forever. You can no longer make love to any of the officers' wives. You will be mine alone. Don't do to me what my husband does who loves to sleep with Ayití's mulatto women. I didn't want to let you make love to me in the sacristy because the sacristan was keeping his eye on me as if I were a wolf in heat! What's more, he used to run his tongue over his parched lips because he was so nervous when he helped me tie my boots. He always wanted to tell me something about you."

She had been practicing what she was going to say to the religious to excuse herself when she could not please him last Palm Sunday. Pauline didn't have to give those explanations to the archbishop. He had massaged her breasts several times while he was confessing her. The prelate of Ireland had heard in confessions from some of the officers' ladies about the erotic secrets that drove their ardent lovers mad. Her intrigue was justified because she knew about the burning and hotness she felt on her tongue every time he passed the host to her. The Countess shuddered up and down every time his fingers touched her lower lip, supposedly to prevent the host from slipping and falling to the floor. That would be an unpardonable sin that would betray the lack of control of the religious or the unbecoming nerves of a Countess.

She did not know how to control her emotions in the face of the archbishop's elegance and the complications of her carnal desires for everything that lay behind that bright green cassock like the Irish prelate's penetrating, hypnotizing eyes.

The Archbishop of Rome arrived first at the cavern. To avoid the effects of the gossip that was already spreading from mouth to mouth, he decided to leave the ceremony in a disguise that only Pauline knew. Elusive, he left the place at full gallop on a black mare that never left him. With three whistles as thin as his lips, the horse almost flew and took off in the direction of the cave already known by the two lovers. He rode away on a black mare as the Caribbean nights. As the evening was cool because of a sudden change in the temperature of the region, the archbishop prepared a fire with dry pine wood and a bath of annatto grains. This had been taught to him by a sorceress from Arcahie who did not hide his support for the rebels but wanted to be at peace with God and the devil. In Haiti, as in all the territories of the world, there are towns that have the reputation of having sorceresses, santeros, and witches of all categories. Puerto Rico has the Guayama city, the Spanish part has San Juan de la Maguana and Samaná, Cuba has Santiago de Cuba, Ayití has El Arcahiea. According to witnesses and evil tongues that almost always go together, in these cities mentioned, spiritual and physical works are carried out by the use of magic. In Saint-Domingue, they make you walk on all fours in no time.

The Irish Archbishop, following the instructions of the sorcerer, was doing a stripping of the cave so that Pauline Bonaparte would not dominate him after they had made love. He had heard what happened to the sculptor Antonio Canova in Italy and to the writer Francois Thalma when they had their amorous encounters with Pauline Bonaparte. The religious was convinced by the information of Tingó Florence and Carole LeBlanche that if he was careless with the eroticism and sensuality of the Countess, he would be at the mercy of her will. Tied up like a meek little lamb for the rest of his life. The Countess had her plan, as did the archbishop.

The religious man heard the story of what happened to the prince of Egypt, capable of satisfying seven wives at once. But he left like an obedient little dog, taking his tail between his legs when he fell under Pauline's sensual dominions. Now, meditating before the Countess entered the cave, he was babbling strange words that sounded like a prayer to ward off the evil spirits that were trying to hinder him in this spiritual contest to which he was preparing to submit himself, risking everything under any circumstances in order to reach the proposed goal in front of the woman he most desired in the world. The corpulent religious man did not want to lose this battle. It was a sexual encounter with a woman he coveted with lust.

His desire to possess her increased when Victor Leclerc came to the sacristy to confess and to tell him everything so that his confessions would not leave the sacristy, reserved for the high officers of Napoleon's powerful army that had arrived in Saint-Domingue to confront and destroy the Slave Revolution, so that the other Antilles would not fall into the new current of Liberté, Igualité, and Fraternité. He also wanted to explain to him the secrets that his wife had shown him when they made love in the tub full of ointments multiplied by the mirrors. He was between intrigue and being displeased by the jealousy that burned his soul as if it were the hell with which he always frightened the parishioners who came to confession because they had misbehaved with God's intentions. The religious remembered the general's parsimonious and hoarse voice when he came to see him in the Cathedral of Notra Damus.

"Votre Excellence. I want to confess because I am in the middle of a battle with the black rebels who, under the pretext that they are being exploited on the plantations, seek freedom. At any moment, the unexpected can happen. Confess me, Votre Excellence! My wife transported me to a world of pleasure and sin. Like an Adam of Eden." Without bothering to commit perjury, the general opened his mouth to accuse his wife of having compelled him to commit one sin after another while teaching him her erotic secrets. "She took me to the ultimate intimate depths. I can't explain anymore, Monseigneur! Take her away from me, Your Excellency, wherever she is! That woman, you know, has driven me crazy after having gone to a voodoo center where she came as if she was bewitched. She's a volcano that burns me like hell. Caribbean women have honey in their waists. Haitian women glue themselves to me until I go to the battlefield. But I fix them.

"God forgive me, Monseñor, with this talent of gravel. Forgive the imprudence, but you are a man even if you have a cassock. I'm not going to show you. But I confess to you that the doctor staff that my brother-in-law the Emperor sent me to take care of me in Saint-Domingue, relaxing, told me, 'You have your talent between your legs, Victor. Let them cut off everything but that member.' You know him, Dr. Francois Duexplesirr, who is the son of the richest and most aristocratic family of Cap-Haitien. What's more, in all the Antilles, there is no such a powerful family. It's for her that we came here. Napoleon ordered me to give you all the imperial protection. I am told that you visit the Duexplesir mansion in Port-Au-Prince a lot. We have many agents throughout the Caribbean.

"But back to my wife, what made me come to you, Votre Excellence! What should I do to control Pauline? In Paris, she was called the Jaina because of her talent and wisdom for her cunning in cornering men as if they were wild prey. Here in Saint-Domingue, they say that she dominates all men, including the military chiefs of Toussaint Louverture's army. She makes women fiercely envious by her presence. Advise me, for the sake of the Pope, who is a friend of our family, Monseigneur."

The religious was as if in a trance. Concentrated. Victor Leclerc's despair went in and out of one ear and into the other. It came out of one ear and went in the other. He was in an internal conflict. His conscience was sacrificing him. Since he did not have a cassock, he dressed himself in a kilt in which he walked in the great ceremonies when he had to play the bagpipes with three pipes. Among them was the largest pipe of the instrument through which he blew until he got such a soft sound out of the bagpipes that the birds fell asleep and the women—white, mulatto, and black—

became zombies to do the will of the Irish archbishop. They all wanted to be musicians to play the flute for him.

The archbishop's bagpipes drove her crazy and awakened all the protuberances in recess. Stupefied. Bewildered. While he was sweeping, he had to take a spectacular leap when a couple of limpkins, with such a confidence that produced the mysterious birds and stayed copulating beyond the usual, flew out of the depth of the cavern. It all happened so quickly that the priest did not expect such a surprise. He never thought that the birds were procreating in the depths of the cavern. The enormous birds came out, one on top of the other, to escape the repercussions that the religious man had formed, making him the spoils of the cavern. Both the male and the female came out terrified, without having concluded their attempts at reproduction due to the disturbance of the archbishop, who was desperately preparing the love nest for the Countess Pauline Bonaparte. The enormous birds began their fluttering, aided by the gravity of the abyss of the ravine next to the exit of Saint Jack's hiding place. The infinite, somnolent, and inoffensive sun passed close to the parsimonious and lazy moon that preceded it this time, the arrival of the invincible night.

Frightened by the noisy passing of the birds, the priest approached the exit of the cave, holding on to the bushes that bordered the ravine. He didn't want to slip into that deep abyss. After all, in Ayití, all the chasms are deep because the mountains brushed against the sky. Down below, both Milito and the religious man's black mare, in their animalistic flirtation, were bumping heads and running their tongues at each other like a prelude to what was to come in Saint Jack's Infinite Cave.

The archbishop saw, in the distance, the almost faded figure of Pauline advancing at a slow pace along the slopes of the mountain. The Countess had listened to the advice of the Irish archbishop: "Pauline, what is at stake is my religious career and your reputation for the crown of France. If we are caught, we will be shot and reported as victims of the war between France and the blacks of Haiti. Do not ride the horse or the mare when you go to go up to the cave. Leave the animals tied up on the slope of the hill. Tie them close so that they can amuse themselves by copulating when they feel like it. If you leave them far away, they will break the rope. The mare is in heat. When she was passing through the savannah of the Mulate, she got mad when she saw a horse whinnying to possess her. I had to calm her down by throwing myself on the ground and rubbing her ass. She almost threw me off the cliff. Remember that Milito always has his member on fire. Standing like a stake. As if it were a burning coal, looking for a place to put it to cool it down. Oh! May God forgive me for what I'm thinking!"

Hearing so many phrases with which the priest painted sensual images while offending the modesty of animals, the Countess loosened the buttons of the cotton blouse she was wearing. She did so because she felt a suffocating heat rising all over her body. Pauline followed the prelate's advice. She listened to him and tied up Milito, her gigantic horse that, with its constantly erect member, wanted to break the rope to follow her uphill. If it had not been for the beauty of the beast that accompanied him at a short distance, the animal would have continued upward so that his owner could mount him. That was what he had come from Europe for. His training in the best stables of Marseilles made Milito the most faithful and obedient horse when it came to the Emperor Napoleon or his sister Pauline. His thunderous whinnies traveled through the hills and mountains of Saint-Domingue. His mistress advanced. She was heading steadily toward the cave.

There, a love encounter awaited her that would mark her for the rest of her life.

The religious's heart stopped three times. It could not be another. He thought. He was excited. For a moment, he forgot that he was a prelate. He touched his body. His cassock was gone. Now he wore the little kilt of Scotland in which he paraded in the cultural processions to play the bagpipes, blowing through the big pipe that, like a member with an obvious phallic representation, shone in the middle of the instrument between pipe and pipe. The archbishop wanted the woman to fly. Her eyes, green as the nature of Hispaniola, grew bigger and bigger. The archbishop knew very well that Pauline was coming to keep her word. She brought the seven secrets of her feminine sex to teach him with the most intense passion in these nights they would spend in Saint Jack's Infinite Cave next to the hill of La Mermelade.

The Archbishop of Rome cared little for the rebellion of the slaves, the annihilation of the colonists, the intense fire of the plantations, nor the fall of Cap-Haitien. The lights of the city and the cannon fire in the distance were signs of jubilation in his hiding place, waiting for his beloved Pauline. She was the only woman who made him lose his mind since he met her giving him the hosts in Basilica Cathedral of Santa Maria La Menor in Florence City. Now was his chance. It was his chance to win or be won in a battle of sex, passion, love, and eroticism. Desperate for Pauline's arrival, he didn't know whether he should give himself a ravage and self-flagellate until he bled with rompe saraguey for the sin he was about to commit or develop everything he knew about lovemaking to satisfy Pauline Bonaparte. In spite of everything, the Irish archbishop knew that hell was not enough to adulterate with his neighbor's wife. The mere guilt that tormented him vanished with the satisfaction of that amorous conquest that began in the sacristy of Rome.

Confused as he was, the prelate did not know what to do. His heart was pounding. It sounded like a drum inside his chest: *PUM! KUTUPUM! PUM! PUM!*

He thought it was the sporadic cannon shots fired by the soldiers led by the husband of the woman he was about to possess. Pauline's every step was followed by his eyes for fear of losing sight of her in the bushes of the ravine. He didn't want this to be part of a dream or a beautiful nightmare. The path was narrow. At the end of the hill passed the Mulatto's Lemon River. Its waters were crystal clear. The moon had stopped like a lamp hanging in the firmament. It looked like a huge spotlight illuminating the mountains, the plains, and the rivers. When the river was calm, you could see from the heights the amount of fish and crustaceans in coexistence with nature, copulating with care, one on top of the other, making love like humans next to the gigantic stones to increase the species. But when the gods of wind and water entered into conflict, the waters swirled, roaring like the mouth of a beast waiting for the fall of its prey to swallow it in one gulp. In a single bite. In a single mouthful.

The whitish foams rose like volcanoes, threatening to erupt the fiery lava from its belly located in Saint Jack's Infinite Cave.

PUM-KUTUPUM-PUM-PUM-PUM!

Each whirlpool was like a huge blowing of the conflicting gods from the depths of the puddles. The water's tongues seemed like whips of punishment for what was about to happen in Saint Jack's Cave. But the passion, the eroticism, and the carnal desires of the archbishop surpassed the divine threats and displeasures.

Pauline found herself at last at the top. She took a deep breath. She breathed in again. She exhaled! Her breasts swelled with heat and humidity, presenting the sharp nipples outlined by the blouse her mother Leticia had given her to combat the high temperatures of the Caribbean. She took deep breaths over and over again. Each breath lifted her breasts in constant struggle against the gravity of the mountainous altitude. Then she uttered some strange words in the dialect of the Corsica Island. It was impossible to understand what she said. She glanced at the place where she had left Milito and Jet, the archbishop's mare. Milito had already ridden the mare seven times after he had been left eating grass on the mountainside. The blowing of the animal attested to that. The beautiful woman smiled at the white horse's antics. She looked back into the abyss. She felt no fear because she was accustomed to the heights of the Pyrenees Mountains that blocked France and Spain. Nor was she afraid of the great ravines that border the Corsica Island.

The bad words she might have uttered about the place chosen by the archbishop were in Creole, language of her native land. Islanders are notorious for eating their words without pronouncing some letters and then repeating what they said over and over again. She repeated it again. Now she took a second breath to enter the huge cave that the Tainos and the slaves have had for centuries as a center for secret ceremonies. With the pure oxygen of the place, her face was turning red. Her cheeks looked like two red apples. Red like Artibonite tomatoes. Her porcelain skin began to blush. She knew she was about to execute an unforgettable love match with the accumulated energy of a thirty-nine-year-old man who followed her from Rome to Saint-Domingue. It was like facing Diana and Poseidon. Body to body.

Just thinking about it made her blush. Her skin looked like gooseflesh. She looked like a mare in heat. Her thoughts now were not on Milito, nor on his prolonged erection, nor on the prelate's mare that the horse was biting on her neck to make sure she endured the pleasurable penetration caused by his extraordinary virile member. Pauline was thinking of the amorous encounter of the man inside the cave. The archbishop of Ireland who played the bagpipes with such mastery that the pigeons and the dastardly lords stopped their flight at the sound of such exquisite high and low notes that they flew out of the middle pipe to ride the hot wind that carried them in all directions with wild freedom.

When Pauline stopped at the entrance to the cave, she looked in all directions. At that moment, a soft breeze was blowing with the scent of the bushes of the Artibonite Mountains. She lifted her chest and inhaled the breeze through her mouth and nose. Her breasts, like two crystal goblets, hardened even more when she heard the deep voice of the archbishop telling her, "Don't come in yet. I'm just finishing making you a snack. You're going to love it. It was taught to me by the Taino Indians of Quisqueya. It's cassava with bee honey! It is the honey of thirty-three queen bees. It is important that the honeycombs are opened at dawn on the first Friday when the moon is full. It is a special snack for you, who are my *sovereiiiiiiiiiiiiiiiiiiiiiiiiiiiiiiiiiiiiiiiiiiign!*"

Like something strange and mysterious, when the religious pronounced the word *sovereign*, an endless echo originated in the enormous cave and escaped from the place, repeating the word *sovereign* over and over again. The word of praise for her Highness, the Countess, left riding on the breeze and in the eternal echo that revives, repeats itself a thousand times, a thousand times a thousand in love encounters. When the immense sun showed the tips of its golden rays like a beast that shows its sharp teeth to frighten its prey as it passed over the back of the mountains of the west, Pauline took the three steps that placed her at the entrance of the cavern.

The archbishop came to meet her while saying, "Welcome, Your Highness, to the cave of love. Come. Sit here by the fire! I want you to feel the warmth that I'm feeling. Feel it, my love, because this will be a burning night for both of us. It will be an unforgettable night, unique and special. Destiny has willed it, and so have we."

He made a signal with his hands. He didn't dare look at her from the front so as not to expose the desire to have her that was burning inside him. The Countess and the prelate were a wild passion that had been repressed for many years, and on several occasions, he was on the verge of making love to her in the sacristy. But luckily for him, the sexual act was not consummated. If it had happened, the religious man's moans would have been heard throughout the cathedral. That's why he looked at her sideways. His light green eyes looked like two miniature torches. He was looking at her with the same eyes that hypnotized her when he first saw her in Rome.

"Sit down, Paolette. Don't be afraid of fire, woman! This is our night. It'll be a special night for both of us. I promise you. I swear it will be unforgettable because of something I've saved just for you!"

He spoke in English with a Scottish accent. Pauline felt vibrations all over her body. The archbishop's tongue was special. His throat was irresistible. With its husky voice like the low voice of a horse in heat, it ate her brain and enveloped her body. It was his tongue that he used with the dexterity of a woodpecker when he wanted to convince the cathedral's parishioners. Pauline's skin was like that of a quality hen when the rooster is about to step on it to lay eggs. Everything that came out of the prelate's mouth dislocated her. When he sang and played the bagpipes, Pauline and the other women swore they could lose their heads for the priest of Ireland any time he asked them to. There were many husbands who felt the bishop's intimidation when he approached their wives. A little attention from the religious was enough for them to feel a pleasant shiver from head to toe. His voice went into their ears and traveled through every cell of their bodies. The women—whether they were white aristocrats, Caribbean Antillean Creoles, or pure-blooded mulattoes—felt that the religious harangues hypnotized them. They felt naked in their presence. Their skin bristled, and the protuberances of their bodies stood up in the presence of this man who had an enchanting magic in his voice and a manly libido that could be appreciated above the cassock.

The archbishop knew the parishioners and had noticed on more than one occasion that many of them were losing their heads over him. That boosted his ego and much more. The archbishop was a polyglot. He spoke several languages, and foreign accents transformed them.

Pauline felt her nipples turning like two rocks from possessing a man as handsome and vigorous as the Irish archbishop. As he gave way to Pauline, the priest flattened himself to lift a bouquet of wildflowers he had lovingly brought her from the ravine. He stood transfixed at the sight of the outlined Pauline Bonaparte's figure that was walking provocatively in the direction of the bonfire. The religious was open-mouthed, petrified at the sight of Pauline's body, so perfect, that in her nakedness, she was looking for the heat of a fire that he had prepared with care. The bishop could not believe it.

"Finally, Pauline is going to be for me body and soul," he said out loud. Deep down, he knew that no one was listening to him. The archbishop was flushed with the intensity of his desire to possess her. His heart was pounding. PUM-PUM-PUM! KUTUPUM-PUM-PUM! His chest was burning like a volcano. The pupils of his sleepy green eyes expanded. In a moment, the conjunction of the two bodies, the passion of their loves and carnal desires, would spread through the huge cavern. The heat of so much love would go out like lightning toward the infinite, toward the unknown.

In the distance, one could see the flashing of the guns of the soldiers of both sides who fought without stopping. The rebels and the French were fighting to death. The slaves were breaking the chains and shackles that the French colonizers had put on them for centuries to bind them to eternal slavery. The attacks could be heard in the distance. But the Countess and the archbishop looked at each other like two wild beasts that were going to devour each other. The fighting mattered little to them at this crucial moment.

Pauline's feminine attributes took on a special whiteness. With the passing of her tongue over her lips, she gave the erotic signal for the archbishop with the little skirt of Scotland to initiate the advance toward the woman whose body was like a volcano in flames. Now it began to open and close to produce the chemistry that would raise her to the top, to the climax, to the infinity of one orgasm after the other. It was then that Pauline saw her lover's erection, and as she had done before, she embraced him in the act of sublime sexual surrender. She climbed up the sturdy tree that penetrated her until, in her desperation, she opened her mouth like a fish that has taken the bait as if the oxygen was running out.

She was gasping for air to the point of pleasurable agony. The woman feared that she would run out of oxygen to continue living. It is a fleeting instant that is felt when ecstasy is reached; both the man and the woman feel that if they die in that final process, what will be, will be. That is why a popular philosopher says, "The one who dies for their taste, their sorrow tastes like glory."

Pauline's body began to bristle as she felt pleasant electric shocks from the emotion of what was entering her beautiful, sensitive, sensual body. Her pupils, like honey, lit up. The archbishop did not move. He knew that in that position, she could not make him succumb. Pauline's body clung to the archbishop's muscular body the way ivy clings to the front of a tree. He lifted her up again with great gentleness. She swung her legs as if she were climbing a mahogany tree. In that instant, they both fell like two pieces of fresh pine in a whirlpool unbridled by the endless explosion of burning bodies. They made love again and again, copulating in the intimacy of Saint Jack's Cave. Man and woman, male and female, they rolled around. At every turn, they were giving way to the unbridled passion of two foals in heat. The somersaults were produced by her to free herself from the lock that the archbishop had placed on her. He knew he had to keep the penetration going all the way in. If he pulled out one centimeter, he would not resist the internal clenching, which would produce an early ejaculation. Each embrace produced animalistic, bestial convulsions. The thunder that repeated itself in sequence among the mountains of Saint-Domingue was confused with the screams and moans of the consummation of that encounter of intense, perennial love.

The boiling eroticism emanating from Pauline's pores combined with the carnal desires of the archbishop created a loving chemistry of such intensity that the couple never left their position. The ups and downs of the orgasms in sequence seemed like an endless wave of lava emanating from Pauline Bonaparte's feminine conformation. The skin had bristled that much more as a prelude to the fusion of tenderness and sensuality that would unleash the swirling waters. The two bodies had merged in the consummation of a love that seemed impossible.

The archbishop remained static in his rhythmic movements at other times with his oak-like musculature, proud of what was happening in Saint Jack's Infinite Cave.

All the parts of their bodies had intertwined to form a single erection, a single swirl, a single spurt of the nectar flowing from a spilled cup. The cavern was like a raging bonfire. The two bodies wallowed. They sighed. They dozed. When the energies surged, stimulated by the honey and the cassava, Pauline and the priest rose again to penetrate again and again, one inside the other. The metal statues melted, only to fall again, fulminated by the intense fire of love. In outer space, a shower of shooting stars were giving account of the concert of love, sensuality, and passion that was taking place in the bowels of the infinite cave. It was a colossal waste of nectar whose taste only the two of them could taste. It was a deep secret of a special love between the Countess and Archbishop of Rome. The place served as a nest for the two sinful, passionate loves. One because of his religious commitment, the other because she was the wife of the commander-in-chief of Napoleon Bonaparte's army that was in Saint-Domingue to destroy the first slave rebellion in the French colonies. That was their nest where the stored passion and energies of their carnal desires as man and woman were wasted.

Seven screams were uttered by Pauline when she realized that the archbishop had succeeded in penetrating to the point where she would have neither strength nor control of her own femininity in order to bend the sex of the archbishop of Ireland. What neither the Prince of Egypt, nor the drama instructor and teacher Francois Talma, nor the ingenious sculptor Antonio Canovas had achieved, the Irish archbishop could achieved it using what he knew and the concoctions of the Arcahie and La Plateau d'Aitibonite sorcerer. This had been the godfather who baptized the religious man when he became a laureate of the voodoo religion of Saint-Domingue.

The seven screams were confused with the pleasurable pain of the woman who robbed him of his virginity in the first penetration; they released into the air the sighs of an act that had been consummated by a loving surrender. In the twilight, they were able to scare away the birds, to astonish the wild beasts, to warm the cavern with their burning bodies, and to provoke a rain of stars. At the end, when the night grew darker and the passions reached the climax producing silent explosions between the fused bodies, the last fiery sighs were heard coming desperately from the throat of Pauline Bonaparte through the immensity of the mountain, pronouncing the true name of the archbishop who had defeated her in the position she had chosen to make love to him, to give him her priestly virginity.

"Jean Paul, Jean Paul, Jean Paul! Je te aime de tout mon coer. No oblie pa que vous cette la'amour de moi vie!"

Her hollowed voice faded as she stammered a few phrases in the Creole language of Corsica in the Ajaccio port town where she was born, like all of Napoleon's brothers and sisters. The words that came out of his half-closed mouth had a melodious, erotic, sensual intonation. But they could not be deciphered because the crickets and cicadas, inseparable companions of the tropical nights, prevented it with their nocturnal singing. To close that scene of such intensity and passion, Milito's neighing and the mare's moans, which were in the final stage of a frenzied copulation, contributed to Pauline's falling into a trance of sexual satisfaction.

The countess snuggled into her beloved's sturdy arms. Lulled by the discharges and the fieriness of that encounter that seemed eternal, she felt the fragility of the eternal beginning. As if she were a little chick feeling cold, she let herself be wrapped between the muscular legs of the one who had just satiated her erotic femininity. Meanwhile, with her mind happy and her body exhausted by satisfaction, Pauline Bonaparte was falling into the depths of a pleasant dream. From her ruddy lips, the name of the archbishop was heard to be whispered once more. She spoke it unhurriedly. Again and again in her journey into her subconscious, he did not want that moment to end. Then a faint smile, lips parted, revealed part of her chipped teeth. With the passage of her red, bristling tongue, she apparently wanted to slowly taste the last kiss of the religious who, in an act of supreme chastity, had kept himself all his life to know Pauline's seven secrets. His concern was not the habits, nor the cassock, nor the implacable punishment of the Vatican for those who violate the legal canons, but to maintain the happiness of having bent the sexual powers of the Countess Bonaparte.

The intermittent flashes of lightning in the distance served as a background to the sighs that came out, pushed in endless sequence by the passion of two bodies that were becoming one. The overwhelming moans, like a love secret and the sharp lightning of the sparkles, stabbed once again the sky of Saint-Domingue. High up there, announcing the imminent arrival of a surprising rain, the sound of thunder was spreading across the geography from end to end of the Hispaniola Island. The clouds and the lightning that intertwined in the sky formed figures that seemed to challenge the imagination and the astonishment of those who saw them traveling at full speed as if they were celestial carriages. Each explosion served as a stimulus for both lovers to remember the continuation of their acts of erotic love that had unleashed the spell of their forbidden relations.

Pauline Bonaparte at thirty-three and the archbishop at thirty-nine formed a couple of volcanic fire as their bodies and genitals melted in an embrace of prelude to a climax of a suffocating orgasm. The immensity of their desires gave no room to let themselves be overcome by the overwhelming sleep of Morpheus because Cupid was on the alert. The honey and the cassava of the three queen bees was his delicacy.

The archbishop now idolized Pauline. He knew he had discovered her secrets. He smiled faintly as he looked at her openly, asking for more, just a little bit more. She wanted him to hook her once on that virile member that was driving her to an agonizing state. To insanity. She begged him to continue what he'd started, even though Pauline knew she could lose her mind in one of the moments of ecstasy. She gave a sign of conscience when she said to him, "Je suis pour vous pour toute la eternité!"

Hearing this confession, the prelate felt something strange. His body began to vibrate again. He took off his kilt. He stood up, and as he knew Pauline Bonaparte's point of pleasure, he lifted her up in the air, carrying her and performing a dance of eroticism that he had learned from the Caribbean Indians of the Dominica Island. The dance consisted of lifting the woman. Leaning her against the wall of the cave, he would use his tongue and make a tour of all the protuberances of her body until she began to discharge the nectar by the force of gravity. When the woman was unhinged, he would flip her seven times. He would receive her in his erection so that she would have no strength or time to flinch. He did so to prevent her from producing a surprise ejaculation due to the effects of the cocomordan she had in her cervix. He waited patiently for her to come on his virile member. It was thirteen minutes that seemed like an eternity. Both of their knees were unable to resist before they fell down in a Kamasutra position hooked to each other next to the huge stone of the cavern, moaning and sighing from the pleasurable effects of the sexual encounter. On the mountainside, Milito and the black mare repeated what they had always done as they neighed and moaned in the procreation of life.

She's gorgeous! he thought, but didn't dare to say it

out loud because it wasn't time yet. Only the chosen ones could be part of the scene that would take place at the stroke of midnight. At that time, there would be a tribute of surrender to the gods. The maidens were to be chosen to begin their lives by coupling with the males who were selected for this purpose. The only condition was that the number of couples could not exceed seven. Through the ritual, the young virgins would be tempted with the test of the flesh. Those who would pass the temptations, and only mate when the gods "mounted" them, when they were stripped and possessed by the spirits, became priestesses at the service of the new queen of the hemisphere, her high Metresilis who had been reincarnated in the figure of Pauline Bonaparte. They were the ones predestined to protect the goddess—three maidens on new moons and three mulattoes when the moon was full. The couples were required strength and abstinence for seven moons to execute the divine mandate on this night of initiation in the meeting of matter and spirit. Those who were not chosen would have to leave the site committed to be witnesses of what would happen as the saying goes. Thus they were disappointed.

PUM! KUTUPUM-PUM-PUM!

9

The Altar in Flames

As soon as the Countess arrived in Cap-Haitien, as a good Catholic, she began to attend the Notra Damus Cathedral. Reverend Jean Cloude LaPeste had arrived with the invasion as chaplain to Napoleon's army. He was a young priest who loved riding horses and building up his muscles by doing extreme exercises. As soon as he hung up his cassock after his religious services, he would go out like a bat out of hell in a marathon race around the bay of Cap-Haitien, on the grounds that it looked very much like the Marseilles port, his hometown. Young and old, white and mulatto girls and women, slaves and freed women, waited behind the sacristy, their heads and faces covered to see the priest in sporting clothes, showing off his muscles above and below for his day-long race. They didn't want to be identified when he gave them the communion wafer and uncovered the desires they held within their souls in search of pleasure. Many women would run their tongues across their lips parched from the Caribbean heat as they watched him pass by. The saliva did not flow to the upper lips. He was a Frenchman careful of his body and his tongue.

Although he had not been Pauline's confidant or designated confessor, he had the opportunity to visit her in the room she had chosen on the lead ship at the head of the fleet of warships that had made the Navy of Napoleon Bonaparte's Grand Armée famous. The priest approached with the excuse that he had come to run his hand to the horse Milito, who had caused him astonishment when he had first seen him. His mischievous mind was always wondering why the organizers of the invasion had put such a big horse traveling for three months without any other animal, neither male nor female, exhibiting his virile member in permanent erection, on such a big ship with the Countess Bonaparte and her court of women and the wives of the highest-ranking officers.

Chaplain LaPeste of the French Navy did not ask many questions. Neither Commandant Leclerc nor Carole, Pauline's personal secretary, liked the questions of the priest who questioned as if he were in the middle of a rigorous confession. As if he were looking for hidden parts in the answers of private confessions. But since the mind is the only free thing a person has, the priest used to mentally masturbate, he masturbated just thinking about the Countess and the mulatto Carole LeBlanche. He knew that the Countess didn't like to be asked questions with double intentions either. That intrigued him even more, and he got horny imagining what the women looked like when they bathed in the Turtle Cascade. He knew about that earthly paradise because the nuns and priests went on retreat, without any supervision, to get rid of the stress and tension produced by the confessions of the blessed, the female and male parishioners in their eagerness to know if they had any hope of going to heaven, when the hour of death arrived in the plantations of Saint-Domingue. The Vatican knew of the existence of this amusement center for nuns and priests with exhaustion and anxiety due to the excess of work in the Catholic dioceses whose churches grew like purslane in all the Antilles, conquering souls before voodoo vanished like a ghost, taking the saint and the alms that the Vatican power was so concerned about in the conquered territories. For his morbid and mischievous mind, however, the fact that the archbishop was coming with an unholy mission to the colony of Saint Dominic never crossed his mind, not even for a moment, the fact that the archbishop was coming with an unholy mission to the Saint-Domingue colony. In fact, the religious became so powerful in the cathedral that the diocese archbishop left him in charge of the cathedral when he had to go away for a long time to the Vatican in Rome.

Father LaPeste was left to cover the absence of the major prelate who had been called to Rome for a consultation with the Pope where he would explain the role of the Catholic Church in the expansionist geopolitics that had begun the French Empire under the rule of Napoleon Bonaparte. But on Sunday, February 13, 1799, the bishop anxiously awaited. He had entered through Port-au-Prince and would officially be back in Cap-Haitien in seven days as he planned to make some stops to visit the dioceses of the interior of the departments of Port-au-Prince, Gonaive, Jackmel, and Uanamendez, which were organizing themselves to increase the contributions of animals and money for the construction of more churches. It was a way to penetrate the structure of the voodoo religion that was not only gaining strength, but also in the whole region of the south west of Saint-Domingue.

Gonaive was growing, and that worried the Pope of Rome. Some women had told Pauline Bonaparte of his arrival. The bishop was very popular among the ladies of all social classes. His career had grown like foam because he was a relative of a pope and had many relations in the Mother Catholic and Apostolic Church of Rome. They said he was a stout man because he had been a professional swimmer. Like his colleague Father LaPeste, he had the same sport inclinations and had a special ability to jump with the dolphins as if he were a skillful fish. He was also a ball player and long-range runner. He was a virtuoso on the bagpipes and fascinated the women he played around him. Whether in the women's parish or by invitation at the cardinal's meetings. The young bishop loved to delight those present because in those events, the chances of playing the flute to the Pope of Rome were very high. There were also the most influential women of the high courts of Europe and the influential religious lobbyists who would reach out to their favorite candidates to give a boost to their favorite's aspirations for the papal throne—even if it meant rubbing the buttocks and breasts of sexually inclined religious of the same sexual gender.

Pauline Bonaparte was so interested in the coming of the Vatican's envoy that every time the subject of the bishop's arrival was brought up, she said without fear of being heard all over Saint-Domingue, "I'm anxious to meet the bishop! His eyes do not let me sleep peacefully! His gaze follows me from Rome to Cap-Haitien. During the three months we spent in the Atlantic, I dreamed of the archbishop giving me the Host. I used to wake up wet with sweat and something creamy, which I think was the cream that Carole LeBlanche used to spread on my skin to take care of it the way I have it: white, soft, and smooth as porcelain. Sometimes I'd wake up in a state of exhaustion because Victor was devising war strategies in the engineering room. The worst thing is that I've never seen him up close. He comes to me in my dreams when

I finish my massages, before falling into the arms of Morpheus, the first thing I see is the archbishop's eyes. It is very strange. If I sin or am unfaithful in thought to my husband, may God have mercy on me and forgive me. It is not my fault that he has bewitched me in this way."

What never crossed her mind was that the religious was the same one who had made her lose her mind in the Cathedral La Menor del Vaticano.

Jean Cloude LaPeste, without wasting time, offered to be the messenger when he heard of Pauline's comments. She was a countess. He was a chaplain priest in the service of Napoleon's army. He did it because he knew that "Saint-Domingue: Domingue and all over the world, he who does not have a godfather, dies a heretic."

The bodies of the dancers formed a whirlpool. The women twisted their curvaceous figures as if they were swirling serpents. The waists of the maidens were stimulated by the erotic chanting of the manly choir's husky voices accompanied by the sounds of the drums scraped with magical mastery by the maestro's fingertips. That's why they put the spy in the Sahara to inform Napoleon's intelligence team of all the steps of the Countess and her husband along with any concerns of the soldiers and high-ranking officers. The rustic instruments vibrated as they were struck with rebellious power by Francois Casablanche. The musician was a twin of Noir Curaçao, and they were separated when they were very young. The two were a mixture of Taino Indians from Ayití, with blacks from Sierra Leone. In that ceremony, the war tradition was being followed so that they would be the priests and advisors who would face the powerful invading army.

The Emperor of France had sent thirty-three thousand of his army's best soldiers to destroy the slave rebellion in Haiti. The invasion was led by General Victor Enmanuel Leclerc, who was Napoleon Bonaparte's brother-in-law. Among those present were priests of different races who aspired to avoid the deaths and bloodshed of their aboriginal brethren and half breeds from the territories of Holland. The seven royal crowns were intervening to negotiate. The sorcerers from Africa who had come to organize the slaves of Bouckman and Mackandal had given a change by orders of their ancestors who reigned in the other world. In a dream from beyond when they used a medium that was mounted on him, a lwa came and told them, "There will come a queen as beautiful as the star of Venus, as white as goat's milk. Do not contradict her or harm her. Woe to him who does not kneel when she removes her veil. The gods will be on the lookout for anyone who uses their imagination to have morbid desires to make love to her. When she undresses, do not look at her attributes with unholy or morbid intent. When she lies down, say nothing because her breasts will be like two arrows. Her nipples will resemble Puerto Rican quenepas and the Quisqueyan lemongrass. If you disobey my will, you will remain in darkness forever. You will never see the light of day again. Did you hear me right? I said you will be blind forever. The devil will tempt you a thousand times so that she will give you a little bit, a tiny bit, of loving attention. Do not be lustful when you are in front of the Goddess who came from the Atlantic Ocean. Pay no attention to her breasts or her almost perfect body. She is for those chosen by the priests of voodoo with the approval of the gods of Africa. The lwas and priests will receive the sign!"

This would be a battle of life and death between the slaves of Haiti and the great French empire. Blood would run to the river. It was a battle between giants like it had never been seen in the history of mankind.

The musicians' eyes were fixed on the undulating waists of the Haitian and Taino aboriginal women who danced past the stage, acclaiming all the gods and saints of the earth and the heavens.

"Mon Dieu, when will you come? Donne moi force to the fight! The women can't do anymore! Sante Socorre, come here! Anaisa and Papa Bocó will help me! Saint-Domingue and Haiti are a single peace! The union makes the force, damn it!"

The phrases were repeated with symmetrical intonation by the presenters. These received, as a background, the rumbling echo of the mountains and hills. It was the message that the Haitian people understood. The ranting of the singers formed, together with the pumpumkutuponing of the drums and zombies. The ceremony was held in the bend of a hill next to the hamlet of La Mermelade. From there you could see, when the clouds allowed it, the majestic imposing Citadelle Castle and its twin, the fortress of La Ferriere. Both buildings, built with the blood, fat, and testicles of the bulls, served as a refuge for the powerful Henry Christophe, the slave and cook who became, overnight, the first King of the New World under the pompous name of Henry I. The slave rebellion raged on as the invaders advanced.

Pum-Kutu-Pum-Pum-Pum-Kutu-Pum-Kupum!-Pum-pum!

The arrival to the place was made more difficult by the curves and ravines that must necessarily be there because in Haiti, as its name indicates, the land is high and mountainous. The mountain of Fonde du Blanc stood out like the erect member of an Arabian horse. Pauline had been fascinated ever since she entered Cape Town. If the colony had not been at war, it would have fascinated her even more her summer home in Mount Joli or on the peak of Found Due North. Pauline loved nature and all the Caribbean West Indies because they resembled the Corsica Island where she ran around with her sisters and brothers until she was sixteen. She was struck by the conical shape with a pointed end, which, from a distance, gave the impression of being the virile member of a Samson of nature. This was how the highest peaks of Saint-Domingue were perceived. If they were seen with the use of imagination and suspicion, they would be described like this:

"I am intrigued by this work of creation!
The mountains look like giant men.
They look like proud giants, showing their muscles!
The caverns look like nymphs showing off their charms like a summons from the gods!
Their forms resembling women's shapes and voluptuous. A true work of nature art."

Pauline said this to the mulatto Carole LeBlanche as they rode to Cape Town to attend the Irish bishop's Mass. Her assistant smiled without saying a word. That was the way her mistress had instructed her. Listen. Look and don't speak. Follow my orders and nothing else. Carole did not dare to mention her mistress's comment to Noir Curaçao, playing with her private part so that the assistant would look at her out of the corner of his eye. To the place one climbed as if one went inside a huge snail, like one who rises in a mountainous spiral, like one who goes into the hollow of a singular and defiant horn.

The pointed horn stood as a password of mockery to the infidelity of the ungodly gods who had defied the designs of the priest. It was a mockery of the Antilles mystery because they thought they were safe from the wrath of the God of gods, the King of kings. Now they would have to pay dearly for their escape to the great plateau, a Caribbean Olympus in the inaccessible geography of Artibonite, a den of the meek and the maroons. That was the only place on the Hispaniola island where the condemned ruled as if they were gods in force in the Caribbean region. There they hide, fearful of being punished by the implacable Papa Bocó.

The renegades did not fight with the necessary courage against the sugar cane settlers against the plantation foremen who had come from France. There also hid the Caribbean caciques who got tired of committing outrages against their race and then chose to stay in the mountains looking at the sea that served them as a stage for combat. Those who were corrupted and fearful fled to the merciless whip of the white masters who had ended up there. The French colonizers had taken over the sugar mills and sugar cane mills with blood, sweat, and fire. Now it was their turn to run to the French stewards, rapists of their females, lustful persecutors of the women, and daughters of the slaves and mulattos in the coffee and sugar cane plantations of Haiti. The tricky thing is that if they spilled the mestizo blood, they would be spilling their own blood. The men used the women as if they were procreation fillies. Their attitude created the wrath of the gods, and the punishment that had befallen them was because they did not listen to the envoys from Africa who had come to calm their fury through the spoils of the sorcerers and priests.

Dessalines cried out for their participation in the battle. They demanded the intervention of the powers beyond to rule the eastern part of Hispaniola. There the idle whites strolled, proud as peacocks in great carriages drawn by well-kept horses. Watching indifferent some, impotent others, change their language, their education, their justice: it was bad, but it was their justice.

Imported like them from the mother country. Now everyone felt the exploitation and annihilation of the aborigines.

Now the false gods were paying for their carelessness against the people of Saint-Domingue. Everyone knew that for the white masters from France, Spain, Holland, England, and Portugal, the Haitians and the aboriginal Tainos were the same. For that reason, they ran unchecked in the great mountains that, for them, had been their purgatory.

"Saint-Domingue et por noi! Let's fight, damn it, the enemy is coming! Long live Haiti! Vivre la revolution! Liberté, igualité et fratenité. Haití y las antilles sont la meme chose!"

I believe, Votre Excellence, that the zero hour is approaching. We are about to clash with the French commanded by General Leclerc." Having said that, Boyer stood at attention. He stared at King James the First. He spun around on his heels and shouted at the top of his lungs, "Long live His Excellency the King! Vivre la Republique de Haiti! L'union faite la force! We shall be free from the slavery of France! The United States of America freed itself from England. We are next."

Commandant Boyer's phrases were repeated by thousandsofsoldierswithimpeccableaccuracy.Thegigantic battalion was heeled and mounted on horseback to initiate the final battle against the invaders. The commanding voices of the officers were expanding. The neighing and galloping of the horses served as a background to the war cry. With a clap of his hands, he ordered his carriage to be brought to him. The symmetrical galloping of the horses dragging King Jean Jacobe Dessalines's luxurious carriage coincided with the nightfall of December 13, 1801.

The earth was boiling. The sun's rays were scorching it mercilessly, without contemplation, despite the fact that the Caribbean winter had just begun. In front of the Presidential Palace, there was an unusual movement. Sitting under an enormous mango tree of the kind called by popular suspicion bull's member, two political military leaders were talking. Alexander Petion was talking with

Boukman, who had just arrived from Kingston, Jamaica. The purpose of his presence in Haiti was to draw up a military plan regarding the threat of the second invasion of Napoleon Bonaparte's army. Rumors were everywhere of a counterattack with a new military intervention being prepared in Paris.

"Mr. President, allow me to inform you that rumors are spreading in Jamaica as well as in Cuba that the French Emperor wants to come and seek revenge. They say that Pauline Bonaparte has gone madder than a goat. The wretch is putting into her brother's head the idea of sending another invasion to punish the Haitians for the death of her husband, General Victor Leclerc. You know well, Your Excellency, that King Christophe negotiates even with the devil himself in order to stay ruling the country of the zombies."

President Petion listened attentively to Boukman's statements.

He continued. "If that crazy woman succeeds and gets away with it, as she has always done, we are lost. This time the emperor is going to come prepared. He will not risk another humiliating defeat. Hmm, what a shame the mighty French emperor must have felt! His face must have fallen when he saw his fearsome and triumphant army leaving Saint-Domingue defeated and humiliated by a small and black nation! Let us not forget," Boukman said to Petion, "that the loss of Haiti means the collapse of the French empire and the disrepute of Napoleon throughout the world. The emperor has said that if another revolution forms in the Caribbean, he will personally come 'to stick hands on it' with his own wisdom. You know that he does what he promises. We can't give him the chance to roll back the independence of Saint-Domingue. According to what I learned in Santiago de Cuba, almost all the gatherings and meetings that are held in Europe are about Napoleon's humiliation and his descent in Haiti."

"I agree, Bouckman," Petion replied. "But what hurts me the most is that they have shamelessly betrayed us. You know very well that although we helped many peoples of the Caribbean and Latin America to fight for their welfare and independence, they have left us alone in the middle of the Antilles fighting the seven-headed monsters that make up the powers that promote and support the plantation system and the enslavement of blacks brought from Africa as a platform to produce wealth, for the powers that represent the potencies with the blessing of the ecclesiastical power. Blacks will fight with blood and fire for freedom."

10

The Tricks of Eroticism

Her icy eyes, like two brown *belludas*, resembled two transparent amber stones. Her gaze betrayed something that caressed the depths of her soul. It was a dream of such intensity that emanated from her radiant face, as if it held a strange and beautiful secret that she could no longer hide. The beauty of her face and the hypnotizing gaze gave her away. From her penetrating eyes, a contagious sensuality came out that invited one to penetrate the depths of that mysterious gaze. It was something strange that she kept like a treasure, hidden in a corner in the chest of her turbulent and passionate soul. It was a fiery volcano that she guarded like the owner of the most precious jewels since she began to grow from a girl into a woman.

In her development, her skin became burning like a bonfire, like a perennial bonfire that very few men could extinguish. Hormonal changes turned her into an erupting volcano. She was a fiery volcano, spurting lava, like a waterfall in the tropics that would make her go crazy. Tumultuous as the Caribbean Sea. Passion and ferocity that widened her pupils that looked like the mouths of two miniature volcanoes about to erupt from the depths of her loins. The pupils of her eyes were like the swirling waters of the Caribbean Sea. The caramel pupils contemplated with the attention of a delicate painter the formation of soldiers with their uniforms and their erect weapons. Bulging from the body definition of the tight uniforms. It made such a strong impression on her that it tantalized her spirit. Her hormones raged, boiling in the erotic ocean that drowned her in pleasure. The impression was so strong that the tip of her reddish tongue protruded from her lips as an extension of her sensual and provocative mouth. Her snow-white face and her blushing cheeks, reddish like the color of roses, betrayed the intention of her interior.

Her cheeks, like two apples, projected a call, a provocation for the sensual thoughts that came out of her imagination from the feverish years of a young and lush Pauline Bonaparte. Her breasts, hard as pears that have not matured due to the lack of time that feminine nature has provided, also trembled with emotion just by bringing with her imagination the aspirations she had so many times to caress the bodies of military men of different ranks and put them under the dominion of her feet, submitting them to her absolute will and domination by the force of her seven erotic secrets with her feminine powers that would drive crazy the most virile males of Corsica.

The man who fell into the nets of her sensual and erotic passion entered a bonfire from which he could not leave until he reached the ecstasy and frenzy that led him to an intoxicating orgasm. He remained in that moment, searching for air to live. Asking for more and more. Meanwhile, burning passion was manifesting itself in her sensual full lips. Appetizing. The porcelain-white face and cheeks flushed with erotic thoughts that flowed like a waterfall from her lush, youthful, restless imagination. They radiated the passion that burned inside Pauline Bonaparte. The desires burned her on a slow fire, smothering her with the flame and the heat of her own feminine sensuality. Her perfect pointed breasts also trembled with excitement just remembering the dreams she often had about having the handsome muscular soldiers and officers under the dominion of her powers cornered in the tangle of her secrets and amorous tricks.

She hypnotized with her gaze, playfully flirting with her half-open lips as an introduction to her secrets of seduction. As she ran her tongue around her lips, they took on a hue like the color of crimson flowers. With her lips half open, she would press the tip of her tongue between her teeth. That half-closed mouth added passion, slow and calculated. The suitors who wanted to flirt their love just gawked. They were frozen in a time that seemed eternal just by looking at Pauline Bonaparte's mysterious face. It was the tricks of her sexual secrets that drove the most virile men of the European courts and of the whole world crazy.

Women, on the other hand, died of envy at the sight of her. It is said that the actor Talma, who was one of the most famous actors in Europe at the time, desperate for love, begged Pauline Bonaparte "not to twist his tongue."

"I swear by what I love most, by all the saints that have been and will be that when Pauline opens her mouth, she drives me to madness. In my hallucination, I see a sensual bonfire when her words come out with the burning fire that drives me mad. The heat of her breath melts my soul. I kneel before you. I give you whatever you ask of me as long as you promise me that when you stand before me, you will show me your tongue. Don't do it to me for the love of Saint Anthony of Padua. Don't teach me that trick if you are not going to complete the work."

Thus he implored her; he begged her not to provoke him with the seductive trick of her magic tongue because he would lose his mind. Her pointed breasts, like two champagne glasses, trembled, vibrating like the tongues of a woodpecker when it sticks its tongue into the bark of a tropical palm to pierce it to make its nest. She was a temper of emotion just remembering the dreams she so often had about having the handsome and sturdy military men instead of the famous actors and sculptors who were dying for her.

She was also fascinated by the high-ranking and highly decorated officers. She wanted to have them under her feet, caught in the tangle of her feminine powers with the strength that came from being the favorite, spoiled, pampered, and protected sister of the great Napoleon Bonaparte. Pauline looked them up and down. Slowly. She watched them. It seemed as if she stopped at each member so as not to miss the projecting details of the muscular bulge proudly displayed by the gendarmes of Napoleon Bonaparte's army. She watched them with a slowness that reached the point of desperate anxiety. She was imbued, self-absorbed, immersed in the parades that the Gallic gendarmes of what would become Napoleon Bonaparte's army, feared and respected around the world, was proudly displaying.

Pauline's eyes were the color of transparent bee honey, caramelized and sleepy. They looked like two drops of honey gazing intently at the formation of soldiers. She stared at them, unhindered by any form of modesty of the women of her time. Her imagination flew with the force of a hurricane. With freedom.

Pauline soared with the strength and passion of her young body at the peak of the incandescence of her carnal desires, drowned in the intense flame that was gushing from her pores. She was an erotic whirlwind that made her a unique woman—special, passionate, and sensual from her feet to her hair. It's probable that the fact of having lived among soldiers from a very young age on the Corsica island put her in the position of looking at soldiers in all their details, which would make her feel a very singular admiration for the military corps of the time. Russian soldiers fascinated her, Arab soldiers on their spirited steeds drove her insane, epic tales of El Cid Campeador, Genghis Khan, Simon Bolívar, and the Mongols who made exhibitions for her brother's delight at military parades drove her to madness.

Her love affair with a high-ranking officer of the Napoleonic forces led her to lose her head over a man twice her age when she was still in her sixteenth year. She was sixteen, and he had passed the four decades. The officer, with the confidence typical of French macho men, confidently bet on his amorous experience with women who, for him, surpassed the erotic and sensual capacity of the young Pauline. The military man boasted of being an exceptional lover, but like Pauline Bonaparte, he possessed more virtues when it came to making love. He went with all the thirst of his manly passion until he was trapped in the passionate ways of a woman. He took her behind the curtain, and there was his mistake or his luck because the atmosphere was so stimulating that it aroused Pauline's sexual desires. The rainy storm, the thunder and lightning that intermittently broke the island atmosphere, was like a stimulant to boost the erotic powers of Pauline Bonaparte and Ramolino. As he was one of the most robust, he waited for her to take a leap where she was caught in an embrace charged with passion and ardent desire to perform a dance of love in the most hidden place of the Bonapartes' mansion. It was in an embrace of love and endless sex where she offered her virginity with a thrill of pleasure. Pain loses meaning when it comes with pleasure. The torrential rain and thunder that pounded the Corsica Island in all directions served as a witness and ally for the woman's moans to be confused with the torrential rain that washed over the island at the precise moment when Pauline gave her fifteen-year-old virginity to a military aide in her beloved brother Napoleon's army.

Her father was a high-ranking officer of the king's court based on the Corsica Island. Apparently, the first lover had hit a dead end when he tasted Pauline's sexual qualities. In his desperation, the military man made the mistake of placing himself behind a giant curtain that adorned one of the wide halls of Charles Bonaparte and Leticia Ramolino Paoli's mansion.

It's probable that Pauline's genius was responsible for selecting the hiding place to give free rein to passions in a mansion that had already been the scene of other passions as strong as hers, and that word of mouth spread all over the island that Leticia Ramolino Bonaparte shared a passionate place hidden from her husband, Charles Bonaparte. Perhaps for that reason, the naughty and sensual Pauline had made of that little corner in the basement of the house a place for them to turn into a secret of love.

The Bonaparte house had many curtains. Although it is probable that the right place was in the basement of the mansion because it was less exposed to the guests who frequented the family. The servants were very conservative; even if they saw something strange, they did not dare to say half a word, especially if it was something that was done for the sake of the family. Paolette or Pauline, because she was conceited and had a very dominant temperament, was stronger than her mother Leticia. Woe to anyone who dared to comment on the moans of pleasure and the breezy movements behind the curtain of the Bonaparte family mansion!

It was never known whether it was the servants or one of the members of the family who, hearing some moans, raised the alarm. They were the howls of a fragile animal that was slowly hurting them. In the end, he gave the news said to hear some moans between pleasant and painful, thinking that the echo of the walls were in charge of amplifying and watering throughout the house as if they were voices of an angel that ascends to infinity and descends to the purgatory of this world, enjoying happiness with the man who, despite their age difference, offered him villages and castles to let him marry the sensual woman.

No one can say for certain what happened afterward to the tall military man who fell madly in love with the beautiful young girl. Nowadays, rumors run all over the Corsica Island among those who dare to say, looking everywhere, as if they wanted to flee from the haunting ghosts of Napoleon Bonaparte, that the soldier was sent to the battle front from which he never returned as the price for his daring to fall in love with the younger sister of the Emperor of France. Many of Pauline's seven lovers met the same fate, which became a mystery to the French. There are others who, with greater freedom and less fear, manifest that the military man walked all over the island for a century. He marched in his uniform and war decorations, making the same moans as when he was making love behind the mysterious curtain to Napoleon's sister. That was one of Pauline's hiding places and secrets. It was a scenario created by her to perform the dances of love that, in the end, ended with an act similar to the Kamasutra.

Looking behind the curtain of the mansion where sensual feelings are born and fed, boiling like a bonfire to increase the fire of the passions of the events that transpired there, the myths and the reality of this exceptional seductive beauty were suffocating from head to toe. The large curtains served as a wall to keep the secrets of Pauline Bonaparte's passionate love.

The events that transpired in Pauline Bonaparte's life were so fast that they ran parallel to her life itself. Therein lies the dynamic of a unique woman with very profound feminine and accelerated characteristics that they brought her to the center of a maelstrom that her destiny created. Pauline Bonaparte's beauty was extraordinary and so mysterious that it absorbed men and women alike. Her body was very close to perfection. This was verified by the sculptor Antonio Canova when he was about to give her the first brushstroke, and he found her completely naked, and the Italian sculptor almost fainted. It is said that after the rumor spread in Italy that Pauline Bonaparte had taken off all her clothes, including her underwear, to pose in the presence of the sculptor Canova. The most beautiful women of the European courts and society begged the sculptor to make them a complete statue of her bodily attributes. When the news spread from mouth to mouth that Pauline was posing nude, the modesty and shame went to the background.

After the news of Pauline's figure became known, all women wanted to undress in front of the Roman sculptor. The interesting thing was that the duration of the artwork culminated in a daily section of sex and passion that became the daily commentary of Parisian society and all major European cities. But the famous sculptor lost his mind when he fell into the net of Pauline Bonaparte's erotic tricks. Her perfect nose compensated for any disproportion in the ears that could be partially covered by his black and soft hair, straight and shiny like jet. But the fact that she was born on an island made her the owner of having the most perfect breasts among the women around her. There were many who neither hid nor concealed their envy and swore that she had breasts as perfect as two glasses of red wine. It was as if the imperial gods had designed the perfection of her breasts as round and hard as two oval porcelain balls. The brown nipples were like two little lemons protruding from the blouse, and as she was fascinated by wearing Chinese silk, it emphasized the perfection of her breasts whose terminations were the product of divine creation.

Among the women of the court, there was a gossip that Josephine Bonaparte was furious when they spoke to her about the perfection of Pauline Bonaparte's breasts and the hardness of her buttocks that resembled two gigantic coconuts of the tropical countryside. This made her enjoy and change her way of loving and perceiving men who loved her with passionate madness when they fell into the trap of her amorous lures. Some of her close friends were fascinated when they had the opportunity to see her naked. The walks in the hills of Corsica and in the family vineyards had hardened her body. The baths in the clean sands of the Mediterranean Sea had developed her body and molded her physical attributes that drove crazy those who saw her up close. Her molded and delicate body was like a living statue.

Pretty sure of herself, Pauline once made a wager on the use of a pair of calabashes to measure her breasts. "Look for the shapeliest woman with the shapeliest breasts in Cap-Haitien. Bring the most beautiful and most desirable woman of the region. Bring the most voluptuous mestizo, the most sensual Creole, the Frenchwoman, or the Taino Indian with the best breasts. I want to prove to you that my breasts are hard as marble. I want to show them all that my breasts are unparalleled in Haiti, Martinique, or Paris!"

The Countess was not much inclined to humility. Sometimes, arrogance came like the thunder before the storm, especially when her feminine charms were questioned. Pauline wanted to take advantage of the meeting of the officers' wives to unmask the one who was carrying information on everything the Countess Bonaparte had been doing since her arrival in Cap-Haitien. She was a double agent in the service of the Empire. Everything that happened in Cap-Haitien in which the Countess Bonaparte was involved spread like wildfire in the palace corridors of Paris. Her cheeks turned as red as two tomatoes every time they brought her the comments of her sister-in-law Josephine Bonaparte. She was so irritated one day while awaiting an audience with the Cathedral Archbishop that on learning from one of his military aide's wives of the rumors spread by her sister-in-law thousands of miles away, in a fit of rage, she cried out, "I'll be damned! I swear by all the saints in this cathedral that if I hear one more lie, I'm going to rip out his tongue if she's a woman! If it's a man, I'm going to pull out his...!"

It was the seven bells of the Cathedral of Our Lady of Notra Damus in Cap-Haitien that did not let listen with clarity the full meaning of her imprecation against his brother's wife. At that instant, before Pauline entered a higher stage, raising her voice so that all could hear the hatred she had for Josephine LaPargerie Bonaparte, Empress of the French Empire, the Irish Archbishop came out, walking as if levitating from the shining mace floor of the church. He came smiling because he made her wait less than three minutes in his own guilt to the beautiful lady; he came to invite her and guide her, holding her left hand, to the church sacristy to make her confession.

As expected, Pauline Bonaparte changed the tone of her voice, and her phrases came out of her mouth this time, with melodious softness to impress the archbishop and appease the evil tongues that had made her lose her patience in a flash. In the blink of an eye. The prelate immediately put his arm around her waist. He lifted her face, letting his soft but robust and athletic hand go down to the neckline of the dress that covered a blanket that gave her the appearance of the Virgin Mary. Thus he carried her stealthily to the sacristy. If the blanket had been wider, the religious would have let his hand go down from her waist to the beginning of her buttocks. That fascinated the bishop and made Pauline lose her mind.

The archbishop liked to be aware of the latest gossip and rumors coming from Europe. Even more so when they came from the fleshy and sensual lips of Pauline Bonaparte. The gossips say that if you want to listen to Pauline's bewitching and sensual voice, all you have to do is go to the cathedral on the last Sunday of every month that falls on the thirteenth day of the calendar. There you will hear, as if in the middle of the repertoire of songs of a heavenly choir, a soft, hollowed voice whose echo repeats, "I'm going to rip off your...your...your...your...your...!"

There are many parishioners who swear and perjure themselves that they have seen Pauline Bonaparte's slender and beautiful figure rising from the cathedral floor like a feather from the sacristy to the bell tower. Many believe that she is the female ghost of one of the female plantation owners who was subjected to a sexual orgy when the blacks came to her estate to sacrifice her husband. She put herself in front of the leader of the slaves with transparent and provocative clothes so that the husband would take advantage of the tumult and escape from the massacre so that he would take his three daughters to Santiago de Cuba before the slaves violently stole their virginities of barely thirteen, fourteen, and fifteen years old.

Rumor has it that there was a white lady known as Madame Marie Chaveaux and that she was one of the few French colonists who managed to escape to Santiago de Cuba by fleeing from the sharp machetes of the black slaves. She makes the sign of the cross every time she mentions under oath that the woman seen floating inside the Cathedral of Perpetual Help is the sister of the Emperor of France. The lady of Saint-Domingue died swearing that Pauline Bonaparte saved her from death and from the lust of unwanted penetration by a black man over six feet and a virile member as hard as an oak bat when she was thirteen years old. She tells how the slave went on top of her, his eyes like two burning embers of hatred. The black man was on the verge of piercing her with a colossal rape. He had lifted the skirt of her wide dress when he pointed his erect manhood in the direction of the petticoat that he had already torn with a mixture of violence and wild carnal desire. The Creole lady, having been born in the colony of Saint-Domingue, swore a thousand times that the white Panama hat she wore had been thrown into the void by the Countess herself as she disappeared up the stairs of the religious center of Cap-Haitien.

True or not, the Countess was idolized by the Catholic parishioners envied by the women of colonial society and sanctified by the lwas and priests of the powerful voodoo religion who gave Pauline special powers because of her resemblance to the Metresa of their religion.

"I don't want them to say that I'm using Saint Jack's baths or the Cave of Marmalade to perform my acts of erotic sensuality or to bathe in the Enchanted Lagoon aphrodisiac mud!"

She said so and did so because news had reached her that among the wives of the French officers, there was an informer of Josephine, her sister-in-law. She worked in combination with one of Countess Bonaparte's servants. That explained why there was no woman in Haiti who could compete with the Countess. She was fascinated by walking around without a bra, a sign of her free soul and her desire to play with the minds of men and the envy of women. In fact, she loved Chinese silk because it highlighted the nipples of her breasts, driving the imagination of men crazy, who would lay their eyes on her breasts and remain enraptured as if they were ravished toads, as if they were zombies.

Some of the women felt jealous that they couldn't and wouldn't hide or conceal. One of those who could not hide the rage of her jealousy was her sister-in-law, Josephine LaPargerie Bonaparte. It is obvious that the changes that Pauline Bonaparte underwent in Saint-Domingue contributed to the increase of her fame, her fortune, and her popularity as the hottest woman of France. For that reason, when she was summoned to her sessions in the baths of Rome or Paris, the women and the men ran terrified to get into the burning thermal baths where the beautiful and desirable body of the sensual woman was submerged.

Among the characteristics of Pauline Bonaparte, there was great self-confidence in her sensual abilities she gave herself while making love from where the nectar with lava and ashes of the volcano of the erotic and sexual passion emanated. Her body was bathed with the aroma of a fragrance that she always mixed in the act of executing the act of lovemaking. She had a trick of fire and flavor. They were powers in her aspiration of greatness and ambition to be like Napoleon.

Pauline started her sexual activity since she became a young lady. Pauline Bonaparte's ability to take advantage of her amorous tricks and combination of natural attributes made her a special woman in French society and throughout Europe. Of course, the knowledge of her fame in lovemaking went beyond the empire boundaries and probably reached far beyond where the sun goes to bed. There were many who swore by all the saints that General Leclerc died of love when he saw his wife Pauline Bonaparte slowly going mad in the land of Ra-Raa, meringue, and voodoo. But everybody knows that that bubonic plague and yellow fever bullshit was a prank by the French Puritans in combination with the English who hated Napoleon Bonaparte and Ramolino to death. They all combined to use the written press to hide what he was doing in Cap-Haitien, the beloved sister of his majesty the Emperor Napoleon, and many officers and civilians came under oath before the holy host to blame the magic African powers as the ones responsible for the annihilation of the Napoleonic army in Haiti.

Never forget, my compadre, that defeats are orphans. There is no one to support them. That is why people say that when childbirth is bad, they blame the midwife. I want it to be noted, in this historical conversation, that my grandfather was an infantry doctor. Salutiano Rodriguez Campoamor was trained at the top of the Spanish crown. He came to live in the city of Santiago de los Caballeros in the heart of Cibao. There he fell in love with a pretty Creole girl from Cibao. As he was crazy about her, he lost his head and did not listen to the advice to beware of the Haitians who were everywhere killing, kidnapping, taking females and males as prey of war.

One night when the moon resembled a huge cassava cake in the Quisqueyano firmament, a military patrol apprehended him for "eating hen" and making out with his girlfriend under a sour orange bush in the backyard of the house. The young man recently graduated from the medical school of Seville and had to go to serve as a doctor for the army commanded by Victor Leclerc. If it were not for his cunning and the fact that he got to know Pauline Bonaparte closely, he would have been sent to the other world.

He was one of the few who escaped with Pauline and her husband's corpse. Thus he avoided being burned alive by the black, mulatto, and Maroon revolutionaries. The conversation would have continued. But a messenger on horseback was coming to report an event, announcing at the top of his lungs, "Brave men of Saint-Domingue, arise right now! I, Felipe Hermosillo, First Lieutenant of Infantry and Cavalry, command you in the name of the Catholic Kings of the Motherland Spain! Fasten your seat belts! Tighten your pants, and don't be cowards. There has been a revolutionary uprising against the Haitian occupation! Let's fight the Congolese! Let's eliminate the zombies of Dessalinne and Louverture! The Haitian capital is on fire! Long live the Royal Crown of Her Majesty, the Queen! Death to the Haitians and the Congolese, the Maroons and all those who sympathize with the rebellion of the blacks of Papa Bocó and Metresilis! Let them go to Africa in the same boats that brought them to the Antilles! They have already taken Saint-Domingue from us. To fight soldiers for the conquerors and the kings to continue to dominate in the hemisphere and beyond!"

The officer continued with his string of epithets, appealing to the bravery of the Creoles, mulattos, and Spaniards to rise up in rebellion against the French occupation. In the meantime, his spirited horse was tumbling, tormented by the shrieking imprecations and stinging spurs of the military man who rode him. Semi-stunned, the animal stood on two legs as he showed his muscles with the erection of a steed that has seen a beautiful mare's tail raised. Raging as he was, he looked like a Trojan horse. Suddenly, just as the Spanish officer thought he had brought the steed under control, it began to neigh again when it saw a luxuriant mare munching grass nearby, indifferent to his blowing. The quiet beast, as if nothing was going on around her, she just wiggled her buttocks. She kept sniffing the grass she was eating with her head down and her tail up. Her copious tail served as a whip to chase away the flies and other insects that bit at her buttocks, sucking her blood. Both rider and horse competed to see who could blow the hardest. When the Spanish officer realized that he might fall off the animal, he drew his sword, which flashed in space like a sharp bolt of lightning.

Immediately, he threw into the air the document that announced the war and the bloody combats that were happening on the other side of the border of Saint-Domingue. Then he drove the spurs into the jaw of the animal, whose neighs changed as if they were the cries of a wolf that has been mortally wounded as it felt the spurs penetrating deep into its ribs. When the horse felt the sting of the steel cutting into the nerves and cartilage of his ribs, in desperation, he took off in the direction of the Santa Barbara neighborhood in the colonial zone, where the officer of the Spanish crown had come from. In his flight, furious as a beast, the officer of the Creole army rushed, sword in hand against three mulattoes and two Spanish onlookers who were playing dominoes under a tree near the Caves of Swallows at the entrance of San Carlos. The man appealed in frustration and vehemence, "Don't be indifferent, the motherland needs you. Don't forget that for the Haitian invaders, color doesn't count! As you are sons of the mother, of the same mother, raise your buttocks in defense of the Crown of Spain! Don't forget that Napoleon is invading Hispaniola!"

The military man was riding in despair. Frustrated by the attitude of a plump merchant who smoked a thick tobacco imported from Europe as if nothing was happening, he shouted at him with diabolical energy, "Don't be stupid, dealer! Gather up your belly, fatty by vagrancy, wrap up your balls. Fasten your seat belts and throw yourself to defend the Queen, the motherland! Stick your hand in the hands of the kings so that the Crown can consolidate in Hispaniola. Let's leave the stupid Spain!"

For fear of being run over by the runaway horse before the cries of war, mulattos, Creoles, and Spaniards ran as if they had seen the Devil. In desperation, one of the chased, who had fewer buttocks than an iron, dropped his pants. As he was more frightened than a goat by the officer's harangue and the horse's enormous legs, he opted to use his acrobatics. He threw himself half naked into a small well known in Santo Domingo as the Laguna del Caiman. The Spaniard didn't care how dirty the water was. He preferred that one of the amphibians devour his ass in pieces before the military man caught up with him.

Lieutenant Felipe Hermosillo, not at all amused by the scene of the rogue, continued brandishing his shining sword and shouting at the top of his lungs at the gawkers of the capital. He said to them, "Get out of my way, the Motherland is on the warpath! Long live the Catholic kings! Fight in the name of Queen Isabella of Castile! Do not be assholes! We are going to break the hearts of the Haitians. We're going to fuck Toussaint, Dessalines, Boyer, Petion, and Henry Christophe. We have to rip their—!"

The neighing of the animal and the noise of the onlookers prevented the last part of the military man's incantations and curses from being heard. At that instant, the body of the handsome Spanish knight was seen flying through the air as he was thrown by a spectacular leap of the steed that kicked and leaped as if possessed by the devil himself. His cries of bravery turned in the blink of an eye into piteous groans, following the body as it descended in a tumble with his legs upward.

The Spanish clerk's whimpers died away slowly with the following sentences: "To the Spanish fight! Death to the invaders of Haiti! By the Virgin of Macarena, I ask you not to be afraid! Don't forget that the zombies come from Africa! And the French have no mercy. Tighten your pants. Spain is no longer the fool! Let's fight like in Granada!"

A big dust of great proportions remained as a sample of the repercussions that formed, covering like a black cloud the streets of the capital.

The military occupation by the French was the dish of the day throughout the territory of Hispaniola. Everyone was talking about the invasion of Saint-Domingue. Several generations had passed with the presence of the invading troops and the indifference of the Mother Country. The blackening of the sky foreshadowed the arrival of a Caribbean storm. The kingdom that was to come did not recognize them as of the family of the pure, of the chosen ones. That was the worst punishment. They were the renegades of the zombie organization. Now the conjured spirits would have to wait for the judgment of judgments until the major tribunal—composed of Alexander Petion, Jean Jacobe Dessalinne, Boukmann, and Jean Bertrand Buitre—would judge them. For the time being, they would have to keep running desperately from mountain to mountain, from hill to hill, lording it.

They turned into three-headed snakes, into porcupine thorns that looked like elephants with only one tusk, into deer that were dehorned, into owls that flew by day, into cows that, instead of suckling calves, suckled men. When they were milked, instead of giving milk, honey was extracted. That was no ordinary night. Everyone who was there had come together to kill two birds with one stone. On one hand, the blacks were celebrating the feast of the zombies, waiting for their liberation. On the other hand, the mulattoes were encouraging the long-suffering Haitians to begin without delay the reconquest of the east. But everything was foreseen, even what was not going to happen. The day had been fixed throughout the country. From the countryside to the city, a single voice was heard: "Les garzons can't anymore! La Isle est un sole paix! L'union fait la force! Saint-Domingue et Haití est la meme chose!"

PUM-KUTU-PUM-PUM-PUM-KUTU-PUM-PUM!

The drums continued their work of warming up and exciting the crowd blackened by the Congolese from Africa and the Creole mulattoes, fruits of the rapes of the blacks by the white masters. This had taken over of lives and properties in the convulsed territory of Haiti. Now, the rebels were attacking everywhere the invading forces commanded by the famous Victor Emmanuel Leclerc, brother-in-law of the First Consul of France and future Emperor.

Pum! Kutu-Pum! Pum! Pum! Kutu-Pum! Pum! Pum!

11

The Night the Planets Aligned

The celestial formation coincided with the alignment of the stars, creating a female figure of extraordinary beauty. The sorcerers, the priests, the lwas, and the followers of Metresilis who led the voodoo in Saint-Domingue came to the conclusion that something great was happening in the universe. That night, with a starry sky and the stars twinkling as if they were enormous necklaces of sea pearls, a beautiful and brilliant figure appeared on the film next to the Big Dipper in the star system. As if by magic, the sky presented a luminous spectacle guided by Mars, Venus, and the Moon. The three stars changed places and positions. They were placed one on top of the other as if they were copulating, like the bride and groom who mount one on top of the other to make love up there on high. In the celestial vault, the Milky Way spilled out into the center of the universe. It was an immense waterfall that expanded in all directions as a provocation to the sensuality and imagination of the earthly men and women. At the moment in which everybody was looking stupefied, the gallop of a gigantic white horse broke the silence and created the astonishment of those who were witnessing the universal spectacle.

The strange things that were being seen in the Caribbean sky caused surprise. Some were astonished; others were in complete doubt. It was the Countess Bonaparte, who passed stealthily along the path of the meeting, arrived mounted on the gigantic white horse. The beast and the woman stopped. The animal reared its legs as if bowing to an invisible figure. The animal whinnied and galloped along. It was striding delicately but with giant strides. The beautiful woman was wrapped in a white cloak. Because of the speed of the steed and the breeze that was blowing at that hour on the plateau of the Mulate, the silhouette of the woman on horseback could be seen naked. As she climbed the hill, the figure of the horse and the rider seemed to be one. The moonlight drew her as if the Creator of the universe had painted every detail, every feminine protuberance. The face, outlined and fine, the hair loose as if floating behind the woman, the breasts like two champagne glasses. The torso, drawing a perfect angle, was an extension of the steed on top of her. The thin transparent robe floated like an extension of her long hair. Many of the priests and priestesses of voodoo who were at the ceremony looked sideways, like they wanted to but didn't want to. Modesty prevailed. Her skin bristled in the cool breeze and the scent of the pine forests of the Mulate Hill. It presented Pauline Bonaparte showing her charms in the light of the initiation circle.

When she had completed the seven turns of 360 degrees, then three forward and three backward, Milito, the white horse that her brother Napoleon had sent her, showed off proudly before those present, showing as always the erection in his muscles. The animal knew that on his back was mounted the most coveted woman in Saint-Domingue and Paris. His neighing was like a song of joy that glided over the hills and mountains of the tropical region. Those present felt the same vibrations every time the horse raised its long neck and cried. The animal attracted the attention of those present.

When the horse lifted its front legs, Pauline slid gracefully and delicately, letting her body slide. She did it smoothly as God brought her into the world, without any piece covering her physiognomy. Her charms were exposed. Not a straw was stirring in the place. Everyone was frozen. Stupefied. Petrified in time. As if they had been hypnotized. Under the huge moon that looked like a huge lamp, illuminating the darkness, her body could be seen almost perfect. It was an extension of the steed that carried her. Pauline. Beauty and the beast had become one. So transfixed were the men and women that they couldn't even appreciate the Countess's feminine charms. Males and females stared at a fixed point. They stared into nothingness. At emptiness. They watched the alignment of the planets in the universe. When Pauline Bonaparte got off the horse, she ran her hand over his face. The animal bared its teeth. He stuck out its tongue. He licked the palms of his left hand and then turned himself around. Milito lifted his tail. She rubbed him from behind.

She patted him three times, and the steed, stomping away like a soldier, placed himself under a huge tree of some mangoes that call him Bull's Cock because of the resemblance they bear to the bulls' member. She was anxious to execute one of her greatest secrets with the archbishop of Rome. But she was, at least for the moment, obliged to remain calm in the midst of the great ceremony of initiation into the voodoo religion that originates in the

African Republic of Benin. Although prudence was not one of her virtues, she had to remain patient. She could not now show despair or interest in the prelate's love. First, she was afraid that Victor, her husband, would find out about her relationship with the bishop, who was running among the courtesans like the overflowing waters of the Massacre and Artibonite rivers. The fuss that was formed slid like the waters of the Seine River that bathes with its abundant waters the capital of France.

There are many who ask, "Why is it that the husband and wife are the last to know when there is an act of infidelity?" There must be a reason why the popular saying goes "Out of sight, out of mind."

The last thing Pauline wanted was for her brother Napoleon to know that she was being converted by the voodoo religion. Nor did she want the Emperor to know about the rumors that the Prince of Morocco had possessed her on several occasions in the mansion and in the cave of Saint Jack. Much less did she want the rumor to reach Europe that she had been seen riding with the bishop while they were making love on Milito's back. She was afraid that the gossip would reach Paris about the bottle of Mamajuana that was sent to her from Santiago de los Caballeros, containing aphrodisiacs such as viní-viní, arrasa con to', rompe saraguey, water of the seven seas, sea turtle member, and shark cartilage. With that drink, both Victor Emmanuel and the Irish priest, as well as the Moroccan prince, were waiting to make love to her without stopping until the day dawned in Saint-Domingue. They all knew that if Antonio Canova the sculptor, the French actor Thalma, and the officer who had stolen her virginity had succumbed to the amorous tricks of Pauline Bonaparte, it was because she was an insatiable and indomitable lover in the act of love. If she wanted to satisfy her amorous cravings and the boiling volcano inside her, she would need more than a bottle of mamajuana to bend the copulation skills hidden in Pauline Bonaparte's entrails.

The first to approach were the seven maidens whose faces were the only thing covered. All of them, with their shapely bodies and buttocks as round and soft as pumpkins, like the jars made by the hands of the Tainos, were not more than thirty-three years old and were guided by Anaísa's representative. Immediately, to prevent the priests present from seeing her naked, they changed her transparent white robe for a Chinese silk blanket with which she would be taken to the throne where the priestess representing the Metresa was located. It was obvious that everything was foreseen, except what was going to happen on that special night. What could be appreciated was the parallelism between Pauline and her sister-in-law Josefina. They both came from an island: Corsica in the Mediterranean Sea and Martinique in the tumultuous Caribbean Sea. Both were accustomed to the ceremonies of extraterrestrial powers, Santeria, voodoo, and witchcraft. Both Josefina and Pauline had received predicted expectant changes in their future lives.

Saint-Domingue, Corsica, and Martinique, although very distant, were possessions of France and practiced religions in different dimensions. They did it with passion like all the islanders, from baptism with water and a candle to a voodoo ceremony with blood and knife, slitting the throats of animals that ran trembling to one side and to the other with no sense of direction because their heads had been severed, detached from their bodies by the sharp steel instrument. The machetes in the ceremonies were like the prelude to the arrival of the guillotine that was invented in Europe, arriving at the final act, which consisted of the raising of the dead called the zombies.

When Pauline Bonaparte arrived at the ceremony, everything was ready for her coronation. This ceremony has been celebrated in Saint-Domingue throughout the centuries, ever since the aborigines began to populate the second largest island of the Greater Antilles. The Catholic religion and voodoo already had a queen. That is why, when the Countess dismounted in her white carriage and her horse Milito, a giant cotton figure ran like a white Pegasus. Stupefied, all present, male and female, threw themselves on the ground with their buttocks up and their heads down. They prayed and invoked their guardian angel, swearing and assuring that their good qualities would help them receive the blessing of the spirits of the afterlife. The new voodoo queen had been crowned in Saint-Domingue.

12

The Archbishop's Flute

The archbishop arrived at the hiding place without much complication. As the night was clear and silvered by the appearance of a very clear moon, the prelate went ahead to the rendezvous.

He could not miss this opportunity to meet Pauline Bonaparte. He was so happy and so satisfied that without realizing it, he was humming a song very popular in the Scottish countryside, which tells the story of two lovers hotter than Romeo and Juliet. To his luck and coinciding with the stars, at that moment, a shooting star lit up the sky, pointing like a fire arrow, the place of the amorous meeting between the prelate and the countess. The atmosphere was charged with a mysterious energy that reached the environment with a soft penetrating hum that took over the place after the passing of the shooting star. Then the light descending from the center of the alignment of the planets settled in the sky of Saint-Domingue.

The Irish religious passed through the Vatican without being trapped by the beautiful women who worked for him and who tried to make him hang up his habit on more than one occasion. Even Pope Julian the Second praised the willpower of the youngest Irish archbishop, also the youngest of the bishops of Rome, to avoid the provocations of the nuns and the beautiful parishioners of the Vatican. Many of them confessed on more than one occasion, telling the priests that this bishop had them crazy. During the nights, they had to bite the pillows so that their moans of satisfaction could not be heard while they daydreamed that the robust religious was stealing their virginity. There he met Pauline Bonaparte in the Italian capital, and he swore that the mysterious silence of that woman impressed him so much that he could not fall asleep. He did not want, in the name of his oath of chastity, to let himself be bent by the flesh that Napoleon Bonaparte's sister offered him. On more than one occasion, he hesitated. He almost gave in. He thought of saying, "Fuck it. Screw my vows of chastity." But he remembered the popular maxim: "For a moment of pleasure, an eternity of torment." His grandparents taught him in parables, in phrases and proverbs that explained to him the philosophy of life. Now, he was on a mountain in Saint-Domingue for the meeting of his life.

That is why he was there. Surrounded by a lush forest where the crickets and cicadas were overhanging the chirping of the birds. The trees swaying as if they were in a reverie dance. On that occasion when he had the chance of a lifetime, he had refrained from making love to her. He felt inhibited because he did not want to risk his meteoric ecclesiastical career neither in Saint-Domingue nor in the Vatican. But the moment had come. When she confessed to him in the sacristy of the Church of Perpetual Help in Cap-Haitien, her voice trembled every time she spoke to him about her sexual life and her erotic provocations to dominate men as much as she did in the sacristy of the Church of Perpetual Help in the palaces of the European royal crowns as well as among the elite of Saint-Domingue.

The archbishop of Cap-Haitien was fascinated by playing the flute. But his specialty was the Irish bagpipes, in which he had become an expert. Whenever he had some free time, he took advantage of it to blow and blow the main pipe of the bagpipes. Through that pipe, with his blowing that bulged his mouth and made his eyes like two billiard balls, he brought out the most pleasing musical tones in the instrument. If he did not play more often in the Cathedral of Cap-Haitien, it was so that the beautiful women would not crowd around him to listen to him and see him play. His fame had spread throughout the French colonies of the Caribbean, and many women from the plantations came to Cap-Haitien to have the Irish Archbishop play the flute and the bagpipes of many pipes for them. The hotels of Saint-Domingue did business with the ladies from the Antilles who came with the excuse of listening to the motivating sermons of the Irish Archbishop.

When he put the tube in his mouth, the bishop of Ireland would pull out notes that showed his great musical talent, and he would make faces that many women mistook as a desire to provoke them to think bad thoughts. Between notes, he would stick out his tongue. He would run it in a circle around his lips. He would turn the mouth of the tube upside down and rub the instrument from the spout to the mouthpiece. It looked like they were sucking Puerto Rican quenepas. Her green eyes were like two embers of fire. Their pupils were wide and on fire like the pupils of an eagle on the prowl. They were reddening with the changing of the hours and the events that were happening in Saint-Domingue.

As for the archbishop, he belonged to a very prestigious family in Northern Ireland. The men of his family were very virile, especially because they were of Celtic descent. The length of his manly member was well known and legendary, thanks to the suspicion of the Scottish women. They were demanding in matters of lovemaking. But instead of carrying on the tradition of the previously males, that entered the brewing industry before they reached puberty. He chose to use his family influence and went to study at a seminary in Rome. In his thirteen years of training, he began to rise meteorically through the Catholic hierarchy. By the age of thirty-three he was a titular archbishop in the service of His Holiness at the Holy See. Pope Julian, who had been supported by Napoleon, opened the doors of his office and bedchamber to him, naming him Private Secretary to His Holiness. That position led him to become an adviser to the Pope in the affairs of the royal crown.

When Pauline went to the Cathedral La Menor in Rome to receive communion, the bishop lasted longer than usual, placing the host on Pauline's tongue. It is likely that the prelate put the host on her as if it were a coin and turned it over several times, as if he were massaging Pauline Bonaparte's tongue as she stood still, amazed, hypnotized by the handsome green eyes of the prelate. Criticisms from the Vatican's envy arose, and they gave him the nickname of the masseur priest. When the other priests saw him passing by, they murmured and laughed slyly between their teeth. It was a smile of hypocrisy like those of the priests who hide behind the habit, behind the cassock, to mock humanity. For many, the priest had the power to anaesthetize the nuns since he had charmed Napoleon Bonaparte's sister.

Another thing that drove Pauline crazy was the religious passion with which he played musical instruments, especially the Irish bagpipes and the Indian flute. Although he paid no attention to gossip, to the crown, or to the

Vatican, he was concerned that such rumors would reach the pope's ears.

What could never be known was who sent him to the cathedral in Port-au-Prince to cover the Catholic jurisdiction of Cap-Haitien. His transfer to the Caribbean was a state secret stronger than the oath of the priests. It is obvious that his transfer to Saint-Domingue was the fruit of a powerful hand both in the crown of France and in the Vatican in Rome. Those who disliked the Irish archbishop's sermons spread the rumor that it was Pauline herself who asked for her brother's intervention so that the Vatican would execute the transfer of the religious to the Caribbean region. The last time they met in the sacristy was on Palm Sunday, May 13, 1800. That day was very special for both of them because they whispered in each other's ears the place where the love date would take place. Everyone in the cathedral thought that the Irish Archbishop was taking too much time with Pauline Bonaparte in the confessional. Rumors and gossip were growing every day all over Cap-Haitien. Many French colonists wanted to tell Napoleon what was going on between the Countess and the archbishop. But the gossips did not effectively reach the emperor's ears. If they did, it is probable that he paid no heed to his agents to protect his dear sister as he had done on other occasions. No one dared to say half a word because, after all, she was the Countess Bonaparte, and the archbishop would not accept questioning from either parishioners or his deacons. For the woman, she would be sent to the guillotine. For the archbishop, the punishment was hell for anyone who dared to defame the Catholic prelate of Cap-Haitien. The sacristan of the church, who had spent his whole life at the service of the archbishops and priests of the cathedral, he sometimes muttered between his teeth, with visible jealousy, that Pauline was leading a double life in Cap-Haitien. But when he suspected that someone might be listening because in Haiti as everywhere else in the world, walls have ears, he would ring out with rabid force the tolling of the bells, summoning the parishioners to the next ceremony at the cathedral of Notra Damus. The archbishop immediately took advantage of the sound of the bells to speak freely.

Pauline listened. It seemed as if she was being lectured for her actions. But the prelate had agreed that they had to have a meeting to strip her of all the influences of voodoo religions and Santeria. Rumor had it that the archbishop was a permanent member of the Cap-Haitian witch council. The priest swore to Pauline that if he appeared at the ceremonial centers of the Mulate, Alcahie, Artibonite, Uanamendez, and Dajabon, it was to understand what the voodoo priests might be doing to her to convert her to voodoo and transform her into the Metresa.

Pauline barely spoke when she was with the archbishop. He promised her that when they met at the Infinite Cave, he was going to bring her a special bottle so that she could let go of her inhibitions and express what was inside her. Despite his virility as a man, he told Pauline that the drink was nothing special as an aphrodisiac stimulant. He brought the drink to lift her spirits when they were together. For her, he would bring cassava with honey. He assured her that she had better not eat anything because with the power of the honey and the cassava bread, she didn't have to put anything in her mouth. What the archbishop did not know was that Pauline Bonaparte had already suffered the spiritual transformation as a fruit of the Santeria and voodoo works. Nor had the priest learned that Napoleon Bonaparte's sister, since her arrival in Haiti, had been recognized as the true reincarnation of Metresilis. That explains why she was never touched by the slaves even when they came very close to kidnapping her. After all, she knew she was protected by the rebels who would never harm the goddess of Haiti's lwas and witches. Pauline was Metresilis herself in the flesh. The spiritists had to take care of her and worship her. For the rebels, she was the queen. Many unbelievers wanted to touch her. But they dared not even lay their fingertips on her. She was the sovereign of voodoo in the Caribbean region.

Therefore, many have wondered why the priestesses and sorcerers felt tremors just by approaching Pauline. They all felt shaking from head to toe. Many of them fell down, rolling on the floor and speaking in strange languages as if they were under the possession of beings from the beyond. It is true that the prince of Morocco almost succeeded in making her lose her head, even if only for a short time. That did not bother Napoleon so much. But if her brother found out that she was making love to the head of the Church in Cap-Haitien, he would be furious as hell. He was jealous of his sister even with the shadow of a man. His protective jealousy had grown since she had given herself in the dawn of her youth to an officer he trusted. That was why both of them would dissemble when they were in front of the parishioners at the cathedral. They also acted like that in the meetings of the club of the frenchified. The mulattoes, who did their best to pretend that they were pure-blooded white Frenchwomen, were slapped in the face when they ran out of words in order to defend the white blood that ran through their veins or when they were presented as Haitian Creoles. In the French colony, everyone wanted to pretend to be something they were not. Everyone wanted to be a frenchified Monsieur or Madame Chic of la societé francois in Saint-Domingue. They were terrified to think that any of the ladies present were either Josephine's agents or Napoleon's envoyed. Pauline was always surrounded by slaves. That explains why she survived such a hostile battle in which the rivers of Hispaniola were filled with half-killed corpses.

For some reason, the black rebels treated her like a queen. They believed that Pauline Bonaparte was Metresa herself in flesh and blood. There were many priestesses who wanted Noir Curaçao to tell them how he felt when he was massaging Pauline Bonaparte. Carole LaBlanche was asked the same questions. They were trusted servants who touched the Countess from her feet to her hair. Both had access to Pauline's most intimate moments. For that reason, evil tongues said that Noir Curaçao knew many of the erotic woman's sexual secrets. True to their loyalty, neither Noir Curaçao nor Carole LaBlanche let out a word about Pauline Bonaparte's unique body, nor did they reveal any of her lovemaking secrets. Despite the offers of gifts of metals and privileges from the Empress Josephine Bonaparte, they never broke their oath to keep all of Pauline's sexual secrets, even if it meant losing their lives.

The Countess had the most faithful servants while she lived in Haiti. She grew to love her servants so much that she took them with her when she returned to France. Pauline Bonaparte did not mind much what they said about the special treatments she received from Carole LeBlanche and Noir Curaçao.

That day it had been decided that the sun of the centuries of Saint-Domingue would rise in the west. Francois Casablanche had been saved from the great extermination, from the great slaughter when they seized and burned Mackandal. Those who witnessed the burning at the huge bonfire in the public square of Cap-Haitien swear and perjure themselves that seven huge birds resembling limpkins and tropical turkeys flew off in an easterly direction. Today, the descendants of Toussaint, Dessalinne, and Mackandal claim that the one who flew on the largest bird was the rebel leader in the flesh. This indicates that the inquisition, the stake, and the fire were not enough to eliminate the head of the rebellion in Saint-Domingue. The twin of Noir Curaçao was handed over to white masters in Brazil. They liked the fact that the black child had legs as thick and long as two mahogany oars. To give him a touch of French chic, he befriended the matron who had been widowed after marrying a mestizo plantation owner. There were many who swore, making the sign of the cross, that the widow's wealth was the fruit of a deal with Lucifer himself. Many came to swear that the smell of sulfur in that plantation that was felt every thirteenth day of every month could not be endured. There were many who said in low voices that the ancestors of the sugar cane plantation had made a contract with the devil.

The lady was accompanied by her faithful stout servant Orine Pierret. The sturdy black freedman and Maroon had been bought by the owner of the sugar cane plantation when her husband built a mill to grind sugar cane in the Cap-Haitien outskirts. She boasted of being Orine Pierret's mistress. But her friends were spreading the rumor that Mrs. Antoniette was a stingy old woman because she had only paid the cheap price of a goat and two little pigs to buy the Maroon. The ex-slave, knowing that he was the center of attention because of the brightness of his skin and the whiteness of his teeth, gesticulated proudly. His gigantic hands looked like two black silk pincers. He was the twin of Francois Casablanche and Noir Curaçao, the greater drummer at the zombie parties. The other was the Countess's masseuse. His velvet skin was proof that he had never "lowered his back or given a blow" to work after his masters bought him.

13

The Countess and the Midwife

Old Francois Lamacanne had received the triplets when his grandchildren were one year old. Their parents them him in the care of their grandfather so that they could "take care of them," to keep them company because they felt very lonely in the little camp of Founde du Blanc. But the truth was that they couldn't keep them with the thirteen other boys they had produced. The triplets were the seventh of the thirteen children born to Marie Rose Rivage and Antoine Pierre Casablanche.

As they were whiter than their brothers, the rumor that these were the three children of Pauline and the archbishop spread throughout Hispaniola and all the Caribbean islands. The fuss of the love affairs of the Countess Bonaparte and the archbishop of Cap-Haitien ran like a seaquake through all the highest and the lowest of Antilles that were part of the Napoleonic Empire that was expanding like a tsunami in the mysterious Caribbean region. There were many who beat their chest for their own guilt and made the sign of the cross.

The parishioners of Cap-Haitien swore and perjured that the triplets, so elegant, were the fruit of the sinful, tormented, and passionate love of the prelate and the Countess Bonaparte. The parishioners of Cap-Haitien swore and perjured that the triplets were conceived from the moment that the Countess and the archbishop lit the altar of the Cathedral of the so-called Paris of the Antilles with the flame of their erotic passion. For the long-tongued people, it all happened the night of the storm when they embraced standing up to make love in which act they revealed all their sexual secrets. No control. Uninhibited in the hiding place provided by La Mermelade Cavern.

He suffered from homesickness when he thought of his family and Cap-Haitien. Although the triplets were born in the Mulate, they often visited who they thought were their parents. They lived in the same place where they were born. They always came down from the mountain with their grandfather, Don Francois Lamacanne. The three of them brought the thirteen baskets loaded with groceries and vegetables for export or to be sold at the Cap-Haitien Municipal Market. Many girls were waiting for the passage of these good-looking young men with their peasant hats, moving stealthily on their beautiful horses, guarding the goods they were carrying. Some of the onlookers made the comment that these were the Irish Archbishop's triplets. Those who heard that phrase would vanish from the place, making the cross as if they had seen the devil. Others would close their doors, swearing that they had neither seen nor heard anything.

Haiti was waiting for the signal to move forward from those in charge of the unifying mission. Everyone was anxious for the message of revenge to spread throughout the nation. Everything was set to begin the announced assault at midnight, which, by coincidence of fate, had fallen on the calendar on Tuesday, January 13, 1801.

The ceremony preceding the great day was about to begin. All was ready in the house of the chief priestess, where, as agreed upon by the Clandestine Congress of the gods, the new reign would be established. The provinces would be reorganized into departments so that the universal constitution of 1801 would be reimposed.

The journey was full of obstacles. Those who traveled along it encountered deep cliffs that stunned the curious with awe. To their amazement, bushes turned into reptiles in the blink of an eye. Plants devoured flesh like hungry piranhas. The journey was a dark one. Cautiously, the travelers had to wade through the rivers of the Artibonite Mountains from where they could see the fabulous Atlantic Ocean, with its waves like giant mountains that hit with the effectiveness of a terminal cancer the northern coasts of the Hispaniola Island. In Turtle Island, which was a favorite place for Pauline to sunbathe, there was a mysterious lagoon that, according to the inhabitants, not only had magic in its waters, but the Countess used it to receive the instructions for her voodoo transformation.

During the rising tide, the lagoon would disappear as if by magic. Then it would appear seven days later in the same place with the same waters of such a special color that had the magic of pure and divine nature of the tropical wonders. It is said that the people who saw the phenomenon of change in the Turtle Enchanted Lagoon were never the same again. Pauline was never the same.

*****

"Matildaaaaaaaaaaaaa! Matildaaaaaaaaaaaaaaaa!" Madame LeBlanche called desperately to her housekeeper. She was furious, in a bad mood, as usual. "Where the hell have you been, Matilda? Don't you know that the ceremony is about to start and I have to be in front!? Woe betide you, *mamasita*, if you make me late for the meeting. Go back to sleep! If you don't want to know what a comb is on bad hair, don't make me fail to Papa Bocó. Otherwise, I'll order the executioner to give you a couple of whacks or a few *garnata*, as the Puerto Ricans say, so that you'll wake up, woman, once and for all. Are you not listening to me Matilda?"

The young maid was running side to side, stumbling to answer her mistress's call. In her scurrying, she almost shattered a naked statue of the Emperor Napoleon Bonaparte that Madame LeBlanche had bought at an auction in Jackmel in the southern region of Haiti. The fright of the mistress and the slave produced a combined scream that echoed in every corner of the estate of the sorceress Marie Antoniette LeBlanche.

"Oh, Papa Mue! Dejavou! Oh, Bon Dieu! Oh God almighty, I think that if the naked statue of my only and legitimate emperor breaks, I'll die of suffering! What the hell do I want to go on living for if I don't have even the rigid statue to console me?"

That said, Madame LeBlanche couldn't resist the shock when she saw the maid staggering next to the manly figure with whom she had collided. The slave lost her balance. She hugged the mahogany statue. She preferred the emperor to fall on top of her. She'd rather she stayed down. The witch LeBlanche became dizzy at the same time. After spinning around three times, she fell into an armchair in the middle of the room, which by now had served only as an ornament and amulet in case of need for unexpected spiritual work. It was an heirloom that belonged to Pauline Bonaparte.

The impact sounded like thunder as the emperor and

the slave fell to the floor. The one who saw them so close together could wrongly think that the housekeeper and Napoleon were fused in an embrace of love, he above and she below. Luckily, the servant Quitasueño arrived, and after freeing Matilda, who was groaning facedown under the weight of the emperor's statue, he revived Madame LeBlanche. The slave made an incantation. He took out a razor that mirrored the reflection of the lights. It was a double-edged razor like the Cubans use. So sharp that it could cut a hair in the air. He raised it. He wanted everyone to stare at the shiny razor. It was like a miniature guillotine. Those present were petrified at the sight of the gleaming razor. The dread in the air increased with the passing of each second that was ticking with desperate slowness on a clock that has been measuring time since colonial times in the French possession called Saint-Domingue.

The slave's lips trembled as he cleared the beautiful neck from the bushy hair of the servant girl who moved her lips as if begging forgiveness for having knocked over the statue, knowing that any slip of the razor would take her throat with the strength and dexterity of the Quitasueño executioner. The atmosphere had become so tense that those present at the ceremony could clearly hear the clatter of a pin falling to the ground, the clock hands announcing the passing of a second, and the breathing of the possessed slave who had no idea what the sturdy Quitasueño one intended to do with the softness of the woman's beauty that brought down the mahogany statue.

The man closed his eyes. He made a strange notch. He ran his tongue across his lips like a painter running his brush up and down and left and right. Without looking at what he was doing, he grabbed the dizzy woman with his left hand. Without hesitating for a second, he cut off a bunch of her hair. Everyone present remained on the edge of their seats, thinking they would hear the slave's death scream, waiting for the final scream of the dizzy girl. In Haiti and in Paris, guillotining and head chopping were the order of the day. The judicial spectacle with the tragic characteristic began in the courts of any French corner and ended on a scaffold for the satisfaction of morbidity in the face of human misfortune.

The razor squeaked because the hair was tough and abundant, like the straw of the great savannahs of the island geography, hard like the guazabara of the Sahara desert that exhibited with an almost macabre pride that they cut the necks to feed the army of zombies that were preparing to form the army of Ayití slaves. Dizzy's hair was like the mares' braids. He asked for a lighted match and stuck it to the piece of hair he had just cut from the slave's lush scalp. He gave it a sniff right under Madame LeBlanche's nose. Still smoldering, he brought it closer to the shaped nostrils of the witches present at the special coronation ceremony. What happened there was written. The events were interconnected by the disposition of the gods of distant Africa and the mysterious Caribbean region. The Antilles were undergoing the most spectacular transformation in the encounters of three worlds since the so-called discovery of the Western Hemisphere by Christopher Columbus and the crown of Spain.

At that crucial moment, the slave rubbed the soles of his feet with snake butter. Even as the scalps smoked, the matron awoke, startled, trembling from head to toe. The lady was reassured to see the figure of the Emperor of France standing erect as always. The woman took a deep breath, enlarging her chest with the sigh. She shook out her skirt. She breathed again.

Recovered from her dizziness, she assumed her haughty position and commanded the servant arrogantly, "Moreno, go and clean the carriage! You know my husband hates to ride in a dirty, dusty carriage. Don't forget to take the horses to the river so that they run shiny as my husband likes. Hurry up, Moreno, today is the coronation of the Metresa. Today is a special day for Haiti. The rebels have triumphed. Toussaint Louverture said, 'Napoleon thinks he killed the tree, but the branches will spread all over the land of Saint-Domingue.'"

Without saying a word, Madame LeBlanche's faithful assistant went to prepare the carriage, taking gigantic strides. He was shaking the ground every time he moved a foot.

Meanwhile, frozen with fear, Matilda Terranova, showing a strange calmness, approached the statue of the emperor slyly. After contemplating the emperor's mahogany figure, she caressed it gently. She rubbed it between the thighs with a delicate cloth. She rubbed it from bottom to top, from top to bottom. She was as if in limbo. She seemed to be praying to the figure that she hadn't broken in her fall. If a scratch had been made, Madame LeBlanche's punishment would have been against the carelessness of all the servants, in the church, and in the neighborhood, for any damage done to the statue of the world and Haiti's Emperor.

PUM! KUTUPUM-PUM! KUTU-PUM-PUM!

The drums boomed in all directions. At the same time, cannon shots could be heard bursting in the sky of Hispaniola. From the mountains could be heard the beating of drums and voices that sounded like thunder with slogans and speeches announcing the arrival of a new order.

"Pum! Pum! Kutu-Pum! Pum! Pum! Pum! Kutu-Pum! Pum! Pum! Anaisaaaaaaaaaaaa! Papa Candeeeeeeeeeeele! Help me with this birth, dammit! Don't die, blessed Haitian! Breathe deeply! Remember when you were making love. Think of the pleasure you had with the one who impregnated you. Breathe and blow out the air so that it doesn't hurt

anymore! Give me the bassinette! I mean the bedpan! Hurry up, the damned thing is dying! Breathe again! She doesn't even know what I'm saying anymore! Remember, you're not a first-timer!"

The midwife grumbled in a mixture of patoi and Spanish. She was, at the same time, giving orders left and right, looking here and looking there with her eyes like two burning embers. From her thunderous voice, one could deduce her intention. The midwife wanted the curious to hear the outcome of this important and strange birth. That was the way to conceal the true identity of the parturient. Neither the archbishop nor Pauline wanted the true progenitors of the children to be revealed, and to top it all off, there were three of them being born at the same time. After each imprecation, her voice dropped drastically in tone. Then the woman babbled a strange language to ask the lwas and San Ramón to bring her safely out of that complicated birth, which, to make matters worse, was a triplet birth. Sweat was pouring down her body like a downpour from the Massacre River. For three nights the laboring woman had been suffering pain after pain, spasm after spasm, which contracted her muscles. She resembled a possessed reptile. Her face changed expression each time the pains passed. His white teeth creaked. They creaked with despair. Her eyes, like her skin, wanted to burst out. They were fixed, fixed in an indeterminate place. The woman was unresponsive. She was in total limbo. But the midwife was afraid of a sudden frenzied attack that would instantly kill her.

During the time she had been in this condition, all the home remedies had been applied: a bath of rompe saraguey, viní-viní, arrasa con to, amansa guapo. As the aim was to provoke her to give birth, the midwife rubbed her belly with a smear of albeaca de muerto, aloe vera with lily, and a cup of donkey's milk sweetened with honey.

However, nothing had happened except the inexorable deterioration of the laboring woman. The babies didn't come out in spite of all the concoctions and salves she had been given. Her belly was growing by the minute as if it were about to burst. The triplets wriggled and kicked inside the woman's bulging belly. Despite all the remedies, they wouldn't go down an inch. The muscle contractions were getting weaker and weaker. It seemed that the woman's moans were more an involuntary reaction to the midwife's insults than the result of the muscular movements that nature intended for birth to occur.

"Push, woman. Keep pushing and don't stop pushing! Push, Marie Rose, the saints will help! Think of the saint who has helped so many women to give birth. Hold on to whatever part it is, Saint Raman will help you! I hope that the Holy Baron will help you, woman! Push harder, harder and harder, *bendite haitiane*! The creatures are coming down now!"

The midwife's concern was growing. Every time she pronounced her name, she did it with energy so that everyone could hear. But everyone knew that the midwife was employing a trick to keep the woman's real name a secret. Although the church was less than a mile away, she sent for Noir Curaçao to go in search of the priest Raul LaPeste, who was the archbishop's assistant. With that, the onlookers thought that it was indeed a mulatto woman who was dying.

What made this birth so unusual was that the placenta was dry because the water had broken in the middle of the night. Doña Tingó Florence was getting irritated with each passing minute.

The midwife hadn't slept for three days because of the laboring woman. It was a triplet birth with two females and a male.

"Keep pushing, you're making me desperate! The

triplets are finally coming, and you don't keep pushing! What kind of a woman are you? Push hard, you're not a first-timer, you damned fool!"

Doña Tingó sucked a huge hookah. She sucked it as if it were the seed of a thin oval-shaped mango that they call a bull's member because of the fruit's resemblance to the bull's virile organ. She chewed the end of the pipe, inhaling the smoke and savoring the tobacco product over and over again, and then spitting a spit into the air with a thin smile that seemed more like a reflex caused by the nerves that were killing her inside. The midwife was so nervous that she forgot she was attending the birth to the Countess's children. She paced back and forth with the unsuccessful intention of hiding her nervousness. In the meantime, she puffed thick gulps of smoke from the unrefined tobacco that her cousin and compadre, Cumandé Le Blanche, had given her. He was in the habit of bringing her what she called "a bite" of andullo tobacco, illegally imported from the Province of Santiago de los Caballeros, which was a place located to several miles from the eastern border. Her ancestors had taught him that Cibaenian tobacco was the purest on the Hispaniola Island.

Monsieur Le Blanche gave it to the midwife Tingó last Friday after giving birth to a mulatto woman near Cap-Haitien. It was an open secret that the landowner lived with the beautiful mulatto woman from Le Cap after his wife died. The good treatment that Cumandé, owner of cattle ranches on the border near Manzanillo, compensated for the bad times that Tingó Florence spent in the Haiti Mountains. Doña Tingó lasted days, weeks, and months in the region where food was scarcer than the teeth of herons. Clients could barely afford to pay for her valuable midwife services because they had nothing to drop dead on. Those who knew the midwife claimed that she was "mouth of the devil and heart of God." If she was paid any money, the midwife would distribute it to those who needed it most.

And so she went along the Dominican-Haitian border, bringing more people into the world, bringing more slaves to serve, more blacks to suffer. Without intending to, perhaps, midwife Doña Tingó Florence was creating an army of zombies. But she had a medical ethic from the University of Rural Life, the peasant coexistence. The only institution that teaches and graduates with practice and theory simultaneously. This was not the time to turn back because the complications of childbirth had the mother and the twins in danger of death. Doña Tingó was also concerned about her fame. Her reputation as the oldest midwife on the entire borderline between Haiti and the eastern part of the island ruled by the Spanish was in danger of being lost. Her work as a midwife was connected to the first settlers of the western part of the island. Many spread the rumor that Tingó Florence was the great-granddaughter of the most efficient midwife in the African territory under the rule of the crown of Portugal. Her skills were passed down from generation to generation. It is said that the first generation of midwives came from Benin and entered the Caribbean through the Martinique Island. Because of her effectiveness, there are many who believe without fear of being mistaken that Tingó was a well-trained slave and that she went from zombie to server in the special missions assigned to her by her superiors.

"Me, Tingó Florence, I'm so pissed off with this childbirth. I can't believe it, damn it! From the frontier, to Jimaní, and all Haiti knows that *je suit la mieur comadrone, bon Dieu.* Oh Papa Mue. Help me, Papa Belier. Come here, Papa Ramon. The Saints can't fail me!" Thus spoke the midwife, mixing English with Creole, sprinkling her language with a few words of the refined French she had learned when she chaperoned the seven daughters of Monsieur Cumandé Le Blanche.

The latter had been widowed after his wife had given birth for him last, who, to his joy or misfortune, was born a female like all the others. He longed for a boy. Now he had one more skirt to take care of because his daughters were the envy of the whole region. From Dajabón to Port-au-Prince, every man had his eye on Cumandé LeBlanche's females. His economic position in Cap-Haitien had forced him to allow the girls to attend society clubs to rub shoulders with frenchified men who had connections in the motherland. Like Toussaint Louverture, all Haitian freedmen or maroons aspired to the French dream of having their children studying in the city of light, in Marseille, or in any European country that belonged to the French crown. Those who envied him said that this was a pretext of the rich man from Cap-Haitien to have more free time. The local fussy spread the rumor that the landowner slept with the mulatto in the bed of the deceased. The daughters seemed fiercely jealous of the father, opposing these relations with the young girl because, as they had confessed, "The mulatto Carole Mounteclaire loved Monsieur LeBlanche out of interest" for his indigo and honey plantation.

Tingó Florence was like one of the family. She slyly advised Monsieur LeBlanche to live with the mestizo, making love as husband and wife. The midwife Tingó swore and perjured that the deceased had appeared to her seven times, asking her to advise her widower Cumandé to find a companion. According to the midwife, the dead woman had appeared to her seven times. Sometimes she appeared in the crowds of the market like a merchant, and other times she appeared weeping on the loneliest roads. She swore by all the saints that the dead wife did not want to see him alone.

As Tingó Florence was a very shrewd woman, the maids never suspected that her relations with Mr. LeBlanche were the result of the work of an efficient French matchmaker. No one denies that the midwife of the LeBlanche family, who was the only one who did not travel to France when Pauline returned to Paris, vanished as if she had been swallowed up by the earth, taking with her the professional secret of who was the one who took care of her to give birth to three babies in the most difficult childbirth of the thousands of children who were born under her care in Saint-Domingue. It was such a complicated birth that if it had not been for a storm of lightning that struck the whole region as if it were the universal deluge, the inhabitants of the city of the Cape would have believed that it was the cries and lamentations of Mackandal when he was being burned in the public square as pigs are roasted.

No one can say for sure if the descendants of Pauline Bonaparte and the Irish archbishop live in Saint-Domingue. The same rumors spread about the descendants of Victor Emmanuel Leclerc and the mulatto Carole LeBlanche, who took advantage of the long walks of the Countess to satisfy the carnal desires of Napoleon Bonaparte's field marshal in Saint-Domingue. The other secret was that the archbishop met the same fate as Tingó Florence. It was as if he had been swallowed up by the earth in a flash, in the twinkling of an eye. Many, including the Sacristan of the Cathedral, claim that the archbishop went into hiding for Southern Ireland where he was not known to them because he came from the north.

"To Monsieur Cumandé," said Tingó, "the deceased, God give her eternal rest, was a very pretty woman, a good woman, and very rich one. But you must have someone to cuddle you at night. As you know, Carole Mountclaire is young, exotic, and lively as a mare in the savannah. She can represent you in Haitian society, which is the most sophisticated in the entire Caribbean area. You know also that she was the damsel who accompanied the deceased to the big events held in Petion Ville, when you could not go to the Capital. She is a female in all areas. The generals of Haiti are crazy about her. That's why they are so envious of you, Monsieur. Don't forget that Carole speaks seven languages, and you like to invite a lot of foreigners to your mansion on the plantation every time a commemoration is held in France."

The midwife Tingó advised the landowner to ensure him a place among the elite of Saint-Domingue. Carole was his daughter. But no one, not even LeBlanche himself, knew it. For that reason, she continued with her advice. "Now that the Countess is leaving for Europe, it's her big chance. Carole learned the seven most important secrets with which Pauline enjoyed and mastered the acts of copulation in Saint-Domingue. But you have to keep that secret from me forever. You can't tell anyone. You're the only one who knows how to tie Pauline's knot. Her lovers were going crazy. I heard the moans of her lovers crying like infants, as if they were children, begging for the breast to give them milk when Pauline was tying the seven knots. Look how it makes my skin crawl just listening to the men moaning for compassion and for a little milk from the breasts that drove them to the edge of craziness every time she unveiled a secret of love. It is true that France enslaved us. It exploited us. But it also left us a racial mix that makes Haitian women the most exotic women in the Caribbean region. Our women—and Carole Mountclaire is one of them—have it all when it comes to making love. They have straps around their waists. Don't tell me they don't, Monsieur Le Blanche, because I've heard a lot of people talking, and in the chambers, you hear a lot of things in private!"

The landowner smiled mischievously. He was surprised

at the midwife's wisdom. But deep in his heart, he knew that the midwife was telling him what he wanted to hear from the mulatto who was Pauline Bonaparte's confidant. He also knew that if Victor Leclerc drank so much, it was because of the treatments the mulatto gave him when Pauline lost herself in the voodoo ceremonies, the meetings with the Irish archbishop, and the baths in Saint Jack's infinite cavern. It was a matter of good luck if the Countess did not take her to France, even though jealousy drove her mad because of the special treatment she gave to Commandant Leclerc and his son Dermide.

Doña Tingó Florence stimulated the love affairs of the mulatto and the master. For the maids she served as chaperone. For Monsieur Le Blanche, she was a confidant par excellence. Moreover, when the youngest called Anne Le Blanche was in a good mood, she affectionately called her Mama Tingó. The midwife saved her from the clutches of death when her mother had a bad childbirth by a sudden frenzied attack, which tore the life out of her. Neither the midwife nor the sorcerers of Cap-Haitien could prevent the tragedy. The midwife's spoken memories came and went. They came and went in the blink of an eye. She kept sucking smoke from the tobacco that burned her bong. Praying to the Metrese, Saint Socorro, and Saint Ramon that the little hope she had of saving the woman from death would not vanish into the border air like the thick flakes of smoke from the aromatic narcotic.

The fame of Monsieur Cumandé LeBlanche's daughters was so great that, according to gossip, a missionary who had just arrived from France had to hang up his habits and resign from the church. The religious went crazy with one of the girls. The scandal that formed in the society of Cap-Haitien was so great that it spread like wildfire and crossed the Atlantic Ocean. The religious fuss spread through the fields, the cities, the markets, the parks, and the churches. After he knocked up the young woman, he did not convince her to have an abortion. The priest abused his physical appearance, his ecclesiastic influence, and above all, Anne Le Blanche's naivety.

Pauline Bonaparte's life was as mysterious as it was fast-paced in Saint-Domingue. Even today, people are still looking for answers to the enigmas created by her erotic and sensual personality. Her secrets will be very difficult to decipher. Pauline's secrets are as mysterious as the multiplication of her mirrors, so much so that not even Victor Leclerc's fellow officers have been able to explain what happened during the three years of the French invasion to crush the slave rebellion. The dead commander and the Countess completely transformed into the most powerful Santeria queen in the Caribbean are more than enough reasons to cause astonishment in contemporary society.

What is known is that all the officers knew that they were on the bloodiest and most violent battlefield of all the battles in which they had participated as members of Napoleon Bonaparte's forces. They also knew that the end of the rebellion of Saint-Domingue could represent the total triumph over the invading forces.

Pauline Bonaparte, who was the symbolic figure of the nascent French empire, had been transformed into the representation of the most venerated saint of the voodoo religion. As the other religions feared her, the news of her coronation spread like wildfire, as if it were a seaquake. The prediction made by a witch to Josephine de LaPargerie, the Martinican, when she was twelve years old was passed on with all its powers to Pauline Bonaparte. What her brother told her when he ordered her husband, General Leclerc, to lead the invasion of Saint-Domingue had been fulfilled. The initial phase of the invasion was a success in spite of the ambushes in which the Leclerc-Bonaparte couple was almost killed by a cannon shot that tore apart the carriage protecting the main retinue. In that attack, the horses flew like light birds, and the men disappeared in the smoke of the cannon shots when they were hit.

With the capture of Toussaint Louverture, Victor Leclerc was in control of the warlike encounters that were taking place in Saint-Domingue. The war reports from the battlefields told of the imminent victory of the French forces at Cap-Haitien. Several commanders were imprisoned under the invading forces. But the tactics of the slaves changed and enraged by the sending of Louverture to a French prison, and this unleashed a mammoth fury among the rebels. Their attacks were of such magnitude that in their wake, they ravaged the plantations, the servants, and their masters regardless of age. The sending of their leader as an exile to a prison in the Swiss Alps infuriated the rebels. That provoked the unification of the rebels, and they destroyed the invaders. This was completed when Victor Leclerc was declared dead because of yellow fever.

To this day, it is an enigma why Victor and Pauline were sent by the Emperor of France to fight the slave rebellion in Saint-Domingue. That was a bloody scenario in which death was an almost inevitable option. Why did he risk them in that way? She was his favorite sister, and he was her brother-in-law and commander of his Grand Armée. Many will wonder the reasons for that decision. Others say that when his most important military man died of yellow fever or a voodoo job as punishment for the imprisonment of the rebel leader Toussaint Louverture, the decline of the mighty Napoleon began.

The maiden with the icy eyes that made the French priest lose his head had a magic that drove men mad. She made women growl like cats in heat from the envy she caused them. Anne Le Blanche was a beautiful and intelligent Haitian. Those who knew her closely swore she was the spitting image of Pauline Bonaparte, the sister of the Emperor of France. Pauline lived in Cap- Haitien and on the Turtle Island with her husband, General Victor Leclerc. The commander of the Napoleonic forces had been sent to the island to destroy the Haitian slave revolution that was devastating the French colonists and bourgeoisie in the Caribbean region. To make it more like her, Anna Le Blanche frequented to bathe completely naked in the river's pools, which, by mere coincidence, was called Quebrada Le Cabronne. There were many soldiers and civilians who aspired to catch Pauline's eye as she would walk lilting toward the river's banks. The beautiful Countess barely stepped on the ground. She seemed to fly, swaying her hips, which she had developed in the mountains of the Corsica Island, and which, in spite of the delicacy of her body, had developed all her protuberances as if they were made of marble. Those who saw her say that both of them had the same taste for nature.

Everyone said that Pauline and Anne LeBlanche were two birds from the same nest. Le Blanche's daughter loved to ride around on horseback completely naked, riding over hills and plains and then going to wallow in a rejuvenating mud during the feasts of Saint James or Saint Jack. The two women had the same bust, buttocks, and waist measurements. Both weighed 125 pounds and were five feet five inches tall. Both were weak for power and opulence. Pauline Bonaparte liked the military to the point of madness for their uniforms and decorations. But what drove her to total insanity was to go on the arm of an officer who had great medals. Pauline didn't care if the decorations had been obtained for their bravery, fighting the defenseless, killing the enemy. In the barracks, there were rumors that Pauline's sensuality was revealed when she was seduced by an officer. The moans that had made her famous when she was a teenager now made her soar through the air. The military went crazy when she ordered them to bring her the "bewitched rope." She learned that trick from Juliette and Noir Curaçao, which consisted of tying herself around her lover's waist until the daylight came out, making love over and over again as if they were in a marathon until one of them gave up. Defeated. It was a fight between titans. Sex, sensuality, libido, and virility collapsed. It was a battle of the opposite sexes until one of the two fainted from an excess of intoxicating pleasure to the point of satiety.

It's told that there was an Arab sheikh who came directly from Morocco to calm the desires of the Countess Bonaparte. That's because of his virility, his seven wives— two Palestinian, two from Iraq, one from Jordan, one from Mongolia, and the youngest being a mixture of Morocco and Spain—had to have special tricks that were able to neutralize the prince's powers when they performed sexual acts. His fame as a fiery lover ran from Gibraltar to Cairo, with the force of the river Nile, taking whatever he found in his path that needed to satisfy his overflowing sexual desires. The prince was the son of an Indian father and a Jordanian mother. But he had learned the Kamasutra from India and used special instruments to perform the sexual acts.

This maddened many women of the European high society and opulence, who, because of their social position in the European lineage, kept their inhibitions and taboos as obstacles not to enjoy the pleasures that made the women of the common society happy. They were not prurient and did not submit to the conventions of sexual restraint that kept them away from the whirlwind of pleasure presented by islanders like Josephine de LaPargerie and Pauline Bonaparte. These were women with the rustic passion of the seas and the skills that nature gave them below the tropics. Rumors reached Paris that before dawn, Pauline had succumbed, and before falling asleep in deep stupor, she pronounced the name of the sheikh seven times to count the times that the Arab made her complete an orgasm of prolonged duration during which she was on the verge of insanity. She herself loosened the knot around his waist as a sign that she had been overcome by the virility of the Moroccan sheikh. It was the first time that a lover had made her loosen the secret knot that tied her around the waist next to the man who made love to her.

According to his aides, Noir Curaçao took him to the boat anchored at the dock of Cap-Haitien, pronouncing the phrase "Al Salam Alykum" (Peace be with you). With the equivalent of a bon voyage and the assurance that the sheik of Morocco would get on the boat, Juliette and the slave Noir Curaçao did not want him to stay one more night in Pauline Bonaparte's mansion. They knew his weaknesses. They knew that the Moroccan Sheikh had accomplished something extraordinary. They had never heard Pauline Bonaparte weeping with pleasure with such desperation. There came a moment with the mulatto and the slave. They wanted to imitate what was going on in their mistress's bedroom and had to bite the rope in order not to let out a cry of greater intensity. The ointments of the baths and the tying of the rope together with other rituals, which only the two of them knew, had come to the conclusion that the mystery of eroticism was about to be discovered. General Victor Leclerc was on a long military mission.

If the man from Morocco did not get on the boat to Europe, what would happen in Countess Bonaparte's bedroom would be unforgettable. Unpredictable. Unexpected. In spite of everything, the faithful servants swore that they never felt jealous of the proximity of the Prince of Morocco, although the sheikh asked many questions about the mulatto Juliette Duex Tetes. And he was also interested in Noir Curaçao. If Pauline had known about the Arab military sheik's inquiries, the screams would have been heard where the devil cast the three voices, and they were not heard. Pauline was a jealous, passionate, and possessive woman. Her conceit led her to believe that every man who approached her had to end up in bed when he so disposed or in the grave if the emperor considered that the reason for his interest in his sister better was to suck Pauline's milk and lick the imperial honey that enjoyed her closeness to the crown of France.

Rumors soon spread in France that the Countess Bonaparte had a tie around her waist. If in the baths of Rome and Paris the rumors of the erotic capacity of Pauline ran, it is necessary to suppose that now everything that was said of the sensual tricks that maddened her lovers were real. The comments told of the six-foot-three-inch man's acrobatics that made her cry and kowtow before completing her amorous mission. The Empress of France, Josephine Bonaparte, never knew of this encounter between the Moroccan sheik and her sister-in-law Pauline Bonaparte. If she had found out, jealousy, envy, and above all the rivalry that the two women had would have made her scream to the sky to show him that, as a woman of the Caribbean, she had a strength of such magnitude that she defeated Napoleon and all the men who came close to her intimacy. What she did not reveal was that the Martinican priestess and sorceress, who foretold her reign in Europe, made an incantation for all men who penetrated her with his virile member and were subjected as meek lambs to her desires and wills, as whimsical as they seemed. The incantations that she prepared by the Martinican witch made Josephine a woman with special powers. She also immunized her against any epidemic, and no metal object could take her life because she made her "swallow the gospels". Those powers served to save her from the guillotine when she was condemned by a court from which not even her betters were spared. For that reason, and other tricks of her feminine wiles, Josephine de LaPargerie was saved from being beheaded by the edge of the guillotine, lacking only thirteen hours before placing her beautiful neck under the mortal shine of the cold steel that did not discriminate when executing the condemned men and women of the transition between the French Revolution and the fall of the Gallic oligarchy.

Pauline's desire to beat her sister-in-law Josephine de LaPargerie made her perfect her qualities and skills. It was a competition of great proportions to dominate Napoleon's empire and the men who supported him. Both were born to dominate. The two women, whose political power throughout Europe and the overseas territories that had fallen under the hegemony of the French empire, came to accumulate influence over the very lives and estates of their subjects and citizens. Pauline and Josephine's power shook the chambers and palaces of the empire, from Martinique and Saint-Domingue to the Far East. Both women were the topic of conversation during their time and beyond.

Today, more than two centuries later, women search for their memories to discover the sensuality of their lives and the mysterious way in which they came to dominate the most powerful men in matters of love. These surrendered to their feet so that they would give them a tiny bit, a sliver, of their attention. In exchange, the kings and emperors would offer on a silver platter the goods and powers acquired in the bloodiest conquests around the world. It is true that since the beginning of humanity, there have been powerful women. It is enough to remember Eve, Delilah, Magdalena, Isabella of Castile, Marie Antoinette, Joan of Arc, and others who made the world tremble. Undoubtedly, in terms of dominance over the male sex, those who truly managed to subdue men with their skills and feminine wiles were Pauline Bonaparte and Josephine LaPargerie, who reached the pinnacle of the greatest power on earth. The might of Napoleon Bonaparte and the French Empire, together with all its possessions in the world, were from the beginning in the hands of the will of Josephine and Pauline—two islanders who came into the world with feminine powers and talents that, to this day, continue to stimulate the curiosity of all sexes who are unable to decipher the spell and the riddle that characterized their relationship with the great Napoleon Bonaparte. The secret, erotic, and sensual powers of these two women have been and will continue to be a mystery for those who delve into the existence and legacy in the domain of the emperor of France.

14

The Secrets That Pauline Never Revealed

To venture into the emotional personality of Pauline Bonaparte is a challenge as great as her erotic qualities and the definition of her feminine figure in terms of the social conglomerate in which she developed her life. It is obvious that from her birth until the seventeen years she lived on the Corsica Island, the second part of her life in the south and north of France, she gained a lot of knowledge related to her palace experiences that existed and still exist in the great European metropolis.

Pauline was facing a changing world in every aspect. It was a challenge of great magnitude if one takes into account that the young Bonaparte came from a very small island involved in the vortex of conflicts between two great nations, Italy and France, which fought for their territory.

It was in the midst of this conflict that Pauline came to the courts as a peasant girl, even though her ancestry overpassed her rural upbringing. The luck she had in her early life was often due to her being protected by the shadow of her brother Napoleon and, other times, motivated by the strength of her feminine personality and physical attributes, combined with her practical development in matters of love at an early age. Analyzing her from an omniscient position, stripping us of unfavorable criticisms for her actions in the historical life that touched her, we can better understand her tumultuous experiences in contemporary society where the powers of the royal crowns were subjected to socio-political changes exercised by new currents that were born of the Industrial Revolution and the expansion of communication that gave account of the excesses of kings and queens against countries and territories where humans were treated worse than animals, enslaved and chained, condemned with laws that were made to favor the powerful and sacrifice the working classes in the world. The fruit of that turbulence in which the whole emotional and physical scaffolding of Pauline Bonaparte was formed presents us with the particularity of a woman who came from an almost-forgotten island in the middle of the Mediterranean Sea, until reaching a city like Paris, which, at that time, occupied the position of being the capital of the modern contemporary world in all aspects.

Entering into her environment and her emotions, we will know what was woven with such an abrupt change. Pauline knew how to take advantage of her physical qualities and her ability to climb the stairs of power, propitiated by the imperial advance of her brother throughout Europe. There has never been a woman born on an island of relatively little political importance such as Corsica who has achieved so much power in such a short time in all the courts of the Western hemisphere.

When Pauline Bonaparte was born, the island was undergoing great social upheavals that had split the territory because of the political changes taking place in Italy and France. Both nations disputed the domination of the Corsica Island, which had a considerable geographical value for geopolitics based on military strategy. Many scholars of history today ask themselves, "What would Pauline Bonaparte's life have been like if instead of being born under the crown of France, she had been born under the dominion of Italy?" Of course, the fact that the Bonaparte family and Ramolino had fought for many years on the Corsica Island to be independent of Italian and French rule has to be considered. Leticia Ramolino supported the guerrillas led by a cousin in the island's mountains. She was pregnant with Napoleon's child and went to meet the guerrilla leader. On her return to Ajaccio, she fell into the mighty river with her horse. The animal disappeared forever, and Pauline Bonaparte's mother survived by swimming and carrying Napoleon in her womb when she was several months pregnant. This created a reputation as revolutionary fighters for the Bonaparte and Ramolino family, who aspired to a free and independent Corsica from the mainland under Italian rule.

Pauline's rebelliousness was evident from her development from girl to woman. The hormones that boiled in her childhood process until reaching puberty exploded with the fire that burned prematurely in her entrails, awakening the conformation of a sensual woman with an erotic capacity of great proportions in the feminine gender. Many women envied her, and others wanted to be like her. Pauline had become a preponderant model in French society, whose strength came to reconfirm the fame gained by the women of France not only in the variety of fashions, but by the contribution of Napoleon Bonaparte's younger sister in the process of the changes that the nation of lights was undergoing from Marseilles in the south to Paris in the north. Pauline was undoubtedly a very advanced woman for her time. Her lack of interest in academic matters opened the way for the set of inclinations that bubbled within her to come to the surface. It was like a volcano that burned her. She was a free, genuine, sensual, original, and hot woman.

When Pauline arrived in Marseilles in the south of France, she brought with her a series of tastes and inclinations that would form her as an island woman, making use of the phrase that made the philosopher Ortega and Gassett famous: "I am already me and my circumstances." The circumstances in which Pauline Bonaparte's life unfolded endowed her with qualities that would later become part of her feminine secrets. She had an enchantment for military uniforms and the men who wore them. Pauline grew up in a military environment because her father, Charles Bonaparte, was an officer, representative of the Crown in Ajaccio, capital of Corsica. This exaggerated admiration for the uniforms got her in touch with the lieutenant of the French Army, who made her a woman and entered into some love affairs that provoked the family's anger because the military man was three times her age. It was this taste for military uniforms that led her into the arms of Victor Emmanuel Leclerc, whom she married. Like many women who come from an island, she developed an exaggerated love for water and mud. It was Pauline Bonaparte who introduced in France what had been used in some cultures as well as in Rome. But it had never reached the sensual creativity of Pauline Bonaparte. For that reason, she felt in her environment when she had the opportunity to be introduced in the ceremonies of Saint Jack (Saint James) in the vicinity of Cap-Haitien.

Pauline was the owner of a very interesting personality. As she loved Cleopatra and Marie Antoinette's beauty, she put into practice many rituals related to the beauty that today is manifested in spa centers around the world and the use of mud, clay, creams, and oils that transform women and increase their power for the execution of love tricks that bind and dominate the men they love. Those centers that were on the verge of vanishing with the debacle of the Roman Empire are maintained with popularity in crescendo, although it was inclined to the observation and the rejection of the hollow words of the French ladies of the belle societé.

As she was Josephine LaPargerie's sister-in-law, wife of the Emperor, the rivalry was between these two women. Josephine, apart from being controlling, had great use of words because of her experience and because she had been married before convincing Napoleon to take her from the bucolic, melancholy, low-activity life on the small island of Martinique to the pompousness of the great palaces of the French empire. Napoleon dominated France. France was the world at that time.

From that meeting, which took place during thirteen days between the prince of Egypt and Pauline Bonaparte, the man whose fame had spread in the Napoleonic courts collapsed like the statue of King Nebuchadnezzar. It was in Cap-Haitien that he found "the corn cob of his ass," as the Cibaenian say of the northern region of the current Dominican Republic.

The prince, overwhelmed and astonished at not being able to win the sexual battle with his coveted Pauline Bonaparte, left the Hispaniola north like a true zombie. Without turning his face, he returned to the country of the great pyramids heartbroken and bewildered. He left with his tail between his legs, as the locals say to refer to the one who has been defeated in an unequal battle.

The seven wives who were waiting for him in seven beds with their faces covered by seven veils for him to make love to them as only he knew how wept with joy to see him arrive. Then they wept with pain when they saw him leave. Obviously, something big had happened to him at Cap-Haitien from where he returned as if he were a zombie. Only Pauline and the member of the Egyptian monarchy knew the secret of his presence in Saint-Domingue. The prince had offered himself as an adviser on war operations to Commander Leclerc and the Emperor of France. But his real motive was to be near Pauline Bonaparte, who had captivated him with her sensual beauty at Napoleon's court. The man put his buttocks where he brought the front. The women were surprised with the change of their virile husband, who, as if by magic, disappeared forever in the Sahara desert without a trace after he met the Countess in the mysterious Caribbean region. Legend has it that in a bend of the Nile River, a tall and handsome man appears, singing to the four winds the seven secrets taught to him by Pauline Bonaparte in the Enchanted Lagoon that mysteriously appears and disappears in the Turtle Island. Those who have seen him say that he appears and disappears mysteriously on the Turtle Island.

After the praise of the erotic and sensual greatness of the Emperor of France's sister and his lamentations for not having completely bent her with the virility of his member, he repeats with sorrow in his soul, over and over again: "AL SALAM ALYKUM!" (Peace be with you!) Adding to his disappointment and bitterness, loudly for all passers-by to hear, he repeats over and over again, "I want everyone to know, Pauline Bonaparte defeated a male from Arabia, for fuck's sake."

When he completes his lamentation, tormented, he

wades naked, as God brought him into the world, into the calm but dangerous and deep waters of the Nile River.

Whether it was kept a secret that Pauline Bonaparte was pregnant with triplets and gave birth in secret from the elite of Saint-Domingue is difficult to uncertain. The veracity or not of this rumor may never be proven. That will add fuel to the fire of intrigue that continues to surround the life of the Countess Pauline. They were comments that slipped through the cracks of the doors and windows of Caribbean high society no matter what empire she belonged to. That was before Pauline returned to France with a coffin full of jewels and her husband's corpse. The mysterious death of Victor Emmanuel Leclerc upon his arrival to the imperial ceremonies swallowed like a gigantic monster the comments that crossed the Atlantic Ocean. This reminded the great Napoleon that in life, everything is transitory. That power, however great it may be, has a Waterloo and a Saint-Domingue.

The maid Carole LeBlanche left with the Countess to France. Tingó Florence, the midwife, vanished from Cap-Haitien as if she had been swallowed by the earth. Noir Curaçao, Pauline's exclusive masseur, went to France taken to Paris to accompany his mistress. No word was taken from him. All that became an enigma because evil tongues also reported that General Victor Leclerc, accustomed to make love every time he went to the battlefield as his brother-in-law Napoleon Bonaparte did, had several children, fruits of his virility. The military man developed an enormous taste for the mulatto women of Saint-Domingue, who gave themselves to him body and soul. That is not known either. What is known is that Pauline's secrets, which made up her magic and erotic attraction, were original.

The Tightness of Her Cervix
With which she squeezed her lover's virile member

while they were copulating, provoking a fast ejaculation but with an unequalled and abundant profusion with which she could conceive seven children and impregnate an equal number of women of different ages. Many were those who lost their heads before the culmination of the sexual act without being able to fully satisfy her.

Pauline Was Fascinated with Making Love While Standing

She preferred that position to avoid pregnancy and to enjoy eroticism and male sex for hours on end. With this act of sensual acrobatics, she subdued her seven amorous partners. Many begged her to repeat the act. Others, more desperate, offered her villas and castles and marriage as well.

Another secret that drove men crazy was...

The Multiplication of Mirrors

Pauline would take seven gigantic mirrors in which her entire body and the body of her chosen lover for amorous encounter could be seen. Of course, the most privileged with the love game of the mirrors was her husband, General Victor Emmanuel Leclerc, since they were brought directly from Europe for him to celebrate the first anniversary of the French invasion of Saint-Domingue.

The beautiful lady appeared in a very fine gown in which all the protuberances of her body protruded profusely. The man was dressed in his military uniform, with the most distinguished gala for such a special occasion. It seemed as if he was going to a swearing in of the emperor or to the coronation of Her Majesty, the queen. As two of them were placed in special geometrical positions, the mirrors created a multidimensional optical illusion in which his lover lost his mind; his sense of time and space took him to a trance where he did not know if what he was experiencing was a lie or truth, if it was fiction or reality.

In that ecstasy of dreaming, the lover entered a tunnel of pleasure from which he did not come out until at the end of the tunnel of the most extraordinary experience of love, he found himself in a bedchamber of such beauty and pleasant smells that penetrated his senses. Thus he went mad, slowly, gently, smoothly as his ego rose to the clouds, deceitfully believing that so much beauty belonged to him alone. Before the naked presence of Pauline Bonaparte's feminine sensuality, the dementia was irreversible.

The Special Baths That Went in through Her Pores
This was to provoke erotic sensations with herbs and scents of perfumes that framed delineated and increased the desires of the couple of lovers to a sexual act of wild culmination.

Make Love Riding on the Giant Milito Horse
Pauline liked to do this, causing her male partner to fall into a trance of transformation of sensual madness.

Erotic Moans
This turned her into an irresistible woman.

The Use of the Bewitched Rope
Tingó Florence had taught this to Pauline to make love until the clearings of the day arrived.

The other secrets will be left to the imagination of the reader who dares to experiment with the application of those tricks and wiles that the Countess put into practice during the years that karmic destiny placed her in the Caribbean region. The reasons that combined to expose

Pauline to this cultural process that is intertwined in the intricacies of religions and beliefs since the aborigines inhabited the highest and lowest Antilles, to the different races that in the present make up the customs of making love between human beings. Many will be able to imagine the tricks she had learned on the Corsica Island until their encounter with each other with the archbishop of Ireland, who is likely to become the true love of her life because of the passionate way in which he let her know the real secret of a sequential orgasm, penetrating her for thirteen hours in Saint Jack's Cavern at the top of La Mermelade Mountain. Above all, because he had kept for the Countess something of incalculable value that is compromised at the moment of the vow of ecclesiastical fidelity when the priesthood is assumed. His manly virginity and the energy of breaking the sexual magic of his seven secrets was what Pauline could never forget about the Irish archbishop, who hung up his sackcloth and threw away his ecclesiastical influence in the Vatican of Rome for the love of the Countess Pauline Bonaparte.

Although some of the sexual methods employed by the Countess are part of the vernacular folklore of Hispaniola Island of the secrets that are perceived and practiced in Saint-Domingue and in the western hemisphere, they are parts of the culture that sees sex as the center of life. That is why man places so much emphasis on the dominance of the male over the female as an axiom of dominance and control. The aborigines of the Caribbean islands use products to harden "the gravel"; the male member has always been for enjoying to the point of madness in the act of love. Because she was such a special woman, Pauline allowed herself to open up so that today, we could better understand her erotic and sensual personality, which she used to attract and enchant the most virile men of her time.

Today, the nude statues that eternalized the most famous sculptures of the sensual skills of the women of the time continue to provoke the evocation of an unforgettable past, bathed by the passionate love of Pauline Bonaparte and of the women who, even without recognizing it, let alone making it public knowledge for the sake of the modesty of the belle societé, continued to wear in the intimacy of her rooms all the magic of the most absolute sensuality. If the Countess had other hidden secrets that could not be deciphered, we will never know. What we do know is that in the intimacy of her bedroom in Saint-Domingue, she left behind the fragrance of the aphrodisiac ointments and oils that were used in the preparation of the erotic baths that drove General Leclerc mad when the din of a pitched battle demanded that he present himself to the arms of the love of his life. Also left behind, without the passage of two centuries having been able to erase, was the smell and fragrance that formed part of the ritual of those baths where Pauline's body became a woman overflowing her eroticism with burning passion and intertwining it with her soft caressing forms as if it were a snake bewitched between her legs in a trick of eroticism that she had learned from an Indian princess. The boiling-hot lover's body, anxious to receive the bath of the volcano's nectar, like an enormous cauldron from where the lava would emanate seven times seven from the very entrails of Pauline Bonaparte with the pheromones, the reminiscence of the sticky lava of the nectar that emanated in a torrent of waterfalls with a brackish taste, unique so that only a chosen few could enjoy, taste the product of each explosion of the perennial volcano that existed in the sensuality of the one who in life bore the name of Pauline Bonaparte and Ramolino. Her secrets were special ways of making love that, being a woman full of sensuality and eroticism, she managed to perfect in a way that until the present has not appeared one with so much power to defeat the most virile men of her time in the copulation encounters. Perhaps in the future, such a complete woman can appear. Until now, the sensual tricks of the Countess remain an enigma that many men and women would like to know. Above all, it was the erotic capacity that made her possess great talents and abilities, learned from the teaching of her tutor on the Corsica Island or by the help and the amorous tricks learned in her incorporation to the syncretism of Catholicism and voodoo.

There were many who spread the rumor that it was the archbishop of Ireland who began to introduce her from the Vatican itself so that she could be incorporated smoothly to the activities of witchcraft, developed by the priestesses and masters of that ancestral religion of Africa that arrived with the first slaves in the transport ships. The same sorcerers and sorceresses who would turn a man into a ferocious bull and a woman into a snake in a second, in the blink of an eye, Pauline combined all these experiences to bring them to the plane of domination that she always wanted to self-impose as if her only interest was to emulate her mother, Leticia Ramolino. She became the power behind the throne of the empire.

Everyone recognized Leticia's absolute power over the daughters and sons of the Bonaparte family. If you ever travel to the Corsica Island, you will hear the legends of Napoleon's mother and her adventures while visiting a guerrilla cousin who had stolen her heart. In the middle of a battle, she ran on her horse at great speed until she jumped off the animal and fell into a rushing river. Leticia, seven months pregnant, managed to save herself, and her horse was never found.

Neither Victor Leclerc nor Camillo Borghese had time to write down the reason why they lost their minds while living with the Countess. The former because he died fighting in Saint-Domingue, the latter because he was traumatized to learn that his wife would bend even the Pope if he approached her to make her fall in love. Camillo Borghese was very connected to the circle of the so-called Holy Father of Rome. He was well known for his economic power in the Vatican.

The knot of her legs enveloped when the man or woman used the limbs as a noose. There was no escape from this amorous trap. In this position—lying, sitting, or standing—the couple was subjected to a form of pleasurable suction as a result of the rhythmic movements produced by the cocomordan. Pauline's clenching and muscle contractions squeezed the virile member so hard that he barely had the strength to gasp for air before he fainted. The lack of oxygen by the emotions and the fatigue of the physical task allowed the man trapped in the sensual knot to give more voluntary pleasure, but in that climatic part in which the woman, owner of the key and the sexual lock, remove the forces and the intention, provoking an orgasm of unthinkable immensity and duration. Afterward, a long lethargy led the man trapped in that sexual trick, overflowed and got dragged without resistance to a dreamlike process that only Morpheus and Pauline could decipher. It was as if several of Pauline's secrets were unveiled to confirm the strength of her erotic sexuality. The vaginal contractions drove the men crazy, and that's why they said they were under a spell from the moment of the penetration.

The coupling of the horse was similar to the first one. The riders reversed while pounding at a slow pace on top of the steed in which the riders were face-to-face while riding as a couple just as the sexual act was done in some regions of the Arab countries.

In the mysterious and exotic Caribbean region, there remained the memory of a slave rebellion that shook the foundations of the French empire under the rule of the powerful Napoleon Bonaparte. When the results of that rebellion are analyzed, it is likely that all those who were behind that campaign with such macabre and harmful results for the black race in Africa should be analyzed. It is necessary to monitor and analyze those who perpetuated this gigantic conquest in the transportation of millions of prisoners from one continent to another. The Catholic Church, governments, kingdoms, empires, and plantation owners in the Caribbean formed an infernal triangle for this tragedy to take place on the slave ships, the French colonists, the buccaneers, and filibusters of Turtle Island that produced for two hundred years what was the richest French colony in the hemisphere.

For that reason, the emperor and then Consul General of France sent his sister together with her husband, General Victor Emmanuel, commander of the most powerful army in the world, to destroy the rebellion of the Saint-Domingue slaves. It is an enigma to discover the reasons why Napoleon gambled everything for everything, sending to the heart of the Caribbean hell with the possibility of certain death his most beloved sister and his brother-in-law, who was the most valuable military man to complete the expansionist plans so that his empire would sweep and restore order in the rebellion of the slaves that had begun in the French plantations established in Haiti. Napoleon Bonaparte never imagined that in that small territory where the bourgeoisie that injected economic strength, social improvement, and political power to the French crown had been born would be the beginning of the resounding fall of the empire. It was a military and political error that, by way of consequence, would multiply the defeats of Waterloo seven times, completing the failure of one of the most powerful empires that the history of humanity remembers and will remember.

The alignment of the planets in the universe was the

sign that something big was happening in the region of the Caribbean. That was the fruit of Pauline Bonaparte's transformation. The Irish archbishop with the presence of a giant looked like a marble statue. His six feet three inches surpassed the figure of Pauline Bonaparte. It all began in the sacristy in the confessional of the Cathedral of Cap-Haitien, when Pauline Bonaparte attended a confession conference with His Excellency, the archbishop, who was transferred after spending seven years in the Basilica of Rome.

The rumors of his transfer to Cap-Haitien were a cause of intrigue. According to gossip, the prelate had been sent to Saint-Domingue on Napoleon's errands or "lobbying" to get the church in favor of his plans for dominions throughout the region. Others close to Josephine LaPargerie spread the rumor that the archbishop, who was Pauline's confessor, was sent to protect her from the voodoo and sorcery that was advancing like a seaquake as it found fertile land among the black slaves and freedmen of the Antilles. What was known was that the archbishop, as if he were a hound dog, did not lose sight on the Emperor of France's sister. Rumors spread like wildfire throughout the region. The sacristy and the confessional listened, as mute witnesses, to the moans and sensual sighs, the suggestive phrases of Pauline and the forced breathing of the prelate, who, in desperation, wept with pleasure each time he penetrated the depths of the beautiful woman's entrails.

Pauline's transformation was total. Her spirit changed, and she let out all the secrets and inhibitions that she had not been able to uncover neither in her native Corsica nor in Rome nor in her beloved Paris. In Haiti, she had the power of a queen. In Cap-Haitien, she was treated like a sovereign.

The vassals, the aristocratic owners of the plantations, and the bourgeoisie who administered Saint-Domingue on behalf of the Crown of France adored her as a goddess as soon as she set foot on the island. In short, the entire population bowed before her presence and treated her as Her Majesty, Pauline Bonaparte. Some swore without fear of being mistaken that this beautiful lady was the reincarnation of the Metresa in body and soul.

In the end, the erotic secrets of Pauline Bonaparte have been captured in the way of life of Caribbean women. The syncretism that took place in the sensuality of the women of the time she lived in Saint-Domingue where the rebels crowned Pauline Bonaparte as the supreme goddess of the voodoo religion was real. The changes formed a union that has continued and will continue through the centuries. Even though Pauline was the symbol of Napoleon's empire and of France, the rebels did not lay a finger on her so as not to cause her any harm.

In spite of the bloody war situation in Saint-Domingue, the rebels allowed the invaders to arrive without attacking with fire while the ships were anchored in the Port of Cap-Haitien. The ships were like sitting ducks, easy to hunt. The plan to set fire to burn the fleet of ships by the revolutionaries was not executed because the rebels' strategists prevented the fire attacks on the ships when they were vulnerable in Cap-Haitien Bay, thus protecting the "voodoo goddess who represented Metresilis" in the person of the Countess.

Nevertheless, Pauline Bonaparte's fame continued to spread throughout the empire. Still on her deathbed, waiting to begin her journey to the afterlife, the mysterious Pauline dressed in the newest and most sensual outfit she had in her abundant wardrobe. Her housekeeper spread the rumor that this was the same dress in which she had presented herself for her amorous encounters with the archbishop of Cap-Haitien. The Countess asked for a mirror to be brought to her, not only to see the attributes that had made her famous, but also to remember some of her most valuable erotic secrets when making love. Perfumed with the exquisiteness of a faint fragrance, she began the route to the eternal. When the bathing ritual was over, her dress was as bright yellow as gold, her makeup light on her still fleshy lips. She put on her hat adorned with black-and-white pearls with three curassow or peacock feathers. She leaned back on the pillows. She struck a pose as if she were modeling for a statue. She looked at herself in the mirror again and again. Her eyes widened, and the movie of her life began.

She heard the drums: PUM! KUTU-PUM-PUM! KUTU-PUM! PUM! PUM! She saw the image of her son Dermide. She remembered Victor Leclerc. She thought of Rome. The sound of the drums was still present. The procession of Ayití blacks bowing to her was endless. Her left hand rose with the slowness of one who is losing their strength; she brought her fingers to her half-open lips. She began to pronounce the name of her beloved: Jean Paul...Jean Paul... Jean Paul. The pupils of her eyes, clear as the honey of the sovereign bees, began to open, looking for the light, the fall of the yellowish leaves. In its descent, the giant reddish moon, like a huge lamp hanging from the sky, the arrival of the bishop of the Vatican beckoning her. He was calling her to ride on a white horse to take her flying through the universe of love.

The Countess left with a smile on her face.

It was a provocative smile as a macabre mockery to her critics and detractors; perhaps she did it as a sign of eternal satisfaction for the confidence she had in herself that her sensual attributes and erotic qualities were of her legitimate creation and belonging. It was a soft smile that was framed between eroticism and sensuality, wanting thus to show to those present in that place where she lived the best and most exciting years, the true trick of hiding in her beauty the tragedy of her demise. If on the battlefields of Saint-Domingue she survived several encounters with death, she would not at this moment show signs of cowardice, of spiritual laziness, or of surrendering her exalted pride.

Many say that the confirmation in the voodoo ceremony and the acceptance that the archbishop of Ireland had chased her from the Vatican of Rome to the mysterious region of the Caribbean to confess his deep love and swear eternal fidelity to her were more than enough reasons to feel strengthened in the face of death as she was in front of men, attracting them through the strength of her eroticism and the passionate sensuality, that through the teaching and the spell work of the Haitian sorcerers, baptized her with the magic power that accompanied her until the last moment of her life.

Pauline's secrets will continue to be the sample of eroticism and sensuality that today is manifested in the cadence, in the walk of the exotic Caribbean woman. Every woman has and will have a secret kept in the chest of nature to satisfy and drive crazy the man who gets into bed. Whoever does so will fall under the spell of the seven secrets that the woman of the Antilles, from the diminished Saba Island to the gigantic Cuban countryside, passing through the Puerto Rican charm, goes through the roads humming melodious songs that with the movement of her buttocks bewitches men and takes them to a world of reverie.

There are seven secrets that have been passed down from generation to generation to confirm Doña Leticia's prediction when she gave them the bewitched undergarments, which she had to wear without further explanation. Therein lay the secret that, combined with the seven secrets, would create an eternal bond so that the man of her choice would be hers and no one else's. That is to say that the Caribbean women would be the only ones who would ever be able to have a man of their choice. That is to say that the Caribbean women not only have melao in their intimacies, but when the spells are combined, the lover loses his senses, his mind heats up, and he falls into a total trance from which he will never be able to free himself. There awaits you in the alcoves of women who give free rein to their sexual capacity to let the explosions spill the fiery nectar of the volcano of their entrails.

The sexual encounters with the men who ignited the incandescent flame of their passion were unforgettable for their protagonists. Saint-Domingue only served as the stage for the great battle that would change the course of the history of the Western Hemisphere. Haiti was the beginning and the end of that empire, which, according to its executor, reached beyond where the sun goes to bed, beyond the horizon. Its rise was as fast as its fall.

No one can deny that Pauline Bonaparte is one of the most interesting women in the courts of Europe and the world. Many were the princesses of the Far and Middle East who were interested in knowing some of the secrets of this intriguing woman who, when she arrived in the realm of this world, they named Pauline Bonaparte. What has never been a secret is that when one travels through the cities, through the countryside and the places where Countess Bonaparte lived, there you see apparitions of a beautiful woman riding naked on a gigantic white horse, proudly showing her muscles as if she were a huge Pegasus flying over the mountains and hills of Saint-Domingue. The animal is jumping over the rivers and ravines of the region. He is showing off his erect male member, like a mahogany club with the resemblance of a ball bat, upright to copulate with the most beautiful mare in the region. In the mind of anyone who sees these erotic figures, the thought immediately arises of a secret that Pauline never revealed to serve as motivation for whoever feels so macho or so female to discover it. Others claim that they have met this beautiful woman who calls them to ride, speaking to them in a form of telepathy. In the message, she invites them to enter Saint Jack's Cavern where she will teach them some secrets of the eroticism that characterizes her femininity and her passion, full of eroticism and sensuality. In this way, she teaches her charms to create lust and passion in the mind of those who see her. Those who have dared to ride on the back of her white horse have never returned to the place from where they left in the mysterious Hispaniola Island. The same island that was called, under the rule of Napoleon Bonaparte, the colony of Saint-Domingue.

THE END